Praise for L

DIS

D0431238

"The personal and the political merge in Yang Huang's debut novel about a college student in post-Cultural Revolution China. Gu Bao negotiates the shifting landscape of a country still struggling toward modernity, as China's education system, family planning policies and the deaths of her fellow students in Tiananmen Square sometimes push her to desperate measures. The story moves from city life to the rural home of Bao's grandparents, acquiring an epic feel in a compact length."

—*San Jose Mercury News*

"This skillfully written work embodies a young woman's journey toward independence and maturity at a time when her country's politics dictate conformity and oppression. The characters are thoughtfully well rounded, the plot lines are true to life, and the narrative focuses refreshingly on the human spirit rather than political issues. Reminiscent of Yu Hua's *To Live* but with a lot less tragedy and heartbreak."

—*Library Journal*

"I feel like I have unearthed another hidden gem. . . . Yang Huang has written a smooth and flowing work of art through words that showcase the inner turmoil of the characters. The vivid scenes that are described transport the reader from their reading chair to the magic and beauty of a country torn apart by corruption and the lust for power."

—Dianne Bylo, *Tome Tender*

"*Living Treasures* is nothing short of spectacular; especially for readers who want a story steeped in Chinese culture, tradition, and politics but cemented by a powerful young woman who emerges as a savior to others."

—*Midwest Book Review*

"Huang's winning novel is more than another work of historical fiction. *Living Treasures* is endearing, extraordinarily moving, and its timely message about life makes it a must read for young and old readers alike."

—*San Francisco Book Review*

"*Living Treasures* expands into a deeply human and sympathetic portrait of people living as best they can in an imperfect society."

—*Foreword Reviews*

"Huang's measured yet evocative novel heightens Bao's journey from timid student to defiant adversary in the midst of personal and political upheaval."

—*Booklist*

"*Living Treasures* is a treasure. Sensual, brave and relevant, the book takes you to a place in China that few of us have ever experienced. I couldn't put it down."

—Patricia Harman, author of *The Midwife of Hope River*

"Yang Huang has written a wonderful first novel. Bao is a complex and appealing character whose harrowing journey through 1989 rural China is told in quietly poetic language that illuminates and reveals. I did not want this book to end."

—Elizabeth Graver, author of *The End of the Point*

"Huang does an admirable job balancing Bao's individual story against the canvas of China's evolution using crisply drawn characters who reveal their layers as the story progresses. . . . A knotty, engaging novel of China's recent history."

—*Kirkus Reviews*

"This is the beautiful and unique coming of age story of a young woman at a moment of history in which her personal journey flows together with that of her generation, a journey of self-determination."

—C.E. Poverman, author of *Love by Drowning*

"Like a young Alice Munro, Yang Huang—authoritative, compassionate, and witty—has a gift for creating characters whose actions, for good or evil, can take even themselves by surprise. *Living Treasures* is a suspenseful, soul-satisfying novel by an impeccable storyteller. I eagerly await her next book."

—Elizabeth Evans, author of *Carter Clay*

"I recommend this book to the permanent library of all readers who enjoy a very well written work of fiction, on a very timely subject, that will keep them entertained for hours."

—*Books and Movies: Reviews*

Living Treasures

Yang Huang

New York
Harvard Square Editions
2014

LIVING TREASURES

ISBN 978-0-9895960-5-3

Published in the United States by Harvard Square Editions
www.harvardsquareeditions.org

To my beautiful family:

My husband, Qin, and our children,

Victor and Oliver

Prologue

December, 1976

GU BAO REMEMBERED the time when she feared disaster. At five years old, she lived with her grandparents at Crystal Village in Pingwu County, Sichuan province. In late spring, she witnessed a rare phenomenon, bamboo flowering over large areas of the Min Mountains. The blossoms dangling from the stems were an eerie sight, for they preceded the death of bamboos. In the following winter months, more than a hundred giant pandas died of starvation.

In August a magnitude 7.2 earthquake struck. The mountains bounded like frightened musk deer, toppling forests and crumbling cliffs. One village was buried alive by a landslide; people, animals, houses, and fields were wiped from the face of the mountain.

Fortunately her grandparents' house withstood the earthquake. The wooden house was pliable and didn't crumble like a concrete building. Even the rickety cupboard had only dropped a few earthenware dishes. Still, they took safety precautions against more earthquakes. During the day Grandma cooked the meals on a coal-cake stove in the backyard. Her tall body bent over the stove, as she waved a fan to coax the flame to rise and spread to the top coal cake. At times her face turned sooty and her eyes watered from the smoke. She pounded her lower back with a fist.

Bao knew how to relieve her of the back pain. "Is it here, Grandma?" She rolled her fist over Grandma's lower back. "All better."

Grandma raised her head and screwed up her eyes. "Now I have a headache, spreading to the left temple."

Bao patted Grandma's forehead and blew air on it. "Cured."

"Aren't you the miracle worker?" Grandma tickled Bao until they burst into laughter in each other's arms.

At night, Bao slept with her grandparents in a shed, propped up by bamboo poles. Its walls were made of straw and bamboo mats. Asphalt felt and plastic sheets formed the roof. Bricks held down the plastic and felted sheets to keep the wind from blowing them away. When it rained, Grandma put out basins and pots to catch water leaking from the roof. At night, rats and mice battled on the roof. Every so often, a rat dropped to the ground or fell into their bed.

In spite of daily hardships, there were unexpected rewards. One day Uncle Wang, a militia leader, brought a dead black bear to the house. The bear had been killed by the earthquake. Grandpa skinned the bear with a long curved knife, his bony hands deftly slicing, tearing, and scraping. With a patient smile on his face, Grandpa looked as though he were giving the bear a loving send-off. Bao could smell blood for days, after he tanned the pelt into an oversize mattress for Uncle Wang. In return, Uncle Wang gave them the bear's heart. Grandma cooked it for a whole morning. It tasted crunchy like tough chicken gizzard.

In September, the village radio broadcast the dirges. Chairman Mao Zedong had passed away at age eighty-two. The news was like a thunderbolt out of a clear sky. For decades people across China had shouted the slogan, "Long live Chairman Mao! May he live to be a thousand, a million years old! May he live for all eternity!" But Chairman Mao had perished like an ordinary man.

Bao saw her grandparents weep, and so did Uncle Wang and other militiamen. Their grief filled her with dread. Some days she was afraid to leave the house; if the sky should fall, who would hold it up above her head, now that Chairman Mao was gone? He had founded the People's Republic of China; all citizens were his children. Suddenly, eight hundred million Chinese people were orphans.

One day Bao woke up at dawn to pee. It was dim inside the earthquake shed. Grandma slept beside Bao with her hands cupped together. Grandpa lay at the foot of the bed, his snores rising and falling like bellows hard at work. Now and then a sharp whistle came from his nostrils and trailed off into labored grunts. Bao crawled out of the bed and slid on her cotton shoes. Making her way to the night pot, she heard leaves rustle and a stem crack outside.

Was it a deer? She pulled back the straw mat door, lined with a thick quilt covered in plastic sheets.

At first she saw only a blur. The hill slope beyond the fields was covered in snow, and fog draped firs and birches on the hillside. In the backyard a large animal lumbered along, swaying from side to side, its head bent low. It looked like a bear, with black and white markings on its body.

It was a giant panda—a national treasure! Her father had shown Bao a picture of one in the newspaper when Premier Zhou Enlai gave a pair of pandas to President Nixon of the United States. Bao opened the door wide. The cold draft made her teeth chatter. She saw a wad of grayish flesh clutched in the panda's mouth. The flesh moved and let out a screech like a banshee.

Bao slammed the door shut. She stood in semi-darkness, trembling and debating whether she should scream and wake up her grandparents. Although pandas lived in the Min Mountains, no villager had ever seen one. Bao wanted to have a closer look. She slid a stool behind the straw mat to keep the door open only a crack.

In front of their house, the panda nuzzled the gray thing on its arm, neck, and head. Covered with silvery hair, it looked like a big rat, yet Bao realized it was a cub. The panda scooped the cub into her arms and cradled it, bit it lightly on the leg as if in play. The cub squirmed and patted its mother's broad, hairy face, as she licked its belly and head. Finally she released the cub, so it slid down her sloping stomach into the hay.

Bao hurried to the night pot to relieve herself and then returned to the door.

The panda sat in front of the chicken coop and reached for the tin basin. The leftover food had frozen. A hen hopped out and made *go-go-go* calls. It was Grandma's favorite, Cauliflower Tail. The panda swiped it with a paw. Cauliflower Tail fell to the ground, flapping its wings. The panda clutched its neck and swung it from side to side. Cauliflower Tail spread her wings weakly. The panda started to devour her, tearing apart her flesh with a ripping sound.

Should Bao wake up Grandpa? He kept a gun in the tool shed, and she was afraid he might hurt the pandas. Grandma would be upset that Cauliflower Tail was dead. Bao hadn't stopped the killing when she had a chance. Now she wanted the panda to eat Cauliflower Tail. After all, the panda was a national treasure, and what better use was a dead hen than to satisfy a panda's hunger?

Grandpa huffed and puffed in his sleep like a locomotive. When Bao peered outside again, the panda sat against the coop fence. Nestling against her chest, the cub appeared to be nursing.

"Are you up, Bao?" Grandma said.

Grandpa's snoring paused and then resumed, rhythmic and loud as usual.

"I got up to pee," Bao whispered.

The panda propped herself up and bit the neck skin of her cub. She moved quickly out of the yard and headed into the woods. Wagging her fat tail, she broke into a trot. In front of the chicken coop there were bloodstains and feathers but no bones or flesh of the hen.

"A weasel got Cauliflower Tail, Grandma." Bao pulled out the stool. The door swung shut and kept the wind out.

Grandma fastened the frog closures of her cotton coat. "Did it leave us the dead hen?"

"There's just blood and feathers left."

"What a year, even weasels are getting meaner." Grandma

grabbed a long-handled broom. "We have to get a dog to guard the coop." She opened the door and went outside, holding up the broomstick, ready to beat any weasels to a pulp.

Bao peered at the mountain slope in the distance. Black stones protruded from the snow-covered slope. It would be hard to spot a black-and-white panda. Besides, Grandma's eyes were poor; she had ruined them by embroidering night after night in the dim light of an oil lamp.

Even then, Bao felt touched by fate that she, rather than anyone else, had seen the pandas and saved them from harm. She breathed the cold mountain air on that almost unreal, yet vivid winter morning. Snow and icicles hung on boughs and logs. When a riffle of wind stirred the branches, the snow drifted down in crystal veils, adding a ghostly radiance to the forest. One of these days, she would hike into the woods and find the pandas, safe and sound.

"The damned thing has big paws like a bear!" Grandma said. "Next time it steals our hen, your grandpa will shoot it!"

Bao was glad she had lied. If people knew that a giant panda ate chicken, would it still be revered as the national treasure? Starvation drove pandas wild, as famine did humans. People in other parts of Sichuan ate bark, rats, even dead babies. If the panda hadn't gotten Cauliflower Tail, would she have attacked Bao and her grandparents? They were indebted to Cauliflower Tail. Grandma came inside and put away the broom. Bao sighed with relief. The panda mother had milk to nurse. At least her cub wouldn't become an orphan.

Bao thought of her own parents. When she visited them every summer, they always marveled at how big she'd grown and what good manners she had. For two months they had lived together as a family. Her father worked on the labor farm. Her mother stayed home and taught Bao phrases like, "East is red," "The people's commune is good," "Parents are dear, but dearer is Chairman Mao."

Of all her mother's lessons, Bao most enjoyed a song called "Finding a Friend." At night she made her parents sit on stools, while she leapt about and sang in turn, *"I'm looking for a friend, a good friend."* She clapped her hands to get their attention. *"I've looked everywhere. Finally I find a little friend."* She tapped her feet. Her father looked interested, although he had heard the song before. *"I take a bow and smile at her. We shake hands and become friends."* She clasped her father's hand and her mother's, too. *"Now you're my good friend."* When the three of them had their arms around each other, she could then stop missing her grandparents.

On that desolate winter morning when she was five years old, Bao made up her mind not to tell anyone about seeing the panda and her cub. She longed for her parents, who wouldn't be with her until next summer. Now that Chairman Mao had died, what would happen to Bao and her family? The series of disasters in 1976 instilled a sense of doom in her young heart. To ward off her fright and keep her family safe, she decided to say a potent prayer.

"Long live Chairman Mao!" Shifting on the bed, Grandpa stopped snoring. He seemed to be listening. Bao raised her voice. "May he live to be a thousand, a million years old! May he live for all eternity!"

She pumped her fist in the air, like a little Red Guard.

Chapter 1

June 2, 1989

THE DEMOCRATIC FERVOR sweeping across college campuses brought Gu Bao ample free time, ever since the boycott of classes started. Early in May, three workers entered Tiananmen Square and hurled the eggs filled with ink at the great portrait of Mao. To students like Bao, this act of defiance was as childish as the bygone faith in the Communist Party during the Cultural Revolution. Bao could laugh at herself for having parroted "Long live Chairman Mao!" thirteen years ago. Although times had changed, many troubles remained the same. Shortly after the three men threw the eggs, students and workers caught them and handed them over to the police. No one feared that the pro-democratic movement might lapse into anarchy more than the students themselves.

Leaving the campus of Nanjing University, Bao merged into the pro-democratic procession. While she didn't shout the slogans, her lips moved to the catchphrases of anti-corruption and freedom of the press. Several bystanders bought popsicles and tea-flavored eggs for the students, but Bao shook her head. She sympathized with their cause, yet she had a different purpose. She made her way to the green canopy of the farmers' market, disengaging herself from the crowd like a wave sweeping onshore. The cool shade was a refuge from the political fervor in the streets.

Her boyfriend Tong squatted on his heels at a fish stand, his leather belt sagging around a red tank top. She tiptoed up. The olive skin of his strong neck was inviting, despite a pimple peeking out from under the hairline. She was too shy for public displays of affection. When a mosquito with striped legs landed on his nape, she brushed it off.

Tong giggled and lost his balance. "Sneaking up on me again?"

"Oh, you're ticklish. You know what that means." Dusting her hands, she was relieved not to have drawn blood from the squashed mosquito. "You'll be afraid of your future wife."

"I'm afraid of you now." He kissed her cheek.

She lowered her head as if she hadn't heard him. Last night they had sat side by side in the red pavilion, watching the wind-rippled lake in the dim moonlight. A security guard had patrolled the area with a flashlight but failed to discover any lewd behavior. After the guard left, Tong had put his arm around her waist without turning his face.

"Are you afraid of me, of what I can do to you?" he had said.

She held her breath until her mind turned blank, and her throat tickled. "Are *you*?" She squeezed his hand.

As if by chance they met each other's eyes. The twinkle in

his eyes told her that he had noticed the heat rising in her cheeks.

Two weeks ago, Tong had slid his tongue into her mouth. Bao had been too mortified to even look at him. This seemed to excite him, for he had kissed her until her lips felt puffy and her chest swelled with strange warmth. After Tong left, she had cried in her bed for a bewilderingly long time. Like her seven roommates, none of whom had a real boyfriend, she believed a girl should only kiss the man she would marry. Then she had relived every single one of the kisses.

Tong wasn't wearing his uniform shirt today. The tan line on his forehead was the only telltale sign that he was an officer, trained at Nanjing Army Commander College. He stood out in the crowd with his straight-backed stance. Unlike some pretty university boys, Tong didn't have a peaches and cream complexion. His face was lean, his cheeks slightly shadowed. He was a two-shaves-a-day man with deep-set eyes. Four years older than Bao, he had an air of ease and confidence.

The poised man in the daylight could become a fervent boyfriend at night. Tong adored her body; to him, every inch of her skin seemed to hold some significance. A week ago he had inserted his fingers into her bra, her underpants, and the soft folds of her skin in all the unspeakable places. Bao had a supreme fear that one night she might lose her virginity to Tong.

Her parents would never forgive her if she did. She would have to hide her secret like a crime.

While a peddler gutted and scaled a fish on a block of cutting board, she wrinkled her nose at the raw odor. Inside a large basin, a dozen grass carp slithered in shallow water as if playing hide and seek. Tong pointed to a medium-sized carp. Its chubby, dark olive body was torpedo shaped with a slim white belly, so it wasn't a female carrying a cluster of roes.

"It tastes good steamed," he said.

"Carp has too many fine bones." She preferred the firmer flesh of saltwater fish. "At 2.3 yuan you could buy a big Belt fish."

"Belt fish is sold dead."

"What do you expect? Ocean fish can't survive in a tub of water."

"Naturally." Tong gave in to her suggestion and turned to look for a better deal.

They ambled down the aisle between the grocery stands. Bao's eyes darted here and there, never resting long enough on one stand to attract a peddler's hopeful gaze. Lily, her best friend, had said that Bao had the quick graceful walk of a dancer. Bao was merely being impatient. She wore short hair that rarely needed brushing and one-piece dress that required no accessories, so she could be the last person to get out of the bed and still be the first to leave the dorm in the morning. Bao was not a lazy person, however. She would never be silent when she could speak. She'd never turn away when she could help, and she would never walk when she could run. She was so prone to trust people that her father was fond of saying Bao had led a sheltered life.

Her white badge printed with red calligraphy, Nanjing University, attracted some admiring gazes. Lately the student-led demonstrations had dominated the news. People often associated the students with political purpose bordering on martyrdom. As an eighteen-year-old law student, Bao had no intention of becoming a martyr. She was preoccupied with her handsome boyfriend as well as her plan to receive an activist from Beijing. Lily said Hongzhi, who was coming to visit, had survived the hunger strike staged in Tiananmen Square.

Tong squatted down in front of a pigeon cage. The birds cooed and pecked at the grain that he tossed. "Would you like to try something new tonight?" He looked up with a smile.

She sighed. "Who has the patience to pluck feathers?"

He put two fingers into the cage to feel their plumpness. "It might be worth the trouble."

"Hongzhi isn't that kind of friend." She dragged him up by the hand. "He's not Lily's boyfriend."

"Let's take him to a restaurant."

"Not that kind of friend."

"How about the university canteen?" Before she could reply, he drawled, "Not that kind of friend. Is he even a friend?"

"Lily was so worried when he joined the hunger strike." Bao had seen a thousand secret emotions flit over her best friend's face, when she spoke of Hongzhi. "They grew up together, like a brother and sister."

Tong patted the back of his head with a bemused smile and then pulled her to a vegetable stand. "Lotus root stuffed with pork." He pointed to its flue-shaped holes. "We can steam it, mmmm, crunchy and rich."

"That's bland." She loosened his hand. "My grandparents in Sichuan make the best spicy tofu jelly."

"Can you make it?"

She shook her head. "Grandma grinds soybeans in a hand mill. Who has time for that?"

He slid an arm around her waist. "Why, you have better things to do?"

She nestled up to him and brushed her lips against his stubbly cheek. Peering over his shoulder, she glimpsed a slim figure at the fruit stand. The woman perused the strawberries, her face shaded by a broad-brimmed sunhat printed with peonies. Bao recognized her by the faux Coach handbag. It was Miss Tan, the political counselor in her department. She was a colleague of Bao's father. Professor Gu was as proud as any father of an only daughter was entitled to be. Being a man of law, he could go on for days citing a mountain of evidence why no man would be good enough for Bao. If he knew Bao was dating a soldier, he would forgo his dignity and have a conniption.

Bao pulled away. "Look out, my political counselor." She flanked a scale with a bloody tray, huge slabs of ribcages, haunches, whole pig and goat heads hung on iron hooks, and hid beside the meat stand.

Miss Tan often described herself as a mother hen, who protected her brood of chickens from bad influences. Bao remembered a game, the hawk and chickens, which she had played in elementary school. Children lined up as chickens, each of whom grasped the shirt of the person in front with both hands to form a queue behind the hen. The hawk dashed and swerved in order to capture a chick, while the hen stretched out her wings to protect her brood.

Miss Tan treated someone like Tong as a predator. Because dating was prohibited on campus, she could give Bao a disciplinary warning for her "indiscreet behavior." Anyone engaged in sexual activities would be condemned and expelled to prevent others from following their example. Good students were supposed to devote their lives to socialist causes rather than indulge in illicit pleasures. Miss Tan's reprimands in Bao's permanent file would ruin her reputation. The longer Bao had waited, the harder it had become for her to disclose her relationship to her parents. They would be devastated that Bao had put on a good girl façade merely to deceive them.

"She's leaving," Tong said.

Walking away, Miss Tan bit into a large strawberry and sucked the juice from it. The hawk had failed to grab a chicken with her talons! If Bao ever became the principal, she would round up the political counselors to teach them some real skills. If they refused, she would assign them janitor jobs or fire them on the spot.

"Good riddance." Bao left the meat stand and dusted her ivory dress. Fortunately there wasn't a stain.

Tong talked with a peddler selling cigarettes and liquor from crates attached to his motorcycle. Tong didn't smoke but enjoyed a drink now and then. He wanted to exchange his cigarette ration tickets for a bottle of wine. This was illegal, but everyone did it in the absence of police. Tong laughed loudly as their bargain grew serious. Bao watched him pore over the wine labels. When she graduated from the university in three years, they could get married. She would get up in the morning to buy groceries and haggle for every penny. If she went home and bragged about the deals she'd gotten, would he praise her for being a clever homemaker? She smiled to herself.

"Do you care for eels, Little Sister? All caught this morning."

A woman held up a fierce-looking eel, and Bao stepped back. Her husband picked out a live eel from a basin, knocked its head on a wooden board, then laid its soft body down, held its head tightly, and sliced a knife through its body three times, throwing away guts, bones, and head in one piece.

"Only 1.30 yuan a pound," the woman said.

Bao stepped back and bumped into something soft. She turned around and saw a boy squatting, his bare bottom showing through his open-slit training pants. He couldn't be more than two years old.

"Excuse me, sir." She patted his downy hair. "I should've watched where I was going."

The boy remained still with his face buried in his lap.

She knelt on one knee. "I said I was sorry."

The boy raised his head, his nose bright red, his face stained with tears and snot.

"Where is your mama?"

His mouth opened wide, as he broke into a silent cry. His small body shook with the effort to control his sobs. Bao felt her own eyes well up. She had to look away in order to think about what to do.

"Is your mama in the market?"

Sniffling, he nibbled at his thumbnail.

"I'll help you find her." She took hold of his wet hand.

"Can you tell me what she looks like?"

He pulled away, his small eyes widening with fear. He turned and ran into a narrow aisle, squatted in front of a metal fence and wept quietly. City children didn't wear open-slit training pants anymore. Bao wished she could win the trust of this bright country boy. He was right not to talk to a stranger.

She approached the eel peddlers. "Did you lose a child?"

The man didn't seem to hear her. He rinsed long slices of eel flesh in a basin of bloody water and piled them neatly.

The woman laughed. "My daughter is almost as tall as you."

"Do you know of someone who might've lost a child?"

"Boy or girl?" The woman ran her tongue over gapped front teeth.

"Why do you ask?" Bao folded her arms on her chest.

"If it's a boy, they'll return for sure."

Bao had heard that some parents abandoned their daughters in crowded market places, and that traffickers stole little boys to sell to people who wanted sons. This had become an epidemic, after the one-child policy was enforced across China. She turned away and stomped off. Tong had bought a bottle of wine. She asked him to keep an eye on the boy but not to approach him, in case he should take off running again.

"What if you don't find his parents?" Tong said.

"I will."

"Don't worry. We can take him to the police station."

"I will find his mama." Bao was angry at his pessimism.

Tong walked to the other side of the metal fence. He dropped a piece of White Rabbit toffee in front of the boy, who failed to see it.

Bao walked through the market looking for his parents. Most peasants had children early, so his parents should be young. There should be some level of family resemblance. His parents were likely to be busy; otherwise, they would've noticed that their son had wandered off.

"Don't miss a good deal." A peddler thrust a basin of pig feet in front of Bao. "Stewed pig's trotters nourish your skin. We give a discount if you buy more than one."

Bao waved away the flies. "I'm looking for the parents of a two-year-old boy."

"Where is the boy?"

The glint of interest in the peddler's bloodshot eyes gave her pause. Bao would rather take the boy to the police station than risk his safety. Tong had a point, after all. She walked away and came upon a large crowd. People formed a circle and were shouting in excited voices. At first she couldn't tell what was being sold. A billboard propped against the fence read, "The Latest Breed from Nanjing Agricultural University," with pictures of a lemon chick nestling against a mottled hen and a basket of eggs in varied shades of brown and pink.

"Pullets will lay eggs in four to five months, at least 280 eggs a year!" A man's voice grew hoarse as it raised an octave. "Guaranteed!"

When an old woman left with her basket, Bao managed to push into the crowd. People hovered over three cages of pullets and made their selections. A man collected money, counted change, and zipped up the black pouch tied to his waist.

"Will they go broody?" A woman reached into the cage to

touch a hen's breast.

"They're not setting hens. That's been bred out to make them lay more eggs." A peddler woman wore an orange apron and blue over-sleeves outside her green shirt. Her hair was pulled back into a bun. "Don't worry yourself. You can get a regular hen to sit on a clutch." A silver tooth gleamed in her mouth when she spoke.

Bao studied her almond-shaped face, a little sallow but endowed with finely chiseled features. She didn't look like the boy with the meaty slits for eyes. Besides, she was middle-aged. A girl about twelve years old helped with hen selections and weighed them for the buyers. She hooked a hen, its feet bound in tight ropes, to hang upside down on a steelyard. When her father nudged the weight on the scale, the hen flapped its wings and made the weight slip off.

"3.2 pounds." He marked the steelyard with a blackened thumbnail.

"Take your pinky off the scale!" A woman picked up the weight and thrust it toward him. "It was 2.8 pounds before you tipped it. You're setting a bad example for your daughter."

"Now auntie, be reasonable," the peddler woman said. "It's hard to do business with city folks, even without dragging our children into this." She glanced at her daughter and then looked again, blinking in bewilderment. While the girl sipped from a green canteen, the woman strode over to clutch her thin arm. "Where's your brother?"

"He went to pee—"

"Why didn't you go with him?" Her face turned red. "How long has he been gone?"

The girl squirmed but couldn't free her arm.

"How old is your son?" Bao asked.

The woman spun around on her heels. Suspicion and fear twisted her face into the startled features of the boy Bao had seen minutes ago. There was almost no need for further identification, but Bao wanted to be thorough, in part to reassure the woman of her good intention.

"Two years old?" Bao said. "Three?"

"Two and four months."

"What's he wearing?"

The woman stared at the school badge on Bao's chest and seemed to find some comfort. "A yellow shirt and open-slit training pants."

"Follow me."

The peddler woman half skipped and ran alongside Bao, looking in every direction and checking under the grocery stands. She veered off to look in the garbage dump and behind the meat stand. When Bao pointed her finger, the woman let out a screech and moved sideways into the gap between the narrow aisles. She threw her arms around the boy to pick him up.

"Mama, Mama." He patted her face with his palm.

"How you frightened me!" She kissed his head and neck. "Why did you wander off like that? There're bad, greedy people out there—"

"He was a good boy and super smart. In fact, he didn't even say a word to me." Bao tapped his pug nose. "That's right, mister. You shouldn't trust anyone but your own family. Stay close to your mother, and don't let her out of your sight."

"Thank God you met the young miss. We owe you a debt of kindness. Do you want an egg-laying hen?" She saw Tong stand beside Bao. "Two hens?"

"Here is what I want." Bao poked the boy's cheek with her pinky. "Give me a smile." He turned to look the other way. When she leapt to meet his eyes, the surprised boy burst into a fit of giggles. "There, that's enough thanks for me."

"You're our savior." The woman wiped her tears on the boy's shoulder. "We can write a thank-you letter to your school."

Bao took out a piece of White Rabbit toffee from her pocket. "You had a good scare and deserve a treat." When the boy reached out his hand, she pulled away abruptly. "Was your mama even more scared? Should you give this to her?" She put the candy in his hand. The boy blinked his eyes, as if looking at a puzzle.

"Sweetie, it's yours. Mama is happy, now you're back."

Bao took hold of Tong's hand. "We have to go. Take care of your boy."

"May you two be blessed with a fat baby boy!"

Bao walked a few steps, then looked at Tong and grinned. Obviously the peddler woman had mistaken her for a teacher, who could get married and have a child.

"I'd prefer a girl who looks like you." Tong kissed her cheek. "My nameless heroine."

Bao nestled up to him. She hadn't just come here to buy groceries, but rather, she had been meant to meet the little boy. If she admitted that she believed in fate, Tong might laugh at her for being superstitious. From the moment she had set foot in the market, slowly but surely, innocent of her purpose, she was walking toward a boy who was in need of her help. How thrilling life was if you could rise to the challenge!

Tong returned to the fish stand and looked in the basin. A stout carp floated with its belly up. He flipped open the gill cover to check its bloody red gill.

"How much is the dead fish?" he asked.

"Sir, you've looked through the market more than once. Don't I have the freshest carp? Only one is about to die. The young lady did a fine thing for the boy. Let's make a deal: for you nice folks, 1.5 yuan a pound."

"That's fair." Tong picked up the carp from the murky water and tossed it into the tray.

The peddler weighed it. "2.8 yuan. Do you want to have it cleaned?"

"Gut and scale it, but don't cut off the fins. Be careful not to break the gall bladder, or the flesh will taste bitter." Tong smiled at her. "The carp is practically alive."

Bao turned away when the peddler thrust a knife into the fish. Tong was right that live carp would make a nourishing dish. Her search was finally over, now that her heart was content to have reunited a family.

Tong held the fish in his hand, its belly slid open to expose the fatty white flesh. Blood seeped into its eyes and pooled in the slightly sunken sockets. Then its head twitched, its mouth opening and closing.

"It's alive!" she said.

"No, it's just muscle spasm." Tong raised it to have a better look. Its tail thrashed weakly, while blood dripped from its mouth. "Does it get fresher than this?"

Bao put her hand in the crook of his arm. "Hongzhi is in for a treat." She squinted in the warm sunshine as they left the shade of the farmers' market.

Chapter 2

COOKING IN THE DORM at Nanjing University was prohibited. Two months earlier Bao and her roommates had been fined for blowing a fuse. Lily, being the most literary among them, had written a self-critique on their behalf. After splitting the cost of the fine, they were pleased with the deal. For seventy cents per person, they could cook hot noodles and boil eggs after the canteen was closed. There was no shame in "stealing electricity," although it would have been nice not to be caught.

Nowadays it was safe to cook. Less than a third of students were still in the dorm, while the rest had joined the 'empty-campus' movement in defiance of the official warnings to stay put. Many students had gone home, and some were visiting their friends in other provinces. Hongzhi had taken a twenty-hour train ride from Beijing, so Lily was flustered about his visit.

Among her seven roommates Bao found in Lily a kindred spirit. They both had chosen to major in law, unlike those who had ended up in the law school after they had failed to win entry to the English department. Lily had a square face that looked masculine at first glance, but Bao could read the softness in her slightly protruding eyes and tiny red mouth. Lily was so sensitive that she had nightmares after seeing children beg in the streets. She was also a good student who respected all her teachers, including Miss Tan.

Lily bought meatballs, tofu, and vegetable dishes from the canteen. Bao took out the hot plate from under the bed to cook the carp.

Tong poured peanut oil in the pot, turned on the hot plate, and added slices of ginger. When he sent the chunks of carp into the hot oil, the fish skin sizzled with the delicious smell of ginger and flesh. The fish turned opaque and juice seeped out. The sizzling grew louder as he turned the pieces over. Finally he smothered it with a few bowls of water and added cooking wine, salt, and pepper.

Who knew her boyfriend cooked like a master chef? Bao loved it when Tong surprised her. After the water boiled, she sprinkled on green scallions and lowered the heat to simmer.

Lily was right that her friend needed nourishment. Hongzhi was thin with a prominent Adam's apple and a smooth, hairless face. One side of his face was darker than the other. He'd taken part in the hunger strike for three days, sleeping in Tiananmen Square.

With a good camera in his hands, conveniently.

Bao scrutinized the photos that Hongzhi had taken in Beijing. One became her favorite. In the upper right corner, a military helicopter was suspended in the misty air. The white statue of the Goddess of Democracy stood against the dawning sky tinted with a rosy hue. She clasped her torch in both hands and thrust it forward, as if she was ready to free a dove.

"How beautiful she is." Bao looked up with a sigh.

"I shot it with a wide-lens. The helicopter is a little warped because it's on the edge of the photo," Hongzhi said, pushing up his wide-frame glasses.

"What an amazing photo." She tilted her head with a smile. "May I have it for a keepsake?"

Hongzhi scratched his head, his brow furrowed.

"You can print more with the negative." Her cheek muscle tensed as she kept smiling.

"I bribed the clerk to get these printed, you know."

Did he have to hoard a subversive photo? The good stuff should be shared amongst friends. After all, Bao had gone to great lengths to treat Hongzhi to a nice meal. She would have called him stingy if he weren't a guest.

Tong opened the lid to check on the broth, which had thickened into milky white chowder. He shut off the hot plate and set the enamel pot on the large desk, flanked by the bunk beds, two on each side. The aroma of carp soup filled the dorm's eight by six meter dimensions.

Tong opened a bottle of white wine. "Made from Xinjiang grapes, the best on the black market." He poured wine into the enamel mugs printed with Nanjing University logos.

"A toast to our chef." Hongzhi raised his mug.

Tong grinned like a child, a little sheepish, as if he couldn't contain his happiness. "To our friends." He clinked everyone's mug in turn.

Bao gulped down the wine, ripe and mellow, which went

straight to her head.

"Are we ready?" Lily lifted the lid from the enamel pot.

Hot steam fogged up Hongzhi's glasses. Lily scooped soup in his bowl and dug in for some fish.

"So, Hongzhi," Tong said. "How was your hunger strike?"

Hongzhi picked up the fish head with his chopsticks, poked out the juicy eyes, and ate them with relish. Bao had heard that eating fish eyes would improve your eyesight, but Hongzhi was the only one wearing glasses at the table.

"Some people deceived the public," Hongzhi said. "They ate and drank as if the strike were only for show."

Tong drank a little soup but didn't touch the fish. "Corruption is the rule, not the exception."

Hongzhi glared at Tong, but Bao wasn't worried. It was good that Hongzhi saw a different perspective. He was a smart guy and might enjoy a good argument.

"There has to be a better way," she said. "Look at the sea of people in Tiananmen Square, as if we're all one, we have one voice, but we're not."

Lily worked on the fish tail, meticulously picking out fine bones from the meat. Bao ate a chunk of fish belly, where the bones were fewest, then tore off the fin from the fatty meat.

"Look, there're four of us here," Bao said. "We each have our own way to eat the fish. It even tastes different to our palates. Isn't it absurd that we should march into the streets shouting the same slogans every day until we don't even know what they mean anymore?"

Hongzhi had disassembled the fish head into a neat pile of bones. He sucked his wet fingers, a habit that Bao found unhygienic.

"The slogans are meant to inspire people," Hongzhi said. "Freedom of the press is a basic human right. Why should we, a quarter of the population on earth, be denied it?"

"I'm on your side, you know I am." Bao fixed her eyes upon his face. "We want to end corruption, but do we even know how it came about? Even some student hunger strikers have become opportunists. If we can't get to the root of the problem, what's the use of shouting?"

"She's a cold hard pragmatist." Lily raised her mug of wine toward Bao.

"We major in law." Bao reached across the table to pat Lily's hand. "The more books we read, the more they all sound the same. It takes a lot of legwork to get real work done. If we insist on talking about big, abstract ideas, nothing gets done. They can simply say it's already done, go read the constitution. Don't we have all rights?"

Hongzhi filled his bowl with the soup and soaked spoonfuls of cold rice in it. "What do you think can be done about it?"

"Work on something small and concrete." She drained her wine and put the mug down with a flourish. "Even a small thing can change society."

"For example?" Tong squeezed her hand.

"There're plenty, if students just focus on campus life. Why do we need political counselors? They could be reeducated and become psychiatrists. What about Socialism with Chinese Characteristics courses? I bet ten years later, the student will ask: you studied what? Do we need that kind of brainwashing, anyone?"

"But it's close enough to . . ." Hongzhi pressed a fist against his mouth to muffle a cough. "The law."

"It's not. Turning law into politics is tragic." Bao bounced a little in her seat. "It should be outlawed! It's illegal."

Hongzhi coughed harder and louder, his face turning crimson. "Is there a fishbone in your throat?" Lily said. Hongzhi nodded helplessly. "Swallow this." She picked up a morsel of rice with her chopsticks. As soon as he ate it, his face relaxed a bit. Lily let out the breath she'd been holding.

Hongzhi cleared his throat and then resumed coughing. "Still there."

Bao had heard that vinegar could soften fishbone, but they didn't have any.

"Try this." Tong cut a meatball in half with his chopsticks. "Don't chew."

Hongzhi swallowed so hard his Adam's apple bobbed. Finally he stopped coughing, and his puckered forehead smoothed out.

"Thank you, brother." He wiped tears from his eyes.

"No worries." Tong put his arm around Bao's back. "Stop attacking your guest. Are you a pit bull or a hostess?"

"Actually she's an optimist. She believes in reform, while a lot of us want a new government. How many more dynasties will pass before we can have a democratic government? Don't we deserve freedom like the rest of the world?" Hongzhi ploughed his chopsticks through the rice to check for fishbones. "Funny I should say this, Bao, but you make me feel old."

Bao stuck her tongue out at Tong. She blushed when Lily stared at them. Hongzhi wasn't a target for an ideological tussle. She owed it to Lily to make him feel welcome.

Hongzhi put down his chopsticks. "I was on a hunger strike, lying on the cold cement ground covered by newspaper. Then my roommate brought me a letter—a scholarship from MIT."

"*The* MIT?" Bao said.

Hongzhi nodded. "I started eating porridge and a pork bun. I realized—to die is human, to leave divine."

Bao stared at his speckled face, hair hanging over his brow. His darker cheek looked a bit older than the lighter one. Hongzhi must be a genius in a million, although he looked like a high school graduate. Why had he let her go on as if she had something important to say? He could laugh at her all the way to the States.

She turned toward Lily. "Will you miss him?"

A coy smile lit her broad face, and Lily looked very feminine. "We're just friends."

Bao wasn't surprised. Lily usually guarded affairs of the heart like a miser banking money. The longer it stayed in the vault, the more interest it would generate.

"Congrats, man." Tong replenished Hongzhi's mug with wine. "You can promise your girl a good life."

"I'm taking the train back to Beijing tonight. I want to check on my passport application." Hongzhi gazed upon Lily's face. "Will you come with me? Tomorrow we'll be home."

Lily closed the curtains to keep the sun off the leftover rice. "But Miss Tan asked us to stay, or we'll be penalized for missing classes."

They hadn't gone to class since the citywide boycott in early May. Still, the political counselor spoke for government policies. Everyone at the table fell silent. The buzzing of a fly was startlingly loud. Bao waved it away. It flew up and circled their heads. Tong tried to swat it with a book, but the fly was quicker than he. Finally they had to ignore it.

"Thank you for a scrumptious dinner. I enjoyed losing the debate to my hostess." Hongzhi dug into his duffle bag to retrieve a photo. "This is for you, Gu Bao."

The Goddess of Democracy! Bao was speechless. Had she made such an ass of herself that her guest gave in to her greed?

"I'll smuggle the negatives to the States and print them there." Hongzhi's tea-colored lenses darkened with the afternoon sunlight slanting into the room. "You deserve to have her."

"I'll take good care of her." Bao leaned forward to shake his hand. "You're a prince."

Hongzhi sat up, squared his shoulders, and made a victory sign with two fingers. Bao laughed and gulped down the wine. A gentle warmth in her belly spread to her chest and face. She hadn't meant to bully Hongzhi into submission, although she enjoyed the Goddess picture even more after their debate. Outside someone dribbled a basketball in the courtyard, crickets chirped in the weeds, and frogs croaked in the nearby pond. In this balmy afternoon sitting with her friends, Bao felt so hopeful she couldn't possibly want anything else in life.

After seeing the guests off and doing the dishes, Bao took a long bath and washed her clothes. She put out the pink saucer-shaped hanger to dry her underwear outside the windows. There were fluffy clouds in the night sky, not a star twinkling. The faint music from the dance hall beckoned to her. It was 9:28 p.m. In two minutes the door guard would let in two people for the price of one, so Lily and she could enjoy the last half-hour of the dance for a bargain price.

"Should we go dancing?" Bao asked.

Lily put down her book, *Madam Curie's Biography*. "Will his train be on time?"

"You miss Hongzhi already." Bao patted her wrist. "Let's go have some fun."

"I know who you're expecting, a certain Ph.D. student." Lily pulled her hand away and picked up the book again.

Bao remembered a baby face framed by curly hair. The Ph.D. student in economics was about her height but carried himself like a large man.

"He's a good dancer, that's all."

"I wasn't blind. Your Ph.D. beau was spellbound by your charms."

Lily wouldn't tease Bao about a dance partner if she knew that Tong had put his tongue in Bao's mouth. Once you became intimate with a man, you didn't look at others with much interest. "Yes, we had fun dancing. He's very intelligent and funny, but it's platonic."

"I won't tell the company commander."

Light wind blew drizzling rain through the open windows. Many rooms in the opposite male dorm didn't have curtains. For weeks, students had donated bedsheets and curtains to make banners. Women gave their bedsheets, while men were happy to part with their curtains. Now their rooms were in plain view. On every floor there were bare-chested men in their boxer shorts. One man sat with his legs dangling from the upper bunk. Another stood and scratched his back with a bamboo claw. None looked like the Ph.D. student.

"Fine, if you don't want to go." Bao retrieved the hanger to place inside her mosquito net. "It's raining."

Lily wet her finger and flipped a page.

"Why didn't you go home with Hongzhi?"

"Miss Tan—"

"Don't use her as an excuse. Six of our roommates have gone home. None of them will be expelled."

"Who says Hongzhi is interested in me?"

Bao put her feet up on a stool. "I saw the way he looked at you."

"He's going to MIT. What have I done for myself? I'm only a freshman. My major is useless in the US. What will I do there?"

"You don't have to be the breadwinner." Bao winked. "A man only needs a pretty wife."

"I'm not so pretty."

"Enough already." Bao grabbed her book and tossed it onto the upper bunk diagonal from Lily's bed. "Why do you build so many obstacles for yourself?"

Lily peered at her book in the bed, with its pages upright. "Do you remember that night your Ph.D. beau took my bicycle?"

"He wasn't my beau."

It had happened one rainy night a month ago. Bao had danced most of the night with the Ph.D. student, who was deft at leading her. Their hips touched as their feet moved in time with the haunting music. She leaned against his chest and felt his starched dress shirt. His eyes, large and almost watery, shone with an innocence that moved her beyond words. She recognized loneliness in his proud face. After the dance, he wanted to talk with Bao. When Lily arrived on her bicycle, he told her to leave. Much to Bao's relief, Lily refused. She got off her bike and stood her ground.

The Ph.D. student didn't talk to Lily. Instead, he grabbed the bicycle and offered to give Bao a ride. When she refused, he rode away, forgetting that it was Lily's bicycle.

"What a lovesick fool, and a robber to boot! I had to chase after my own bike by jumping onto the back rack. Then he said so many rude things to me." Lily screwed up her eyes and pursed her mouth. "Why are *you* on the bicycle? You think you're so pretty? You're such a catch that I want to take you home?" She pulled a long face. "I was going to slap him, but instead I said, 'This is my goddamn bike!'"

Bao burst into laughter. She was prettier than Lily, and she was flirtier, so she'd gotten herself into a little situation. She owed Lily a favor.

"Forget about that jerk." Bao sat on Lily's bed and held her hand. "Hongzhi is smitten with you. You are the goddess in his eyes."

"What makes you an expert on men?"

"I'm not, but you grew up with him. Don't you know him best? Now be honest, he's more than a friend." Bao brushed the hair back from Lily's forehead. "You must have a ton of memories. You're so *pretty*, Lily. Do you know that? In Hongzhi's eyes, you look like Helena Bonham Carter, but younger and prettier."

Lily bit her lip and stared at the ceiling. Her eyes enormous, she looked like a little girl coveting an expensive doll in a shop window. She sighed, then got up and removed a few books, a photo album, and a sandalwood fan from her bed. She began to pack her travel bag.

"Are you leaving?" Bao said.

"I have a long trip tomorrow."

"Way to go, lover girl! Don't disappoint Hongzhi, after he took an overnight trip just to see you."

"If Miss Tan asks about me, tell her that I can't stay any longer. When martial law tightens up, I won't be able to get home."

"Don't worry about Miss Tan. If Hongzhi will leave in August, you need to marry him."

"Very funny."

"Why not? Do your future in-laws object to you? What?"

Lily put her clothes inside the duffle bag and zipped it up. "He wants to have three children in the States."

How sly Lily was to pretend that Hongzhi was just a friend after they had talked about having children! Despite his political views, Hongzhi had the old-fashioned values about the family. Bao should warn Lily about the dangers of marrying into a patriarchal family.

"Have mercy!" She reached out to pat Lily's flat belly. "You'll be stretched out like a sack!"

Lily beat away her hand. "Having three children is scientifically sound—this way the population can sustain itself."

"But is it fair to you? I mean, you'll have three times the housework, sleepless nights, and the pain." Bao had only heard about the birth pangs, and it made her shudder. "What does he have to do? It's so easy to be a father. Will you go abroad to suffer the bondage of our grandmothers?"

"Isn't it a woman's right to have children?"

"It's also a burden. You know, my mother is so glad about the one-child policy. She said it relieved her of the duty to bear a son."

"Don't worry about me, Miss Popularity. You'll snag a husband long before I get lucky." Lily put down the wings of the mosquito net and fastened them with two wooden clips, then changed into her jewel-necked pajamas.

Suddenly the lights were shut off. A clamor rose from the male dorm.

"Turn on the lights!"

"Down with Li Peng! Abolish martial law!"

"March immediately! March immediately!" several people yelled in unison.

Bao crawled into her bed and closed the mosquito net. "Will you become a housewife? How will you be happy then?"

"Who says he's going to marry me?"

Lily could be a prude. Bao wasn't sorry to see her go, because she would have the dorm all to herself.

Chapter 3

BAO LOOKED AT HER FACE in a cloisonné hand mirror—no makeup, no pimples, just the way Tong liked her. She brushed her hair with a buffalo horn comb and scratched her scalp with its blunt teeth. This helped her grow fuller and shinier hair, so claimed the peddler who had sold the comb for an exorbitant eight yuan. Beside the pillow, she placed a sandalwood fan, carved with wintersweet blossoms and two magpies signifying double-happiness, a symbol for newlyweds. She bent and smoothed the white bedsheet over the cotton mattress.

Inside the mosquito net she attached a photo of her and her roommates wearing olive green uniforms, while Tong stood beside the group as their company commander. During the month-long military training last year, Bao had thought she had little hope of enamoring Tong, who was in charge of training a hundred and fifty freshman girls. In the canteen, Tong had usually sat beside some pretty girls, eaten and laughed with them. The ones Bao hated the most were the tall girls from the English department and the flirty girls from the Chinese department.

The first time she was alone with Tong was in the

infirmary. She had felt sick and was excused from the parade-step drill. After two penicillin shots and being on an IV for a night, she woke up finding Tong by her bedside. She rubbed her sore eyes in disbelief.

"How are you feeling?" His face was creased with worry.

"My head's stopped aching."

"Don't get up." He pulled his chair closer. "I can hear you."

She wondered how long he had been watching her, and why he wasn't tending to the company's drills. Then she remembered it was Sunday. How wretched she was to get sick on the only day she was free! She felt homesick and missed her parents.

"You're a national treasure."

"What?"

"Your name, Gu Bao, sounds like national treasure."

"No one's ever said that before."

He looked flattered, as if Bao had handed him an unexpected gift. "The name suits you, because university students are our national treasures."

What a cliché! Granted, only four percent of high school graduates were admitted into universities each year. Students were educated with the guarantee of future jobs, so female students were not short of admirers. Still, the compliment made Bao uneasy.

"You're giving me goose bumps." She tossed him another cliché. "I'll have to call you 'the most lovable man.'"

Tong blushed like a peony. "I hope you mean it." He stood up and left.

The nurse came to give Bao a shot. Lying on her belly with her pants down, Bao thought of the handsome company commander. In high school she had listened to reports by veterans of the Vietnam War; they all spoke of the heartbreak of losing young comrades and glorified the cause of defending China's border from Vietnamese invaders. A book of war stories titled *Who Is the Most Lovable?* was widely quoted. For years the People's Liberation Army had been called "the most lovable."

After the military training Bao grew restless and lost weight. Tong would receive disciplinary punishment and even lose his job, if he asked her out. She had to take the matter into her own hands. Finally she wrote Tong, "The weather is cooling down, but my heart begins to warm up to you." When he stood before her panting from having ridden twenty kilometers on a bicycle, she was surprised that the pretty girls in English department hadn't snared him. For seven months she had seen Tong mostly on Sundays. Thanks to the citywide class boycott that left the campus increasingly vacant, they'd grown intimate with each other in the last few weeks. Now for the first time she had the room all to herself. Looking at her roommates' empty beds, Bao was afraid to imagine what could happen tonight.

Hearing a familiar knock on the door, she tentatively opened it. Tong entered and closed the door. She couldn't meet his gaze. Her heart beat a little faster, and her cheeks felt warm.

"Have you heard?" he said. "An emergency announcement

warned Beijing citizens to stay off the streets."

"Again?" She sat on the bed and crossed her legs.

"This one is serious." He sat beside her.

"Lily went after Hongzhi. She left this morning."

"Good, they have each other. You're staying here alone now?" He moved close so their thighs touched. "Why didn't you tell me?"

"What're you going to do?"

She was surprised to hear herself laugh: provocative, unabashed. They used to steal kisses and touch each other hastily before one of her roommates burst inside. Now she didn't have to worry. The privacy excited as much as frightened her.

"I missed you." Cradling her in his arms, he sniffed her hair, cheek, ear, and neck. "You smell so good. I dreamt about you last night."

"What were we doing?"

She trembled when he slid a hand into her blouse. His hand swam downward into her underpants. Moaning, she squeezed her privates to make them shrink into a small pear. Yet, she had the unsafe feeling that her bottom spread out like an oversized pumpkin.

"You have no idea," he said, "how beautiful you are."

The wooden bed squeaked as he leapt to kneel above her. Watching his eyes, she felt naked and vulnerable, but at the same time powerful and absolutely confident about her body. He peeled off her underpants and then parted her legs wide.

"Wait." She grabbed his hand.

"Let's make love."

"But I—"

"I won't hurt you, I promise."

The word "hurt" made her head clear a little. Having sex could cause her to be expelled from the university, and she'd never set foot in the classroom again. Anyone could be an informer—including Tong, who might flaunt his conquest.

"I can't do it," she said in a clear voice.

"But I love you."

"Then . . . you'll wait for us to get married." The pain in his eyes brought her remorse. What hypocrisy! She loved Tong, and she trusted him come hell or high water . . . didn't she?

Something touched her thigh, and she looked down. It was his thing. She hadn't noticed when he took off his pants. His legs were hairy, his muscles pink and firm. His crotch was black with dense, curly hair. When he put her hand on his privates, she couldn't look anymore and closed her eyes.

"Rub it," he said.

She moved her hand up and down his erect penis. He kissed her gently, barely touching her lips. She opened her eyes and saw her face reflected in his pupils.

"Don't be afraid."

Could she give it—was she even allowed to lose her virginity? Her body wasn't hers alone. It also belonged to her family, the university, and many years of dedicated work, without which she wouldn't have an identity, no future to speak of, just an outlier whom Tong would have ignored rather than called her a national treasure.

"Are you safe?"

At first she didn't know what he meant. Her legs were

parted. She felt him push inside her and then slowly withdraw. The depth of penetration told her it wasn't done by fingers.

"Will I get . . ." She bit her lip. The word "pregnant" seemed petty somehow. He was inside her body, and she became his woman. Their desire for each other was stronger than their virtues. Passion had no fear, and she wanted to believe it was pure, loving, and beautiful.

He pumped away vigorously. The pain was so acute she felt dazed. Fleeting visions ran through her mind. She saw the Ph.D. student's glittering eyes and shy smile. If she'd gotten on his bicycle that night, he would have courted her with witty words and carefree laughter. Not doing this, flesh grating inside flesh. She let out a half sob.

"Does it hurt?"

Nodding, she bit her lip and sniffled.

"Just a bit longer, you're so tight and sweet."

He pushed up her blouse and undid her bra. He kissed her breast, caressing it with his tongue. Her nipple rolled around in his mouth. He licked and sucked as if to draw milk. Nobody had touched her body before. Now she felt like a goddess, a wife, and a mother, all at once. When he thrust into her again, she became open, pliant, and wet between her legs. He propped himself up on his elbows. She raised her leg to put a heel lightly on his back, her breasts jiggling as he thrust deeper. Her pain diminished into a longing for him, more of him.

"Oh." He shivered above her. "You're a dream."

She lay there, perfectly still.

Shouts sounded from the opposite dorm. "Brothers and

sisters, go to the streets and protest! There's bloodshed in Beijing!"

The cacophony was accompanied by the beating of washbasins and enamel food basins.

"Down with Fascists!"

"They're killing students! Arise, everyone, arise!"

"Bandits! Animals!"

Bao sat up. Sticky stuff flowed out of her, tainted by blood. She wiped it with her underpants and cried.

"It's okay," he said. "I'm your first."

She was too mortified to ask if he'd had other women before. "What if I get pregnant?"

"No one gets pregnant their first time. It isn't as easy as you think, honey. Now let's take a nap." He walked to the door in bare feet and shut off the lights.

The moonlight, streetlight, and light from the opposite dorm illuminated the white curtains. A boombox blasted 'The Internationale':

> *Arise ye workers from your slumbers*
> *Arise ye prisoners of want*

Glass bottles broke on the cement ground like firecrackers, punctuating the sonorous, stirring music.

What happened in Beijing? Why had she given in to temptation at such a tumultuous time? A week ago a student activist couple had gotten married in Tiananmen Square. They might've done it for publicity. Bao had given Tong the most precious gift a woman could give a man. When he returned to the bed, she let him hold her. Her eyes brimmed over with tears.

"I love you, Bao."

"You do?"

He stroked the sensitive skin on her lower back. "I'm afraid you will find out—how much I love you."

She wept quietly in his arms.

Sometime later, Bao opened her eyes with a start. The mosquito net quivered in the breeze. The lights in the opposite dorm were still on, so it must be before eleven p.m. Her head felt clearer after a nap. Her fear had vanished, and in its place, an unidentifiable anger flamed in her chest.

"What're you doing?" She grabbed Tong's hand from between her legs.

"Let's make love."

"No, never again!"

"*Never?*" He saw her face and draped his arm around her back. "All right, we'll lie here, like the dearest couple in the world."

"Let me go." He ignored her, so she pushed him. "Why didn't you use some form of protection?"

He pulled back and folded his arm under his head. "I didn't expect it to happen. When was your last period?"

"Why didn't you ask earlier?" Her voice trembled. "You couldn't wait."

"Don't cry, sweetheart. We won't do it again until I have a condom." He kissed her shoulder. "I want to stay with you tonight. I'll say I visited my friends at Hehai University, if my roommate asks."

"What if you told the truth?"

"I would be discharged from my training program. How about you?"

"I'd be expelled, and my parents would never forgive me. My teachers and classmates would think I'm a slut—"

"Hush, don't think so much." He wiped away her tears. "We won't tell anyone."

She took a deep breath. "Why did they say killing? Do you think—"

"I hope it's not true."

"But is it true?"

"What can we do?" He stroked her cheek. "I'm here with you. Would you rather we meet in the streets?"

"Hongzhi was right—it's a horrible country. I wish I could go away—"

"Leaving your home, leaving *me*?"

"Take me now, before I say no. Tomorrow I may hate you—"

He was inside her, teasing, thrusting, pounding, until her angry thoughts vanished, and in their place was a blissful oblivion, thickened into pleasure. Her hips trembling, her throat emitted a guttural sound. She seemed to grow wings and rise into fluffy clouds that tickled her between the legs. What was happening?

"Do you love me?" He collapsed beside her, sweating profusely.

She opened her eyes but was unwilling to speak.

"I can't bear it if you don't love me."

"I do." She whispered into his ear, "And I saw stars."

His eyes softened. "Congratulations, you're a woman."

She put her chin on his shoulder. "Have you done it before?"

"I was seduced by an older woman." He sighed. "I was seventeen, studying for my college entrance exams. She was thirty-five, married, with a twelve-year-old son."

Bao hadn't suspected Tong had a past. Why hadn't he told her before?

"She moved away years ago, when her husband threatened to divorce her."

Tears welled up in her eyes. Why was Tong not ashamed for what he'd done, with a married woman?

"It was a turning point in my life. Instead of focusing on my studies, I began to think about women, sex. Confused and distracted, I failed the college entrance exams."

She sneered. "You think?"

"I'm not stupid."

"Did I say you were stupid?"

"My brother went to the Second Military Medical University. We went to the same high school. My teachers expected me to go to a university at least as good as SMMU. If not for that woman . . ." He pounded the pillow. "I wish I'd never met her. I wish her husband had divorced her."

"So you joined the army."

"My father is a division commander of the Nanjing Military Region. He has influential friends in the military. It's a good place for me to be. The best part is . . ." He kissed her temple. "I met you, sweetie."

Her heart warmed at the endearment. She smiled through

her tears. "You haven't had other girlfriends, have you?"

"After I joined the army, several married women tried to seduce me. I was weak and went along with them." He ran his fingers through his hair. "I was like a dog that couldn't stand the temptation of pork buns."

"You're worse than a dog." She'd only had fleeting thoughts of the Ph.D. student when she was in bed with Tong. What could he have thought about when he brought her to cloud nine? She couldn't bear to imagine it.

"Bao, that was before I met you." His eyes were filled with contrition. "You may think I'm a dirty old man. But I can tell you sex is easy, it's cheap. Sex is nothing compared to love."

"Say whatever you want."

"You've known me for nine months. You know I wasn't just lusting after you."

"What else were you after?"

"I love your passion, your wit, your beauty, and most of all, your trust in me. I can do without sex if that's your wish."

She wrapped her leg around him. His skin, warm and salty, made her a bit drunk. Would her love grow stronger or diminish into a physical need? She touched the ribbed cotton of his tank top and felt his firm, supple muscles. She found his hand and clutched it tightly.

Bao woke up several times at night and listened to his rhythmic breathing in the dark. How could Tong sleep like a log after making love? She was afraid that the whole world would look different, when she opened her eyes tomorrow. Tong got up at dawn to catch the first bus, before students would blockade the streets. She sprawled her legs to the warm spot where he had lain. Inexplicably the morning came, just like any other day. The sun gilded the eastern wall of the male dorm. The cement ground was littered with broken glass, torn paper, worn-out shoes, and discarded food. A janitor wearing a gauze mask swept the ground with a bamboo broom.

Bao looked into her cloisonné hand mirror and saw a pasty face. Her pores were more visible, and she had dark rings under her eyes. This was a woman's face, tainted by lust. Where was that chaste girl with a peaches and cream complexion? She couldn't bear to look anymore and thrust the mirror under her pillow.

She was hungry but didn't want to go to the canteen for breakfast. She added milk powder to a mug and poured hot water, then sat down with the drink and two almond cookies. After a few bites, she heard people shouting slogans.

"Give us back our fellow students."

"Blood for blood."

"Try the murderers!"

A group of students marched through the alleyway between the two dorms. Those in front played dirges on a boom box and carried wreathes and banners that read, "Mourn the victims in Beijing," "The army proved with tanks and machine guns that they entered Beijing to repress students and the masses," "Marshal Xu and Marshal Nie, what happened to your promises?"

She couldn't read anymore. After finishing her breakfast, she went downstairs to call her parents.

"Dad? Dad, what happened?" She turned her back on the

doorwoman.

"Bao, should I come get you?"

"No, there's no need." She wouldn't go home because she had dates with Tong. "I'm fine, so don't worry."

"Promise us: Do *not* go into the streets."

"I promise." She heard him cough. Her mother had tried every means to make him quit smoking, but none lasted more than five days. "Are you okay, Dad?"

"Some said 20,000 died, some said 5,000, and some said 900." His voice was hoarse. "CCTV said about a handful of civilians, nobody died in the Square."

"Any students?"

"No. Only thugs, rioters, looters, and riffraff."

"That's what they call them." She tried to blink away tears.

"The CCTV said the People's Liberation Army was heroic, and the thugs got what they deserved. Our anchors wore black suits, and the lady was in tears. It was open defiance, since they mourned the victims despite the official verdict. Sure you don't want to come home?"

"It's only a fifteen-minute walk home. I'll come home on Friday." She cleared her throat. "Oh, what happened to the Goddess?"

"Toppled, like a piece of trash."

She hung up the phone. For a while she couldn't move. The Goddess had been a beacon of hope for the students like Hongzhi, who considered themselves revolutionists. Now that she was gone, what would happen to the young people who could have become trailblazers? The peaceful demonstrations ended in bloodshed and shameless lies to cover up the murders. She hoped Hongzhi would be able to smuggle the film to the States, so the rest of the world would know the truth.

Bao ran to her room to gaze at the photo. The Goddess's face was as young as the day, her rough plaster features blending with the rosy hue of the rising sun. She clasped her torch in both hands and held it out slightly forward to her right. Her eyes looked ahead, the flame not far from her line of vision. She was stepping forward to face the portrait of Mao Zedong on the Tiananmen Gate, as if to say, "Behold what we have been denied all these decades."

Bao ran her finger on the plastic protective sheet. She stared and stared until her vision turned into fog. Tears splattered on the pedestal adorned with fresh bouquets, two bullhorns, and university flags.

Bao changed her bedsheet. The bloodstain was pinkish brown, like a peach blossom. She wouldn't bring it home to wash. Outside, a male voice startled her.

"Are you a soldier, asshole?" someone in the opposite dorm shouted at a man downstairs. "Surrender your gun and ammo to the people."

A man in an olive green uniform stood in the courtyard. He took off his broad-brimmed hat. "Excuse me," he said with a northern country accent. "Where is Dorm Number Two?"

"Are you visiting your girlfriend?" a man on the fourth floor asked.

"My sister, actually."

"Man, that excuse is getting old," someone on the second

floor said.

"Eat shit, dumb soldier!"

Bao couldn't tell where the voice came from. The male students seemed equally surprised. They rushed to the windows.

"Let's be civil, now. I've taken a whole day's train ride to see my baby sister. Our parents are mighty worried she—"

"If bastards like you hadn't opened fire, why should you worry about her safety?" The speaker was on the second floor, a scrawny man without a shirt. He pounded the desk with a wooden T-square. As he lifted his arm, black hair flashed under his armpit. "Murderer, leave the campus!"

A bottle popped on the ground. Red ink splashed the gray sidewalk. Then newspaper and food scraps flew at the soldier. Someone threw a thermos bottle and missed the soldier by a few inches. Shards of the glass liner glittered on the cement.

Bao watched with a hand on her throat. The students were deluded to think that venting their anger on a lone soldier stood for justice. Yet, when the CCTV lied about what had happened, what else was left for the students to do? Amidst thunderous beating of enamel basins and furious table poundings, a girl appeared in the courtyard.

"Stop it!" She ran to the soldier and held his hand. "He *is* my brother."

There was an awkward silence. The girl's auburn skirt fluttered in the breeze like a butterfly's wings.

"Whose side are you on, sister?" a gruff voice said.

"I'm *not* your sister. Now listen, my brother wasn't in Beijing, and neither were you. The well water does not intrude into the river water—mind your own business."

As she turned to leave, a basin of soapy water drenched her from head to toe. "What are you, animals?"

"Get this, whore!"

A pair of worn sneakers hit her shoulder. She would've fallen had her brother not held her tightly. She wiped her face and squared her shoulders. Before she could open her mouth, her brother grabbed her arms and dragged her into the female dorm.

Tong might get a broken head if he passed under there now in his uniform. The bullies, though loud and righteous, were cowards in Bao's eyes. Being in a certain group didn't make you a good person. She had learned last night that people didn't remain whom they were. When her body was connected with Tong, she had lost a precious part of herself to share a moment of ecstasy, and thereby be imbued with the passion and spirit of a man who loved her deeply.

She shuddered as lightning ripped through the sky. A clap of thunder muted young men's cheering in the opposite dorm. She closed the windows. Raindrops splattered on the dusty glass and left muddy stains.

She hoped the demonstrators found shelter on their march.

The downpour turned into dense, mild rain, and the sky began to clear up. A shaft of sunlight penetrated the clouds. Downstairs, colorful umbrellas gathered in front of the female dorm, like mushrooms sprouting from an old tree. The clanging of spoons against enamel bowls resounded in the courtyard. It was almost lunchtime. A drenched quilt weighed down the nylon clothesline. Sycamores shook their damp leaves in the breeze like thousands of waving hands. The cherry-colored quilt dripped water that collected into a pool on the cracked cement.

In the hallway of the male dorm, Bao dropped off her bedsheet and a poncho as donations. It was the first time she donated to the students' cause. She had to show her support, now that innocent people had met their bitter end. The faint bloodstain on the sheet wasn't offensive. They could overwrite it with a brush-pen and splatter red ink for effect. Bao wouldn't join the demonstrators, but her bedsheet, which would become a banner, was a heartfelt gift.

A girl was cutting stencils. Two men printed leaflets, one of them nodding thanks to Bao. She quickened her steps toward the bathhouse, her heart pounding in her chest.

At the bathhouse entrance, Bao gave the dozing doorwoman a bath ticket. Then she undressed and put her clothes inside a locker. She walked to the shower, turned on the hot water, and twisted the cold-water knob. All around her stood naked bodies in different sizes and shapes. One girl had stout thighs and a slim waist. Her belly bulged with folds of fat. As she scrubbed behind her ears, the flesh on her upper arms flapped. When she shook water from her head, Bao turned toward the tiled wall. She didn't want to be caught staring.

"Gu Bao."

She jerked her chin up and saw Miss Tan. Naked and dry, Miss Tan turned the water knobs. The water spraying noise drowned out Bao's sigh. Couldn't she have some privacy, when she scrubbed off Tong's scent from the cleft between her legs?

"It's a good day for a shower," Bao said. "Not too many people here."

"I always come at lunch." Miss Tan closed her eyes as water splashed her face. "It's never crowded."

Bao nodded, even though Miss Tan's eyes were shut. She had never met Miss Tan in the bathhouse before, so her naked body was a revelation. Miss Tan was tall, her breasts small and far apart. Her ribcage indented her torso as she threw back her head. Her hips were wide and bony. Her legs were long, graceful cylinders that joined her body at a triangle of black hair. Undoing her braids, she cut a sensual figure with long hair rippling down her back.

"Why don't you go home?" Miss Tan said. "There's mayhem on campus."

Bao bent her arm to scrub her back. "But you told us to stay."

"Now the situation is different." Her voice dropped to a low whisper. "Some protesters were arrested for setting up blockades on the Yangtze River Bridge."

"I won't go to the protest." Bao wanted to wash her vagina but was afraid to arouse suspicion. She rocked her body back and forth in hopes of catching the warm stream in her crotch.

"Are you dating someone?" Miss Tan peered at her with half-open eyes.

Caught by surprise, Bao sucked in air between her teeth. "No."

"Last semester a girl spent a night with a student of the opposite sex. She was expelled from the university, no questions asked."

"I told you already: I'm not dating."

Miss Tan ran the comb through her wet hair. "I feel like a mother hen protecting her brood. I often worry that if I neglect you girls, something unfortunate might happen."

"Don't you worry." Bao scrubbed her collarbone until it hurt. "My father is stricter with me than you are."

"Professor Gu is one of the finest men I've known." Miss Tan began to sing. "*Quietly I'll leave you, please wipe away your tears, dear.*"

Bao breathed a sigh of relief. The pop song "Perhaps in the Winter" was a hit on campus.

Miss Tan hadn't always been a prude. Two years ago, Bao's father had helped her with a nervous breakdown. Her boyfriend had gone to study physics in the United States. At first he had sent her gifts. The mahogany Coach handbag was her favorite, although someone told her it was a high-quality faux bag made in China. A few months later her boyfriend stopped writing. One day he called Miss Tan and told her not to wait for him anymore.

Bao's father was usually tight-lipped about other people's secrets. In this case he must have thought Miss Tan's experience could teach Bao, then a junior in high school, an important lesson about life. "Naturally a man wants to possess an attractive young woman," he had said. "It's her responsibility to stop his advance. If she gives herself to him once, her feminine mystique is lost in his eyes."

"Oops!" Miss Tan dropped the comb on the wet tile floor.

Bao picked it up. "Here you go."

"Thank you."

Bao must've miscalculated their distance. Her hand touched Miss Tan's breast when she handed over the comb. She blushed deeply, although Miss Tan didn't notice the collision.

"*You ask me when I'll come home, I ask myself the same thing.*" Miss Tan's voice was supple and ripe. The water pouring down her face added to her air of dejection. "*Not yet, I don't know when, but I think it'll be in the winter.*"

The poignant song echoing in the shower gave Bao chills. Turning up the hot water, she stood with her back to Miss Tan, rubbed soap on her privates, and rinsed quickly. No matter how long she showered, Tong's semen clung inside her body. A woman could never be pristine, her body like a vessel for a man to deposit his fluids. This was the price of growing up. She turned off the water and said goodbye to Miss Tan, who answered her with a light nod.

Bao got dressed and went outside, the breeze caressing her warm cheeks. She carried the washbasin on her hip and walked slowly. Several men stared at her in passing. Did she walk with a rolling gait? She glanced down at her legs and tried to keep her knees together as she walked. That didn't feel right, either. Perhaps her plastic slippers tapped the cement too loudly. She placed the balls of her feet on the ground, instead of letting her heels drop.

She had a new body. A part of her enjoyed it, while another part was ashamed and wanted to hide. From a distance she saw Tong waiting for her at the dorm entrance. He read *People's Daily* framed in a window strung with iron wires. He must have brought a condom this time. Could she remain a good girl after losing her virginity? Tong looked up from the newspaper and took his hands out of his pockets. She walked toward him and swayed her hips a bit. Her feminine mystique wasn't lost to Tong but changed somehow—no longer a barrier that kept them apart but a force that drew them together. She lowered her chin with a grin. She wanted Tong, come hell or high water. Let their intimacy sweep her off her feet and give her wings. Together they would rise above the heartache and isolation each felt as being a nonentity in an unjust society.

Chapter 4

BAO NEVER ASKED TONG about his work. For several days, he had joined the police squad to keep order in Drum Tower Square, while angry protestors collided with the police. One day Tong came to her with a handprint on his face. He threw her on the bed and ripped off her clothes. Without a kiss he thrust into her and pressed his chest against her breasts. He was heavy, almost crushing her with his weight.

"You're mine, mine."

He stabbed her so ferociously she didn't think it was possible, until he fell off her, drenched and spent, lying motionlessly in her arms. She stroked his hair, basking in her love for him.

Tong sighed. "I can't bear to go back if I don't have you."

"You aren't a victim."

"I want the same thing they do." He touched her cheek. "I want to love you, with dignity and honor. Not to be expelled, called a hooligan, cannon fodder, kicked, spat on, and pelted rocks—"

She pressed a finger on his lips. "You have me."

His eyes misted up. She kissed the eyelids as if to draw tears. They rolled in his eyes, around and around, not a drop spilt.

"You have me." She could say this in the bedroom.

On Friday Tong was gentle. He kissed her lips for a long time, never once trying to push his tongue into her mouth. Then he kissed her face, her breasts, her belly, and her thighs until he reached her toes. She tried to pull him up, but he crouched between her legs. His tongue found her vagina, playing with the sensitive organ.

"How could you? Oh please, don't . . ." She couldn't reciprocate the favor. There was a matter of dignity even in the bed. What he did was so odd and yet exciting, she couldn't stand it anymore. "Take me, take me."

He made love tenderly and never stopped kissing her. When her head bumped against the bed frame, he cupped his hands around her skull like a helmet.

Afterwards they lay in each other's arms. She felt a tear and wiped it on the pillow. Was this true love? They had better be each other's destiny, because she couldn't take another man into her arms.

Rubbing her cheek against his chest, she overheard his strong, steady heartbeats.

They got dressed. Bao needed to see her parents, while Tong had to return to the Army Commander College.

"I don't have to keep order anymore." He smiled for seemingly the first time in days. "I can be with you all day tomorrow."

"I'll get out as soon as my parents release me."

She felt a bit wobbly walking downstairs. Her whole body was sore—her thighs, her belly, her vagina, her lower back, even her breasts. Her legs wanted to stay open even as she tried to close them. Tong walked alongside her. They didn't hold hands like they used to. His face was radiant, his eyes happy. He strolled with his hands in the pant pockets.

"I'm sore." She looked down at her breasts.

"You're blooming into a sexy lady." He licked his lips. "So your two sisters are growing bigger."

She didn't want larger breasts, which made her look curvy and matronly. Near the school gate, she glimpsed a familiar figure, short and agile. It was the Ph.D. student she'd danced with. He looked older in the daylight, his face pasty and lined, his permed hair a fluffy mess. Seeing her, his eyes shone with recognition. She stared at her open-toed sandals. Her cheeks were flaming, and so were her neck and ears.

"Who is he?" Tong asked.

Bao ignored him and continued walking. The Ph.D. student was no fool. He could see she had trouble keeping her legs closed. She stepped outside the university gate, a concrete arch twenty meters high. In her heart she said goodbye to an old friend—let their memories remain on the dance floor that rainy night.

"Your old flame?"

"You're my only flame."

Tong folded her into his arms. He kissed her face and pressed his cheek against her forehead. They stood embracing each other as if they were the only two people in the world. If the sky should fall, he would protect her with his body. She was grateful to have lost virginity to Tong.

"I'll miss you." A chill went down her spine as she heard herself say it. It was dreadful to love so much.

"Let's not say goodbye." He kissed her temple with his eyes closed. "See you soon." He went toward the bus stop, never once looking over his shoulder.

She stood on the sidewalk alone. Gone were the days when the protesters had waved their banners and made stirring speeches in the streets. Now life seemed to have returned to normal. The ringing of bicycle bells, honking of buses, and puttering of motorcycles assaulted her ears. The policeman didn't enforce the function of traffic lights, as vehicles crossed the intersection at all times. She jaywalked along with other people, dodging the buses, bicycles, tractors, and motorcycles.

Her mother usually bought produce on her way home. Grocery stands lined up on the sidewalk, selling strawberries, pears, grapes, tomatoes, cucumbers, carp, trout, and river snails. Bao entered the apartment complex for tenured professors. In the six-story buildings, many families were cooking supper. She heard eggs sizzling in a wok, mushrooms wilt in heated oil, pork fat crackle and hiss amidst smoke. Her mother used to extract lard for cooking. Bao liked to eat zesty dregs of pork fat, dabbled with salt. In recent years their rations of soybean oil increased, so her mother stopped using lard and bought only lean pork.

When Bao was in middle school, she had come home and

helped her father with lunch. She had picked the vegetables and snapped them into chunks. Her father could rock the knife to cut a cucumber into thin slices and retrieve bent fingers just before the blade fell, but he never let her touch the cleaver. Instead he taught Bao to use a hand vise. Live river snails, much cheaper than fish and shrimp, were poor people's seafood. After being kept in water for a few hours, they could eliminate the dirt and sand from their entrails. Bao used a hand vise to clip off the pointed end of a river snail. She preferred clipping the large ones and did the small ones last. Every clipped river snail was a result of her labor, and she enjoyed the dish even more for it.

She could help her parents with supper, and this cheered her up. Climbing up flights of stairs, she heard rhythmic clashing noises as a spatula flipped river snails in a wok. The aroma of soy sauce with ginger and scallion tickled her nose. On the fifth floor, she unlocked the burglarproof steel gate. Inside, the mahogany door displayed a picture of a head-down bat, a sign for prosperity. When she fumbled for the key, the door opened, and her father appeared in his pajamas.

"Just in time for supper," he said.

There seemed to be more gray hair on his temples. By age forty he had lost his teeth to irreversible pericoronitis. Now he had a full set of false teeth. The effort of maneuvering the false teeth changed the contour of his face. His prominent jawbones and a short chin made him look like an old woman. Blue veins, thick as earthworms, stood out on his arm as he reached for her backpack.

"We talk about you every day. Do your ears burn?"

Fortunately he didn't notice any changes in her body. Bao put on her bamboo slippers. "Can I help with anything?" The hardwood floor greeted her soles with solidity, completing her homecoming.

"Try the river snails." Her father carried a large bowl, filled to the brim, to the rosewood dining table.

"What would you like to drink?" Her mother opened the fridge.

"7-Up."

"You two start eating." Her mother was making kelp and rib bone soup, a summer tonic. "Don't wait for me." She wiped her hands on the apron and smiled at Bao.

At forty-three, her mother kept her slim figure and had few wrinkles or gray hairs. Bao hoped she'd age gracefully like her mother. Her father, at forty-five, looked ten years older than his wife. As a young man he had been handsome, albeit a chain smoker with the nickname Chimney, and exiled to the mountain area of Sichuan to do manual labor. Cigarettes stained his fingers and etched wrinkles around his purplish lips.

A hiss escaped as he opened a large plastic bottle. He poured 7-Up for Bao and a glass of beer for himself. She sipped the cold drink, a luxury not available at the school canteen. She picked up a river snail and sucked its opening. The leathery meat flew into her mouth. She chewed off one third of its length and discarded the entrails.

"Is it bland or salty?" her father said.

"It's just right," Bao said.

He smiled, like a schoolboy being praised by a tough teacher.

"You can't buy river snails at the canteen," Bao said.

"Clipping river snails is time-consuming," he said. "Of course it isn't on the canteen menu. Cooks have to feed hundreds of people at mealtime."

Bao sucked another river snail but got nothing. The meat hid in the back of its shell. She sucked its small end to pull back the meat. With a forceful suck at its large opening she extracted the meat. Relishing the salty river snail, she reviewed her strategy: taking a small step back in exchange for a huge leap forward. She fiddled with her hearts bracelet, a gift from Tong after their first kiss.

Her mother noticed it but said nothing about it. "Be careful." She sipped the soup. "It's hot."

Her father sucked a river snail from its shell. His false teeth clattered as they clamped down on the leathery meat and sawed its round head from the entrails. Sighing with relief, he pushed the bowl toward Bao.

"A young man gave me this as a gift." Bao showed her bracelet to them.

"Is it aluminum?" Her father ate a spoonful of tofu.

Bao gulped down 7-Up. "Sterling silver."

"Is he from your department?" her father said.

"No." As the carbonated drink settled in her belly, she covered her mouth to suppress a belch.

"Does he work?" her mother said.

"He's training at Nanjing Army Commander College."

"That's a military camp." Her father put down his chopsticks.

"He's a company commander." Bao wrung her hands

under the table. "He likes me."

"Do you like him?" Her mother, usually the voice of reason, sounded sharp and critical.

"I think . . . Yes."

Averting her eyes, Bao pick up a river snail. She sucked, and the river snail splattered fetid juice. It was rotten. She went to the sink to spit and rinse her mouth.

"You're very young." Her mother gave Bao a napkin. "A man may pursue you because you're sweet and chaste. You shouldn't mistake your gratitude for love."

"Where did you meet this Big Soldier?"

Bao was angry with her father for using the disparaging term. Tong had a fine physique, but he wasn't stupid.

"We met during the military training. Lots of girls liked him, but he only—"

"How typical!" Her father's face grew blotchy. "The military training is a waste of time. Were you brainwashed? Do you know what soldiers did in Beijing? They even shot a nine-year-old—"

"Tong would never hurt anyone. Like me, he sympathizes with the protestors."

"You've known him for a while," her mother said.

"Nine months." She saw the pain in her father's eyes and added, "We didn't date much, every other Sunday or so, and always in a crowd." This had been true until the citywide class boycott in early May.

"Is he allowed to date a trainee?" he said.

"I'm not the only one dating." Bao lost her patience—better to lie and distract them. "Lily is seeing Hongzhi, her high school sweetheart. She says they'll have three children."

Her parents looked at each other in puzzlement.

"Hongzhi applied to the universities overseas."

She didn't offer more details, which would cast Tong in an even poorer light. Her parents had met all her roommates. Her father had predicted that Bao was most likely to attract a perfect man: erudite, enterprising, and honorable. So far Tong had done little to recommend him.

"I almost forgot," her mother said. "Lily wrote you a letter. I put it in your room."

"Oh! Let me go get it."

"Finish your supper," her father said.

Bao fanned her cheek with a hand. "The soup is hot."

She entered her room and left the door ajar. She heard her mother suck a river snail and her father slurp soup. Bao wasn't discouraged. If she could finish her supper without arguing, in the morning she might show them a picture of Tong in civilian clothes.

Lily's letter was as thin as an empty envelope. Bao sat on her bed to open it.

"You wouldn't believe what I found out when I got home—Hongzhi was killed."

Not comprehending the news, she reread the first line and continued reading with a hand covering her mouth.

> He went to Tiananmen Square on June 3rd with his sister to see what was happening there. He brought a camera. They were separated by the crowd. Hongzhi didn't return by 4 a.m. on June 4.

His sister woke up their parents, who set out to look for him. They headed toward the Square, but it was overrun with soldiers. They went to nearby hospitals and worked their way through the sickrooms to the morgue. The bodies were in the drawers. His father pulled out one after another looking for him. They finally found Hongzhi at the Number Three Hospital. Doctors recalled a young man wearing a white tee shirt printed with the Great Wall, like his parents described. Two students had carried him in. His camera disappeared, and he had two rolls of unused films in his pocket. He was shot in the head.

I went to comfort his parents but didn't know what to say. They didn't have one picture that Hongzhi had taken. His sister consoled her parents, saying they should pretend that Hongzhi had gone to MIT.

Nobody blamed the poor girl, but she blamed herself.

Bao shuddered when a hand touched her shoulder.

"The soup is cool," her mother said.

"Not now."

"We won't talk about him. Don't worry about your father."

"Mom, why don't you go back?"

"All right." Her mother backed away. "Don't take too long."

Bao returned to the letter.

Why didn't I go home with Hongzhi? If I were with him, I would *never* have let him take any pictures—with a flash! He was so naïve.

I couldn't bring myself to go to his funeral. He is alive in my heart. I remember our last dinner, and it was also our first. We never kissed. I could give him three children, or ten, whatever suits him.

Someday the murderers will be on trial. I want to become a lawyer.

–Lily

Bao folded the letter in half, then a quarter, an eighth, a sixteenth, until her fingers could no longer bend the paper. Strength left her suddenly. She fell upon the pillow, drew up her legs, and closed her eyes.

"Come back," her father said. "I'll behave."

She shook her head, even though they couldn't see her from the dining table. Chairs moved, and footsteps approached her room. She pulled the quilt to cover her head.

"Don't make me beg," her father said.

"Lily's boyfriend is dead, shot in the head." No light penetrated the quilt. She felt alone, safe with her misery.

"Oh baby." Her mother sat on the bed.

"Hongzhi was going to MIT. He looked fifteen years old, his one cheek darker than the other, and he wore those big orange-framed glasses." Her voice broke. "I coaxed a photo of the Goddess from him."

"How his poor parents must be grieving!" Her mother tugged at the quilt and let in a shaft of light.

Bao threw down the quilt and knelt on the bed. She stared at the hardwood floor. Its beautiful even grains shone in the dusk. She heaved and retched up 7-Up and river snails.

"It's all right." Her father rubbed her back.

"Let it all out now." Her mother laid a basin in front of her bed.

Inside the enamel basin printed a ship in blue rippling

water. The caption read, "To sail the ocean we need a helmsman." It was a relic of the Cultural Revolution. Bao gazed at the rust spot on the hull of the sailboat. Shuddering, she spat into the basin. The picture of a ship breaking the waves made her feel seasick.

Bao vomited again after catching a whiff of the river snails. Her mother put away the leftovers in the refrigerator and turned on the electric fan to blow away the smell in the kitchen. Bao came out of her room, after her mother made fermented glutinous dessert soup.

"This doesn't taste fishy, baby. You'll feel better, if you aren't hungry."

Bao chewed a sweet rice dumpling. Its hot filling squirted out and scalded the roof of her mouth.

Her father stood beside the open windows. His flabby mouth clutched the filter tip of a Big Front Gate.

"Was he an only child?" he said.

"He had a younger sister."

"There will be a day," he said, "when the so-called ruffians will be mourned as victims, even honored as martyrs."

"That won't bring him back," her mother said. "If he was going to MIT, what was he doing in the streets?"

"Taking pictures," Bao said.

"Stupid kid," he said. "Some tenants in the apartment buildings were shot down because they had lights on."

Her father pressed the cigarette butt into a piece of watermelon rind. It sizzled before the ember died. Nobody talked. The fluorescent light hummed like a hundred dragonflies. Every so often a moth flew toward the light to bang its dusty wings against the tube. Bao heard a spoon scrape the bowl and realized she'd finished the dessert. She had hardly tasted it. Now she was full, nauseous with fatigue, a bone-weary exhaustion that she had never experienced.

"I'm going to bed," she said.

Her father took the dirty dishes to the sink. "You don't look good. Stay home and rest, because there's no school. We can feed you better food than the canteen meals."

Bao was supposed to have a date with Tong the next day. It would be hard to keep the appointment. She couldn't make love to him as if nothing had happened. A few days ago Hongzhi had eaten with them and argued with Bao. Surely Tong wouldn't mind her mourning for a few days.

She washed up and returned to her bedroom. Her mother put down the wings of the mosquito net and secured them with two wooden clips. Bao only had to crawl inside and sleep. She looked through the screen windows. Yellow lights shone in the apartment building ten meters away. There were no passionate outcries or loud music. The opposite windows were serene and indifferent. Her parents were next door, making no noise except for low conversation and an occasional cough.

Finally they closed their bedroom door. The light beam cast on the hardwood floor vanished, replaced by pale, soft moonlight. Bao walked to the living room in bare feet and picked up the phone in semi-darkness. She dialed Tong's number from memory. When the doorman asked her to hold, she rehearsed what she had to say in her mind.

"Hello?" Tong panted. He must've run down the stairs.

"It's me."

"I know, sweetie—"

"I can't see you tomorrow. I want to stay home for a while."

There was silence on the other end. Suddenly she felt a pain. It was her heartbeat, shifting into the wound he had made in her a few days ago, he, who had taken her innocence and given her desire. Now she wanted to distance herself, it felt like duty.

"Hongzhi is dead."

"What! Are you sure? How do you know?"

"Lily wrote me a letter. Hongzhi brought a camera to Tiananmen Square. He was shot in the head."

"Oh my God! I'm so sorry, Bao."

Hot tears streamed down her cheeks. It was easy for her to cry in the dark, away from her parents.

"We're cowards," she said. "We were in bed when Hongzhi was shot."

"We did nothing wrong."

"I know, we're immune. Let's look the other way and enjoy ourselves."

There was a long silence. When he spoke again, his voice was a barely audible whisper.

"What about the soldiers who died? Some of them were teenagers. They're not people?"

"They had guns."

"In case you don't know, mobs do kill. Do you watch TV? One soldier was disemboweled, castrated, burnt, and hung from an overpass."

"I wonder what he did to the others." She bit her lip hard. No amount of quarreling would bring back Hongzhi. He had taken a picture of the Goddess, whom had been toppled and crushed.

"Bao." He raised his voice. "When can I see you again?"

"I told my parents about you, but they weren't pleased. Dad doesn't like soldiers."

"You didn't—"

"No! They'd be horrified."

"What did you say?"

"That I like you."

"Did they turn you against me?"

"Don't talk like that. They're my parents."

He sighed. "Give my condolences to Lily. I'm devastated."

"I know, bye now." She waited to hear the phone click, but the line stayed open. "You go first."

"No."

She listened to his breathing for a while longer and then gingerly put the handset over the phone. She watched the beige phone gleam in the moonlight. Hongzhi's death tamed the passion in her heart. In its place, she felt a sense of adult responsibility growing like a tree sprouting new leaves.

Chapter 5

TWO WEEKS AT HOME FELT LIKE two months at the dorm. Bao was sick of the evening news. Every day some activists or student leaders were arrested. One woman boasted after she turned in her brother, a student activist. Bao went to bed in tears. She tossed and turned and dreamt that she was the young man's sister. She would hide him wherever she could— in her bed if that helped. Then she would find people to smuggle him overseas to safety.

The next day she wrote a long letter to Lily, starting with "Your loss brought the tragedy so close to home. Tong and I are devastated." Then she threw down the pen, curled up in her bed and wept, wishing that she'd known Hongzhi better to justify this sadness. She sent the picture of the Goddess to Lily. "At least you have one photo of his to keep. Don't despair, Lily. You will become a lawyer who fights for victims."

She didn't speak to Tong again. When she missed him, she tried to imagine how heartbreaking it must be for Lily, who'd never even kissed Hongzhi.

During the day Bao resumed a disciplined routine under her father's watchful eye. After breakfast she sat down with *New*

Concept English Volume 2, a textbook for English majors. She chewed a pencil and spied on the neighbors ambling in the garden. Retired folks complained about the prices of eggs, pork, and snakehead fish. Some held the hands of their grandchildren to keep them from tottering away. She looked forward to eleven o'clock, when she could help her father with lunch.

"Can I get a hand with the broad beans?" her father said.

"You bet."

Bao had learned to shell beans when she was a little girl living with her grandparents. She snapped a pod and squeezed out two beans from their pockets, working with both hands nonstop.

"You're as fast as Charlie Chaplin in *Modern Times*," her father said.

He threw whole mushrooms into hot oil. The sizzling noise was deafening. He flipped the mushrooms with a spatula until they were wilted, then added a dash of salt and two bowls of water, and put on the wooden lid.

The steel gate clanged. Her mother was back for lunch.

"Mushroom soup again?" she said. "I'm losing weight on this diet."

A dizzy spell seized Bao as she raised her head. Her eyes went dark. The last thing she heard was her mother changing into her slippers and walking toward the living room. Bao sank into oblivion.

When she opened her eyes, the light in the kitchen was as blinding as the darkness. She was lying on a pile of broad bean shells.

Her mother was wiping her forehead with a damp towel. "What happened, baby?"

"Nothing." Bao couldn't explain it, either. "I'm fine now."

Her father pressed his cheek to her forehead. "You don't have a fever. How is your stomach?"

"Fine."

"When is your period?" her mother asked.

Bao thought about it. "It should've started already. Is this PMS?"

"Probably." She cast her husband a sidelong glance. "I'll take her to the infirmary. She may need some herbal medicine."

"Good idea," he said. "Herbal medicine may be slow-acting, but it has few side effects."

Bao sat at the dining table opposite her mother, who pushed the mushroom soup toward her.

"This is good for you." Her mother's face was creased with worry.

They were making a big deal out of nothing. Her father was overly protective, while her mother seemed to be plagued by some terrible suspicion. Bao didn't believe she could be in any serious trouble. Tong had said no girl ever got pregnant her first time. There was no need to panic.

Averting her eyes, Bao bit off the stem of a mushroom and sucked its juicy cap.

After lunch Bao left home with her mother. She didn't take Bao to the university infirmary for a free treatment. Instead she went to a pay phone and called her office.

"I had a bout of stomach flu," her mother said. "My legs are so weak I can't walk down the stairs."

It was the first time Bao heard her mother lie. She sounded convincing and obtained permission to take an afternoon sick leave. They boarded a bus for the suburbs.

"Where are we going?" Bao said.

"A clinic for women." Her mother's face was impassive.

Bao felt the floor under her feet sink. How could her mother suspect she was pregnant? Bao watched a girl sitting on her mother's lap. She wore a pink bow and a purple skirt with a lacy hem. Her small naked legs swayed as the bus jolted and heaved on the bumpy road. If only Bao could crawl onto her mother's lap like a little girl! Gripping a handlebar tightly, she wished the bus would never stop.

Soon her mother patted her shoulder. Bao stepped off the bus. She decided to remain silent until proven guilty. They walked toward a bungalow with whitewashed walls, the faded Red Cross sign amidst graffiti.

When her mother went to pay the registration fee, Bao sat on a wooden bench and folded her hands on her lap. "A hospital is full of germs," her father had once said. "You mustn't touch anything if you can help it." A pile of vomit on the red brick floor emanated a sour stench. She stood up and walked into the courtyard. Passing tractors raised dust from the road. The odor of diesel and hot asphalt were a welcome relief from the pervading dead-fish smell of antiseptic.

Her mother came to give Bao a plastic cup. "Go to the bathroom and collect your urine."

"Why?"

"Just do it."

Bao went to the bathroom. The cement stalls had no doors. A woman held a boy as he sprayed pee around the squat toilet. Bao walked to the end stall beneath a water bucket. She pulled the string to flush the toilet, but no water came out. She loosened her pants and squatted. A throng of flies rose from the excrement covered by soiled paper and sanitary napkins. A fly landed on her bottom, tickling her. Another slid over her privates, rubbing its forelegs with relish. She got up and fastened her pants. She went outside, her face flushed and throat parched.

"What's the problem?" her mother said.

"I can't do it." Bao was nearly in tears. "Can we go home?"

"No." Her mother bought a tube of orange juice at a grocery counter. "Drink it."

"What for? I'm not pregnant."

Her mother seemed stung by her words. Averting her eyes, she peered at a woman nursing a baby at the curbside. The woman had sparse hair that barely covered her pink scalp. Her swaddled baby sucked serenely at her breast, like a worm sapping life from a diseased tree.

"We shall see in a moment." Her somber voice discouraged argument.

So what if anyone eavesdropped? Most of these people looked like country folks, with their tanned faces and bluntly chopped hair. "Do you think I'm a bad girl?"

"You have nothing to fear if you were good."

Unable to retort, Bao burst into tears.

"Don't worry." Her mother showed Bao the lab slip. "The pregnancy test bears my name, not yours."

Her mother had prepared for the worst. This knowledge calmed Bao somewhat. She bit off the plastic seal of the juice bottle.

"When I was pregnant with you, I had the same symptoms: nausea and fainting spells early on. Then I missed my period, like you. If you're in trouble, Bao, I'd like to find out early."

But Tong had used condoms, except for the first time. To keep herself from talking, Bao slurped the orange juice. It tasted salty and tart, like cough medicine.

"If you fooled around, I hope you took care of yourself." Her mother lowered her voice. "Have you done it?"

Bao pulled the bottle from her mouth, clumsily squirting juice on her blouse.

"I won't tell your father." Her mother gave her a hanky.

"But he'll find out—"

"If you're not pregnant, I won't tell him, I promise. But if you are . . . how can we keep such a secret from him? We have to think of some way to help you." She wiped sweat from Bao's face. Her hanky was soft and warm.

"But Mom, he used . . ." Bao was too ashamed to say "condoms." "He used stuff. He wouldn't get me into trouble."

Her mother crumpled the hanky in her fist, while tears welled up in her red eyes. "Did you do it with Tong?"

Bao nodded. She felt as if she were standing on an ice floe in a wide river, broken in two. Her mother drifting away, Bao looked on like a deserted child. She was less afraid of being drowned than disowned.

"How old is he?" Her mother wiped her eyes with a swift brush of her hand.

"Twenty-two."

"Lusty as a tiger, I bet. How could he enjoy himself without any concern for you? You're a freshman." Her mother bit her lower lip but couldn't stop it from trembling. "If anyone finds out, you'll be expelled."

"But he used condoms." This time, the word flew out of her mouth like gospel.

"Now go, get me the urine sample."

Bao finished the juice and then took the plastic cup to the bathroom. This time her pee came easily. She collected a half-cup and snapped on the lid. Her mother took the cup to an office marked "Gynecology." Bao sat on the curbside to wait. How easy it was to treat the matter like a medical procedure! Her heart swelled with hope, as she prayed she wasn't pregnant.

"Be merciful, young miss." A girl about eight years old knelt and held out an enamel bowl. "Spare me a little change. My mother needs money to have an abortion."

Had Bao been confronted with the plea any other day, she would have walked away. But today she wanted to do a kind deed—the good karma might help. She found some coins and a one-yuan bill. She gave the coins to the girl, who bowed deeply.

"Thank you, Miss. May you be blessed with good health and fine fortune!" The girl knelt down in front of a middle-aged man wearing leather shoes. "Be merciful, kind sir. My mother needs money—"

The man fluttered his newspaper. "Stop pestering me!"

The girl looked up at him. There wasn't a trace of annoyance in her eyes, only patience and silent hope. She was a dainty girl with soft, pale skin. In a few years she would grow up to be a winsome maiden. Would she quit begging before it became a habit? If not, what would become of her?

"Go away. Are you deaf?" The man folded his newspaper and stormed away.

The girl rose, too, as if to follow him. Bao hastily took out a five-yuan bill to put in her hand.

"Take this, Little Sister, don't follow him." There was so much she wanted to tell the girl, but she couldn't find the words. "Don't follow men, Little Sister."

The girl nodded, her face glowing with surprise and happiness at the windfall.

"Thank the young miss!" a woman said.

The girl dropped to her knees and kowtowed, touching her forehead to the floor.

A middle-aged woman carried a baby in a cloth sling. Bao's eyes were drawn to the baby's red, puffy, pear-shaped face. He had none of the good looks of his sister. The woman must have disobeyed the one-child policy and been subject to a considerable fine.

"Bao," her mother said. "I'm expecting."

Bao was confused for a split second, before she understood the news. Her pain and shame were so great she couldn't face her mother. Meeting the girl's eyes instead, Bao had a delirious thought that the young beggar could be her daughter. Her maternal instinct awakened. Bao stooped to lift the girl from the ground.

This must be the reason why parents told their daughters to keep their virginity until marriage. Why had Tong said that no girl got pregnant her first time? He couldn't have known that, because he had never been with a virgin. His ex-girlfriends were married women who knew how to take care of themselves.

How foolish Bao had been to believe him! What was worse, she'd deceived herself, thinking that passion should be pure, spontaneous, and carefree. She wasn't a man, after all. Her body was as much a burden as an indulgence. She massaged her flat belly. All was not lost. Inside her womb was a seedling of love. For now she could call it Soybean. If it was a daughter, Soybean would be smart like Bao and good-looking like her father.

She went to the refrigerator and poured a glass of 7-Up. Her mother had told Bao to drink warm beverages during her menstrual period in order to minimize cramping. Perhaps an expectant mother should heed this advice as well. But if she heated the 7-Up, the carbonated drink would be ruined. She pressed the sweating glass to her forehead and cheeks. Then she held a small sip in her mouth until all the bubbles burst on the tip of her tongue.

She glanced at the closed bedroom door. Her parents had been talking behind it for over half an hour. Their interference gave Bao comfort. Like most of her schoolmates, Bao had never held a job in her life. Her parents sheltered and provided for her, so that she could become a lawyer in the near future.

Although Bao loved children, she had no idea how to raise a baby. Was it animal instinct that a mother could care for her young? But she wanted more than a struggling life that reduced her to a female mammal. What was more, she wasn't alone in this trouble. She would have to drop out of the university in order to marry Tong. But would he become a faithful husband? He had philandered with married women before. Would they earn enough to eat, let alone give Soybean a future?

Bao sucked in her belly and held her breath, until the carbonated drink caused her to belch.

The bedroom door finally opened. "Bao," her mother said. "Let's talk."

Her father stalked out like a sleepwalker. His shoulders were stooped, and his head hung low. The glasses were about to slip off his nose. He sank into the sofa and lit a Big Front Gate. His lips trembled as they gripped the filter tip. He seemed afraid to look in her direction, as if Bao were stark naked.

"Your father and I—"

"We need to see him," he said. "Give him a call, Bao. I want to meet this Big Soldier—"

"The situation is quite simple." Her mother pressed a hand on his wrist. "If you want to continue your education, you must have an abortion as soon as possible. We need to arrange . . ."

What about the baby? Soybean was snug and safe inside her womb. How selfish they were to only think of Bao! Should her career take precedence over biology and human nature? A mother ought to fight for the survival of her child. She had no choice—her body ached to nurture Soybean to a safe delivery even though her mind had reservations.

"It's my baby! You can't rip it out like—" Bao met her father's glare and lowered her voice. "It isn't a tumor."

"I understand what you're going through," her mother said. "When you fainted this morning, I saw myself in you. Your father and I will want to be grandparents someday, when you are married."

Her father gripped the arm of the sofa and looked at the windows. He must have been told not to speak. Her mother had rallied his support because they were a family. Bao's privacy and her pride had to be set aside, as they were discussing a matter of life and death.

"I want to keep my baby."

"Think it through," her mother said. "Do you want to be expelled?"

"If I marry Tong—"

"Students are prohibited from dating or marrying. You'll be expelled and never return to the university." Her father leapt up and bumped his knee against the sharp corner of the coffee table.

They were talking about the only thing that was truly hers in this world. Keeping the baby would cause Bao to lose everything that she had worked for her entire life. Having an abortion would tear her apart. She started to cry.

"We're on your side no matter what you do." Her mother tried to blink away her tears. "You're our only child."

"Do you want to become a lawyer?" her father said.

"Yes, yes!!"

Being a straight A student, Bao could have studied science or engineering, which guaranteed high-paying jobs and even opportunities to study overseas. When she was in middle school, she had read a story in the newspaper. A woman had an alcoholic husband who beat her and cheated on her. She filed for a divorce. The case was communicated to her work unit, where the female cadre persuaded her to "patch up the marriage for the child's sake." Six months later the woman was beaten blind, and her husband was arrested. One day she asked her three-year-old son to cook porridge. The pot slipped from his hands. The picture of the boy with severe burns on his arms, stomach, and legs was etched in Bao's mind. There were few prominent woman lawyers. Once she became one, Bao would protect women's and children's rights.

"Do you want to give up your law career?" her mother said.

"Why do I have to choose?"

"You always have to choose, it's life." Her father struck several matches before he lit a new cigarette. "A life without a choice isn't necessarily a happy one."

"But I already have Soybean." Bao put a hand on her belly. "I'm not free to choose whatever I want."

"Bao, you should look at your life from a long-term perspective," her mother said. "You're eighteen years old— now it's the time for education. In a few years you can have everything you want: a career, husband, and child. Do you want to throw away your future for instant gratification?"

Bao winced at the last words. Honest advice was hard to

take. Her parents meant to guide and support her during this difficult time.

"If I . . ." Her throat clamped up, and she couldn't say the terrible word. "I may regret it all my life."

"I'll see you through it, baby." Her mother stroked Bao's forearm. "You won't be alone."

"I'm so sorry, Mom. I let you down."

"It's not your fault. People in love do foolish things. Remember, don't let your heart do all the thinking for you. What kind of a lawyer would that make!" Her mother brushed the loose hair to the back of Bao's ears. "Will you make a call and tell him your decision?"

Bao gripped the windowsill to stand up. She already felt heavy and moved awkwardly toward the phone. The doorman asked her to hold. She wrapped the cord around her wrist until it was tight enough to stop her blood. She felt a flutter in her belly. Was it her imagination that Soybean cried for help?

"Hello?"

"It's me, Gu Bao."

Her mother pressed the speaker button.

"Sweetheart, when can I see you? I miss—"

"My parents are here, *listening*." Bao cleared her throat. "You must come to our apartment tonight. We have an important matter to discuss."

He was silent for a while. "Are you all right?"

Bao would've told him the news if her father weren't staring at her.

"We'll talk about it later." She told Tong the address and which bus to take and then added, "We're expecting you, so don't be late." Without waiting for his answer, she hung up the phone. She was afraid to make her father listen to Tong's voice longer than necessary.

Her father put on his glasses. "Have you met his parents?"

Bao shook her head. "His father is a division commander of Nanjing Military Region. I don't know what his mother does."

"So he's the son of an official. No wonder he's brazen and immoral, preying upon innocent girls—"

"I'm not so innocent."

Her father froze as if struck by lightning. His eyes were enormous with shock, shame, and grief. Her mother started setting the table, banging the bowls around.

"Good, let's have supper," her mother said. "Tong will be here in an hour."

"What're you telling me?" he said. "Did you seduce him? Did you take him to your bed?"

A large tear left a glistening trail on his cheek. It disappeared between his purplish lips. He was not a fainthearted man. During the Cultural Revolution he had been paraded and beaten in front of a crowd. He had slept in a cowshed and been starved for being a Stinky Ninth Category of intellectuals. Even then his eyes had been dry—now Bao made him cry. She longed to save her father from the misery she had caused him. She would forsake her own life, if necessary. What was her young life compared to that of the now frail old man who had given her life?

"Don't worry, Dad." She knelt on the floor and held his shin. "I'll have an abortion, like you said."

The hardwood floor was cool and unyielding beneath her knees.

Bao wanted to meet Tong downstairs and explain her decision, before her father pushed the buzzer.

"You stay here. Don't run around in your condition." His voice was gentle, but she knew his command must be obeyed.

Tong stood, holding a large box. Bao was dumbstruck to see him in his army uniform and a wide-lipped cap with red and gold trim. Thank goodness he didn't have on his pistol belt! She blushed when she saw the derision in her father's eyes.

"Professor Gu, it is a pleasure to finally meet you." Tong bowed deeply like a pupil meeting his tutor for the first time.

"Come in." Her father pulled the steel burglarproof door shut and closed the wooden door.

"This is a nice apartment." Tong scanned the apartment. The balcony was transformed into a dining room. Plaster cornices decorated the ceiling. "It's cozy and elegant."

"These are cramped quarters, I'm sure, compared to your father's mansion." Her father lit a cigarette. He didn't offer Tong one, as he usually did to his male colleagues.

"My father lives in the military compound. I haven't been home in a while."

"No doubt you were busy seeing my daughter."

Tong peered at Bao, but she was unable to advise him on how to approach her parents. Tong held up the box with both hands, when her mother stepped forward.

"It's good to meet you." He paused, uncertain how to

address her. "I didn't have time to buy a gift, so I picked up a cream cake on the way. I hope you'll enjoy it."

Her mother thanked him. She seated Tong in the sofa chair, opposite Bao on the love seat.

"A cream cake is all grease with little nutrition," her father said. "We have to watch our cholesterol and blood sugar. You'd better take it home."

Neither of her parents had cholesterol or blood sugar problems.

"Sorry, I didn't know what else to bring." Tong flushed to the roots of his hair.

"Do you want a cup of tea or plain boiled water?" her mother said.

"Please don't trouble yourself. Tap water is fine." Sweat wilted his collar.

Bao wished to offer iced beer or cold watermelon to calm his nerves. She only had to open the refrigerator, but this gesture would be interpreted as disloyalty in her parents' eyes. So she remained seated, ashamed for having put Tong in the position of being the enemy.

"I took Bao for a test today." Her mother set down a glass of water. "Sadly, we found she is expecting."

"What?" Tong slapped his forehead. "Are you sure the test was accurate?"

"Yes," her mother said. "She has all the symptoms of being pregnant."

Tong pressed his temples with his fingers, as if to squeeze his brain into comprehension. Then he raised his head.

"With your permission, I want to marry Bao."

Both parents turned toward Bao. Under their insistent gaze, she had no choice but to take their side.

"I want to finish school," she said.

"She's only a freshman." Her father flicked ash from his cigarette. "It's both her and our wish that she finishes her college education. She will have an abortion."

"Will you please hear me out?" Tong clasped his hands in front of his chest. "I'm in love with your daughter, and she loves me." Bao looked at her lap and pressed her knees together. "I'll graduate from Army Commander College in a few months and be promoted to a battalion commander. Officers are allowed to marry. If we live on the military base, we can raise our baby and make ends meet."

"What about her studies?" her mother said.

Tong wrung his hands and cracked his knuckles. "Bao has to choose me or the university."

He wasn't making this easy for Bao. She had never earned a salary. She didn't mind so much about having money as being financially independent. If an able-bodied woman relying on her parents led the life of a parasite, then depending on her husband for livelihood would amount to prostitution. She thirsted for a career.

"I want to become a lawyer," she said.

"What about our baby?"

"You asked me to do something very hard, to choose." She tried to keep her voice steady. "And I did it."

Tong buried his face in his hands and remained still for a while. "I'm the father, and I want my baby." His eyes were red when he put down his hands.

If only they could be alone! Bao would have a good cry in his arms. Tong wanted to marry her. How could she turn her back on his love? When their eyes met, she saw pain, despair, and fear reduce him to a helpless boy. Did she look distraught and guilty to him? Her mother was right—if she was to become a lawyer, she shouldn't let her heart do all the thinking.

"You have to be reasonable, young man." Her father spoke with the pleasant cadence he used in his lectures. "Think of it from Bao's perspective. If she sacrificed her future for you, what sort of a life could you give her in ten years, twenty years? A marriage based on obligation won't work. You might persuade her to quit school and marry you. She might live with you on the military base, raise a child, and become a middle-school teacher, or whatever else she's qualified for. In twenty years' time, your child would be grown. What else would be left for her? Her youth, her potential will be gone. How will you keep each other happy then?"

"With all due respect, love will find the way." Tong clenched his teeth, as a blue vein stood out in the middle of his forehead. "My grandparents had eight children. They scraped and begged to feed their children. Five of them survived, and three went to the university. Where there is a will, there is a way."

"Being older than Bao, you ought to understand our concerns." Her mother's voice was gentle. "She's our only child, the apple of our eye. We haven't spoiled her, but she's young and inexperienced. She may speak her mind like an intelligent person, but in many ways she's a child who has seen little of the world."

"I'm not a child." Bao slid to the edge of her seat. "I love you, Tong, and I love our Soybean." She started to weep. "I need time to think about all this. But if I allow myself to mull it over, I'll hate myself even more for having done this to myself. I had no right to be so irresponsible, and neither did you, but we're not the victims. Soybean is the one who will . . ." She covered her mouth with a hand.

"Listen, Bao." Tong got down on one knee without moving closer. "We can get through this. I will help you the best I can. I love you so much—"

"You talk about love as if you know what it means." Her father stubbed out his cigarette in the ashtray. "Bao is not only talented but also has a passion for justice. She'll become one of the top woman lawyers. In a few years she may meet and fall in love with a man truly worthy of her. If you love her, set her free. This is the best you can do."

"I won't love another man." Bao wiped tears with her palm. "I can't even stand myself."

"Whatever you decide, Bao, please don't give up on our child. I'll get my parents to help us—"

Bao had heard enough. She ran into her room and slammed the door. Then she threw herself on the bed, wrapped the quilt around her head, and burst into tears.

When she calmed down a little, she heard soft knocking on the door. "Will I see you again, Bao?"

"We prefer that you don't bother our daughter from now on," her father said.

How could she run into his arms and beg for his forgiveness? The love that had given her pleasure now caused her so much pain. Feeling a dull cramping in her lower belly, she drew up her legs and moaned.

The burglarproof gate clanged. "We have reached an understanding, young man," her father said. "Let me see you out."

"I beg for your forgiveness, Professor Gu. I love your daughter, and I never meant to hurt her." Tong's voice echoed in the stairway. "Take care of yourself, Bao. Goodbye."

She threw away the quilt and stared at the windows. She had robbed Tong of the right to take care of her. She had sinned against Soybean, only because she wanted to become an independent woman. Why was the price of love so high?

Her father shut the burglarproof gate and then closed the wooden door. "If he weren't a Big Soldier, he might make an okay son-in-law." He opened the screen windows. "You forgot your cake, Big Soldier."

Bao heard Tong's voice but couldn't make out his words.

"Why don't you share it with your cadets? Consider it a donation from us grass people."

The cake landed with a plop.

"Who's throwing stuff?" a shrill voice called from downstairs.

"Help yourself. It's a free cake from the PLA man." Her father closed the window.

Chapter 6

BAO WORE A WHITE RAYON DRESS with red-and-blue polka dots. Its elastic waist wrapped gently around her torso. Thank goodness she wasn't showing, or she would be too ashamed to leave home in daylight. She exchanged her heeled sandals for cotton socks and sneakers. It would be a long train ride, and she wanted to be comfortable.

The dawn sky was overcast. A draft through the open kitchen windows raised gooseflesh on her arms. After combing her hair, she put on a pair of dark brown sunglasses. She felt like wearing a gauze mask to cover up her face. After all, Bao was going to the abortion clinic.

Her mother appeared with a duffle bag on her shoulder. "Will you see us off?"

Her father nodded, picked up the canvas suitcase, and held the door open for Bao.

"Take her arm," he said, "in case she has a dizzy spell."

"I'm not an invalid." Bao skipped down the stairs as if she were in a race.

"Bao, slow down." Her father's voice echoed in the stairway. He finally emerged at the bottom of the stairs, his eyes crinkled with a smile. "You make me feel old."

When her mother joined them, they walked toward the bus stop together. Outside the gate of their apartment complex, a peddler fried long doughnuts, while his partner baked sesame seed cakes. A young girl holding an enamel cup waited in line. She wore a sleeveless blouse with a jewel neckline. Her bobbed hair looked a little boyish.

Her father peered back over his shoulder. "She looks like you when you were little, but you were prettier."

"One day I took you to buy vinegar." Her mother hoisted the duffle bag onto her shoulder. "An old woman in front of me bought a bowl of soy sauce. When she saw you, she stared at your face. Then she tripped over a cobblestone and spilled soy sauce over her white blouse." She stroked Bao's cheek. "You were a fetching girl."

Bao slowed her steps to lag behind her mother.

"You might be too young to remember," her father said. "I worked on the labor farm in Songpan, and your mother taught elementary school in Nanping. You lived with your grandparents. We missed you so much we longed for the summer when we could be reunited as a family."

Bao pushed up the sunglasses that slid down her nose. Nothing could put her at ease about going to her grandparents' house for a secret abortion. She hadn't seen her grandparents in Sichuan for six years. A few months ago Grandpa had written and asked how Little Bao was doing. She could never be that girl who had massaged Grandma's aching back or blown air on her forehead to cure her of a headache. From a sense of obligation she wrote two paragraphs at the end of her mother's letter, but finding the words was like squeezing toothpaste out of a nearly empty tube.

The crowd began to move as the bus pulled into the stop. Her father held the suitcase to his chest and elbowed his way onto the bus.

"Sit here." He pointed to a seat where he had laid the suitcase. He lifted it when Bao got close.

The doors of the bus heaved shut.

"I have to get off!" he shouted at the top of his lungs, his face red and glowing with sweat. "I'm not taking the bus."

The ticket seller pressed a button to open the doors. "Hurry up."

Passengers stared at her father. Even a baby let go of her bottle and gaped at him, drool trickling down her mouth. Her father stooped to kiss Bao.

"Take care, baby." He backed away. "Write to me." He stumbled off the bus.

With a jolt the bus began to move. Her father waved both hands over his head. His white hair fluttered in the breeze as he grew smaller and more distant. The cigarette scent lingered on Bao's cheek. She could bear her own humiliation, even the pain of ending Soybean's life, but her father's desolation seemed overwhelming.

"Why doesn't he come to the train station?" Bao was in tears.

"He's afraid he would want to accompany you to Pingwu." Her mother clutched the overhead bar. "You can't blame him, Bao. Last night he couldn't sleep. He said it was our fault, not having raised you when you were young. You don't trust us enough to confide your secrets to us."

"It wasn't your fault." Bao raised her voice, not caring that other passengers watched and listened. "I let you down."

The bus honked furiously each time it approached a crowded intersection. Bicycles weaved their way through pedicabs, buses, tractors, taxis, and trucks. Jaywalkers were undeterred by the ding of bicycle bells and the constant honking of automobiles. The ticket seller slapped a metal clip against the window as the bus pulled over. People swarmed and jostled each other at the door. Children and old people weren't able to get on the rush-hour bus. Nanjing was miserably congested. If half of its population were relocated, the remaining residents could get around the city in relative comfort and greater safety. Perhaps she was doing Nanjingers a favor by having an abortion.

Bao knew she was rationalizing. She wanted to feel justified in her decision, wanted to believe that her sacrifice was noble and for the common good.

Bao wasn't allowed to help when her mother lifted the duffle bag onto the overhead rack and pushed the suitcase under their seat. Several men were smoking in the carriage. Bao opened the window. Luckily she had a window seat for the next thirty hours. She gazed at the platform with longing. She hadn't phoned Tong since their meeting. Two weeks ago she had been so madly in love they were inseparable. Now she was too mortified to even speak to him.

"Do you want orange juice?" her mother said.

Bao nodded. Her throat felt constricted, and she wasn't in

the mood to talk.

Her mother waved a peddler to the window and bought a pack of juice. The train started to move. Sipping the juice, Bao watched the tall buildings fall behind. The train sped through open rice fields dotted with farmhouses, ox carts, farmers on foot and bicycles, and children playing in the fields and tending to chickens, ducks, and geese.

"Dad seems to hate Tong, but he's a good man."

Her mother cast Bao a sidelong glance. "He's good-looking."

Her sympathy gave Bao courage. "He was good to me." She took off her sunglasses. The world suddenly lit up, and the green fields dazzled her eyes. "He loves me."

"I saw the way he looked at you. For a moment I thought, what a beautiful baby you would make!"

"I named it." She took her mother's hand to put on her belly. "Soybean."

The hand trembled. Bao tightened her grip so her mother couldn't pull away. Her warm palm pressed against Bao's stomach.

"Little One, don't blame us. We'll always remember you."

Her words brought tears to Bao's eyes. "We should save a piece of moon cake for Soybean on the Mid-Autumn Festival."

"Any flavor Little One likes, Grandma will see to it."

Bao drank up the juice and flung the empty box from the train. It rolled off into a ditch. She permitted herself to rest, as if she had arranged a decent funeral for Soybean. She napped with her head resting on her mother's lap. She woke up to eat, drink, and go to the bathroom. The train chugged through fields, villages, towns, cities, and provinces. She changed positions to sleep: leaning against her mother, folding her arms upon the tray table, and crouching against the high back of their seat.

When Bao woke up again, it was morning. The loudspeaker blared out the morning news from the Central Broadcasting Station. Several student activists had been arrested, one of them turned in by his former teacher. All travelers were advised to be on the alert and report wanted criminals to law enforcement. Bao was disgusted. Lily was right: they should become lawyers and fight to free the political prisoners.

Outside, rolling mountains dominated the landscape. Terraced fields and valleys stretched out in the rising sun. Herds of cows grazed. The farmhouses were few and far between. Suddenly the train was enveloped in darkness. Rhythmic chugging echoed inside a tunnel. She listened with trepidation and reverence. A part of her wished the tunnel were short, while another part of her wanted it to last forever. Soon, sunlight illuminated the end of the tunnel. The train roared on and left the tunnel behind. Bao felt refreshed and full of energy. She was far away from home; her father and his tearful exhortations were a distant memory. In the mountainous Sichuan province, she felt like a new person.

Her mother stirred.

"Have some tea." Bao put dry tealeaves into two glasses. A train attendant carried a kettle of hot water to fill passengers' glasses and mugs. Another attendant pushed a cart with hot breakfast. "Can we have sweet rice rolls? I'm starving."

"Two rolls." Her mother handed Bao a hot roll. "You sound chirpy today."

"I slept well." Bao bit into the rice roll, filled with a fried long doughnut and shredded pork. As the train approached another tunnel, her heart swelled with apprehension. "Here it comes again!"

Darkness shrouded the train. The attendant grabbed the handle on Bao's seat. Some passengers stopped talking. The rhythmic chugging drowned out the radio broadcast. The resounding noise pounded in Bao's ears and made her heart race with nameless longings. Soon, the train shot out of the tunnel into bright sunlight. The attendant released the handle and pushed the breakfast cart forward.

"Remember those tunnels?" her mother said. "When you were little, you were so scared you climbed into my lap until there was light again. Your father said we were in the belly of the mountain. You asked him if we crossed the mountain like an earthworm digging through soil."

"Did I?" Bao was pleased with the anecdote.

"You were only two and half years old, so sweet and precocious. Your grandparents doted on you." Her mother put down the rice roll, as if she'd suddenly lost her appetite.

"They'll be surprised to see me again."

Bao had trouble swallowing the wad of food, so she kept chewing. Her eyes grew wet, but her throat was dry. She put her glass beside the open window to let the wind cool the tea.

"I telegraphed your grandpa and told him we're coming." Her mother sipped tea and took a savage bite of her rice roll. She chewed vigorously and with determination. "Don't worry.

They love you to pieces."

Bao's heart sank. Right now she preferred indifferent acceptance to smothering love. Her father's tears had persuaded her to have an abortion. What would she do to answer for her grandparents' love? She didn't want to imagine.

"When will I see the doctor?" Bao said.

"I'll take you there this afternoon."

"Is he good?"

"He's performed thousands, probably tens of thousands of cases. In fact he was awarded the National Model Worker advocating the one-child policy." Her mother gulped down the tea.

Bao smoothed out the wrinkles in her skirt.

"Will it hurt?"

Her mother wrapped her arm around Bao's back and rocked her like a baby. "Not to fear, daughter, I'll see you through it."

Bao cupped her hands around the sweet rice roll, crushed into a pancake between her hands and her mother's bosom. As the fragrance of fried long doughnut oozed from her palms, she knew this was the last good breakfast she'd ever have. She still had her mother's love while carrying Soybean inside her.

Outside Mianyang train station they boarded a tired old bus headed for Pingwu County. The aisle was already packed full of sacks and bundles that had been stacked up almost as high as the seats. Her mother said it was going to be a bumpy ride and advised Bao to take an aisle seat near the front. Bao stretched her legs out atop the bundles. The passengers were mostly peasants with swarthy faces. Men smoked pipes and cheap cigarettes, while women peeled hard-boiled eggs and shelled peanuts for their children. They ate, spat, and grunted. Their loud voices crackled in the air, as if they were shouting at one another across the hillside.

Bao understood about half of the Pingwu dialect. She heard women talk about the prices of printed cloth, ready-made coats, and shoes in Mianyang. A boy reached out a hand to grab the leaves brushing the bus windows. His father slapped his head.

"Go, get your hand chopped off." He pulled the windows shut.

Bao had heard that peasants in Pingwu weren't a bright lot. Isolated in the mountainous region, they often married their cousins, and a high percentage of couples had borderline retarded children. Her mother, a schoolteacher who had married a university student from a metropolitan city, was considered a phoenix flying out of a chicken coop. Bao was dismayed at the prospect of staying at her grandparents' house for a month. She hadn't brought many books to read. How would she kill time?

The bus heaved and jolted on the potholed road, which wound along a rushing river. Every now and then Bao glimpsed the mountains in the distance, their snowy peaks shrouded in heavy mist and cloud. With every bend of the river the road grew more perilous, reminding her of the saying, "The road to Sichuan is more difficult than the road to Heaven." The road was littered with huge slabs of granite and rocks that fell from the mountains. Many of the mountains were terraced all the way to the top. The soil looked thin, and the dense green crops appeared tyrannical in their resilience.

When the bus pulled into a dusty parking lot, Bao saw her grandpa's ruddy face. He fanned himself with a straw hat.

She sat back. "Grandpa is here."

Her mother reached outside and waved her hand. "Dad!"

"Yinyin!" Grandpa called out her nickname, his voice hoarse with emotion. "Where's my granddaughter?"

"Right here beside me."

Bao had to lean forward. "Grandpa." She managed to smile.

"She looks thin. What're you feeding her?"

"She eats at the school canteen most of the time." Her mother pulled out the suitcase from under the seat. "Let's go."

Bao grabbed the handle to step off the bus. Standing on the ground, she still felt the rhythmic rocking in her body. Her feet seemed to dance to invisible steps, and her blood undulated in her veins. Her mind felt watery, and so did her eyes. Although the air was cool, the sunlight was unrelentingly bright. She put on her sunglasses.

"You left wearing pigtails. Now you're all grown up. I wouldn't recognize you if I saw you on the street. Who's that pretty lady?" Grandpa took the suitcase and carried the duffle bag on his shoulder. With his shirtsleeves rolled up, he looked brisk, strong, and almost youthful. He hailed a pedicab and placed the luggage inside it. Then he unlocked his bicycle and told the pedicab driver, "Follow me."

Bao climbed into the pedicab.

"Are you comfy?" her mother said as she squeezed into the

narrow seat beside Bao.

"I'm fine." Just then the pedicab started to move. Bao was thrown back and hit her head on the wooden beam that held up the awning.

"Did you talk to Doctor Li?" her mother said.

Grandpa cycled alongside the pedicab. "He's going to visit his newborn grandson in Chengdu. He leaves tomorrow."

"Why didn't you tell me?"

Grandpa hunched his back to pedal uphill, his face reddening with exertion.

"I gave you my phone number, Dad. You should've called me."

"Do you know how expensive a long-distance call is?" He held the handlebars with one hand, his back upright. "It could buy us tonics like longans and ginseng."

"Dad, I'd buy you tonics, if only you asked me."

"We don't want your money, and we can look after ourselves."

"Now listen, Dad." Her mother stamped her foot. "We must stop at the clinic before we go home. I have to see Doctor Li today."

Grandpa cast them a sidelong glance. There was apprehension in his eyes. He must've known that Bao needed an abortion. Was that the reason he appeared reluctant to take them there? Bao pressed her neck against the wooden beam. She wanted to make herself disappear.

"The clinic is on the way home," Grandpa said. "Just twenty minutes by bike."

Her mother pressed Bao's hand gently. Bao grew afraid and

grabbed a handful of her skirt. Soybean was not yet a month old. How would the doctor scrape it from her womb? Would Soybean thrash for life, like a baby fish? She pressed her belly with a fist. Could she have another day, another hour?

"How's Mom?"

"She couldn't sleep last night. Today she got up at daybreak and killed an old hen, then went to the market to buy pork and shrimp." Grandpa grinned at them. "When you lived with us ten years ago, we couldn't afford to eat much meat and seafood. Now you must eat your fill and grow some flesh on your bones."

"I'm stout enough." Bao's voice, shrill and childlike, made the pedicab driver glance at her. Why was Grandpa so fixated on fattening her up? "I need to go on a diet."

"It's fashionable for young women to stay thin," her mother said. "Bao thinks she's too fat."

"Humph!" Grandpa flung a white towel around his neck and wiped his sweaty face with it. "A plump girl is healthy, healthy is pretty."

Every now and then a man on a bicycle passed them by. He peered into the pedicab to see who the visitors were. Bao stared at her lap. These were her last moments with Soybean. A slice of Tong traveled a thousand miles with her. Could she bear to let it go—let Tong go? Put their child to death, and let their love die? With a moan she put her head on her mother's shoulder.

The pedicab stopped at a crumbling brick gate. Grandpa got off his bicycle. Bao's mother jumped down to stop him from paying the fare. They quarreled in angry voices as the father and daughter pushed away each other's hand and thrust their own money toward the pedicab driver. Bao took down the luggage. The momentary exertion didn't trigger a miscarriage, as she had secretly hoped. A portrait of Chairman Mao with sunrays emitting from his head caught her eye.

On the whitewashed wall, a picture of a couple holding a chubby baby girl was painted over old slogans. "It is good to have one child," the caption said. The family of three wore identical smiles on their faces; only their hairstyles and outfits were different. Bao knew enough history not to be misled by the new brand of propaganda that flourished after Mao's death in 1976. Mao Zedong had never promoted the one-child policy. With a typical peasant mentality, he had encouraged countrymen to have as many children as they were biologically capable of, awarded women with five or more children the title of "glorious mother," and given their families economic subsidies. During the Cultural Revolution, Mao had persecuted the renowned economist Ma Yinchu, who promoted family planning. If not for Mao's policy in the fifties, China might now have a manageable population and wouldn't need the restrictive one-child policy.

There were no trees, lawn, or shrubs in front of the clinic, an L-shaped bungalow with a dozen rooms. The courtyard was overrun with short, dense weeds. In the corner, a garbage dump contained rusted bicycle parts. There was a deep rectangular cement sink with three faucets. A nurse washed her enamel bowl and chopsticks. Two women scrubbed bedsheets against wooden washboards propped against their chests. They chatted in the local dialect and stamped their feet every so often to drive away mosquitoes. An old man lifted a bamboo curtain hung in front of an office. With his prescription, he went to a small window to buy medicine. He had no teeth, not even false ones.

A flock of geese honked and waddled out of the road when the pedicab left. Her mother took Bao's hand. Grandpa squatted beside his bike and draped the white towel over his head. On the ground inches from his foot, an army of ants was moving a dead locust. Bao glanced at Grandpa before she reached the gynecology office, but he didn't look up from the ground.

The office door was open. Bao heard the slurping sound of someone eating noodle soup. Her mother lifted the bamboo curtain.

"Doctor Li," she said. "I'm Yinyin. It's good to see you again. Congratulations on your becoming a grandfather!"

Doctor Li bit down on the noodles clutched between his teeth. He chewed noisily while studying their faces.

"What wind has blown you here, Yinyin?" He put down his chopsticks and stood up. "Your father talked to me the other day. I wasn't sure what he meant." He gazed at Bao from head to toe. "Your daughter is the spitting image of you. You two look like sisters."

"You mustn't flatter a middle-aged woman. Gu Bao is eighteen years old and a law student at Nanjing University." Her mother nudged Bao toward Doctor Li, a short man with stubby fingers. The white coat wrapped around his stout torso like an apron. "Say hello to Uncle Li."

"Uncle Li." Bao hadn't called a stranger "Uncle" since she turned fourteen. In Nanjing she'd call him "Mister." Now she greeted her abortion doctor with a term of endearment that she'd normally bestow upon a male relative. The humiliation was complete; somehow, this relaxed her. "Please finish your noodles, Uncle Li."

"We were rude to barge in on you," her mother said. "Your noodles are getting cold. We aren't strangers. Why don't you eat while we talk?"

In the courtyard several women rocked with laughter. A man tapped his enamel bowl with chopsticks as if beating a gong.

"Take your seats. I'll be done in a minute." Doctor Li lowered his face to a bowl almost as large as his head.

"I have to trouble you with an urgent matter. I heard you're going away tomorrow."

"I'm going to see my grandson." He ate slices of beef and onion and drank the brownish soup. "My wife went to look after our daughter. She said after June 4th there were demonstrations and riots in Chengdu. People torched a government building and firebombed police stations. Actually many stores were closed for a while. I've waited until the situation became stable. Now I'll take a month off to be with my family."

"I'm happy for you." Her mother unzipped the duffle bag and took out two small packages. "I brought you some silk fabric. Royal blue looks good on you. Bronze is a favorite color in Nanjing this year. There's enough fabric to make two dresses, for both your wife and daughter. It's a hundred percent silk of the top quality."

Doctor Li glanced at the silk with perfunctory interest. "You shouldn't spend so much, Yinyin. We're old friends."

He studied Bao with surprise and evident understanding. His heavy-lidded eyes expressed pity, concern, and silent reproach.

"My daughter has a little trouble." Her mother brushed Bao's hair back from her forehead. "Perhaps you could perform a procedure on her. She's about five weeks, I believe."

Doctor Li lifted the bowl with both hands. His lower lip sucked voluptuously until the whole bowl was drained.

"This is just a token of our appreciation." Her mother gave him a white envelope.

"Put away your money. I'll help your daughter." He wiped his mouth with a crumpled hanky and then reached under his desk to grab a thermos bottle. "I need to get hot water and make a cup of tea. Then we can get started."

After he left, Bao stared at her mother.

"Don't worry, he's a very good doctor. I'll go tell your grandpa—you stay here."

Bao wanted to follow her. This was her last chance to hop onto a pedicab and get away from here. The whole journey was a mistake, triggered by a moment of weakness. She should be in Nanjing with Tong instead, sharing the news with his parents and making plans for parenthood. There was so much to do she'd better not waste her precious time.

Doctor Li returned with a thermos bottle. As if being caught for doing something wrong, Bao backed into the office before he entered. Seeing her alone, he gave Bao a nod and smile.

"There's a political study meeting this afternoon. I can skip it, because I'm leaving for vacation." He poured hot water into an enamel mug, its inside stained by black tea.

Bao lowered her head. "You're very kind."

"I need to take your temperature and blood pressure."

The bamboo curtain lifted, and her mother returned.

"Your grandpa will go home and get the wheelbarrow. He'll tell Grandma not to wait for us to have lunch. After you have a rest, we'll take you home."

Bao was glad that with a thermometer in her mouth, she didn't have to say anything.

"Your blood pressure is normal, so is your temperature." Doctor Li rubbed the thermometer with alcohol, shook it, and returned it into its shield. "Let's get started." He took his tea mug. "Follow me."

Bao wore her sunglasses as she crossed the courtyard. In the dumpster flies feasted on rotten melon rinds, chicken bones, and vegetable leaves. A few hens pecked at the garbage and wiped their beaks in the dirt. After they entered a room, Doctor Li closed the door. He turned on the fluorescent light and drew the yellow-checked curtains. There was a narrow table covered with white sheets.

"Take off your underwear, lie on the table, and put your feet in the stirrups." He gave her mother a white sheet. "Put this over her lap." He went to a sink to wash his hands.

Bao crawled onto the table. Doctor Li came to raise it so her rear was higher than her head. He saw her high-topped sneakers.

"Do you play basketball?" He pressed a stethoscope to her chest and listened.

"She's a swimmer," her mother said.

"It shows, you're well-built." Bao blushed as he looked at her bare bottom. "Take off her shoes and put her feet in the stirrups. Pull up her skirt, so it won't get soiled."

Bao held her knees together when her mother slid her feet into the stirrups. She fantasized that Tong would break in and tell her to get up. How grateful she would be to have a second chance to make it right! Pick herself up, take Soybean, and run away to board a train. If other women could learn to become mothers, so could she. Forget about her parents, the university, and a career. She was a woman with a ripe body for childbearing. Why fight the purpose of her own existence? Tong was right—he knew she was fit to be a mother even when she doubted herself.

Doctor Li put on rubber gloves. His fingers probed around her vagina while his other hand pressed lightly on her abdomen.

"It's good that you do this early, the aftereffects are minimal." He slid a cold instrument into her vagina. "It's the speculum, which allows me to look inside you."

Her mother sat on a stool. "Thank you for looking after her." She sounded nervous and short of breath.

Bao saw a giant mosquito cling upside down to the ceiling. Its striped legs were as long as her finger. It might give a person a serious ailment. She'd warn Doctor Li and her mother if the mosquito took off.

Doctor Li filled a syringe and pulled some equipment from under the table. "I'm going to give you local anesthesia. You'll feel a little sting."

He nudged her knees apart with his wrists. Her mother held her hand when he pushed a needle deep inside Bao. A dull ache brought on a numb feeling in her lower belly.

Could Soybean feel it?

Bao couldn't keep her own baby. How could she stand up for anyone else? She wasn't a free woman but a slave. Her intellectual ideals were empty words. In real life she was powerless. Without a penny to her name, she lacked a backbone. On this table she lay down without a word and gave up her own flesh.

"I'll use syringe suction. It'll be over before you know it."

She heard suction, soft murmurs, a whooshing noise down a dark tunnel. A pinch, some scraping, more murmurs, whoosh. Out of the corner of her eye, she saw blood and tissue going into the collection jar. A low moan escaped her lips.

It was too late to scream out NO. Her mouth agape, she witnessed the death of Soybean.

"Shhh, it'll be over soon." The soothing voice of her mother, her touch. Bao squeezed the offered hand.

Was it a boy or girl? For the first time she wondered. Then it started hurting, not physically but spiritually, like she was losing a real and important part of her being. She would hate Tong forever. It didn't matter that he loved her and wanted to marry her. She'd always associate him with this horrible loss. It was so cruel to strip her body like this; it seemed so unfair.

Feeling dizzy and sick, she wept in silence.

The mosquito flew away from the ceiling. The suction noise stopped.

"Get dressed. I'll get you a hot-water bottle."

Doctor Li lowered the table so she was flat again. He left the room with the collection jar.

Her mother took her feet from the stirrups and slid on her panties with a sanitary napkin. She helped Bao down from the table and put on her shoes. Doctor Li took them to a sickroom and told Bao to rest there for an hour or two. Then he'd check to see if she had stopped bleeding.

After Bao crawled into the bed, her mother pulled a quilt over her body. Lying on her side, Bao held a hot-water bottle against her belly. At first she felt numb. Then her legs started to cramp up, and so did her uterus. She groaned like a wounded animal. Her mother stroked her hair.

"Are you all right, baby?"

Bao started sobbing. She was sad Tong wasn't there to mourn her loss. Why had she let this happen? Was a moment of pleasure worth this pain and a lifetime of regret? She pulled up her skirt to rub her belly. It felt tender and empty. She stretched out her legs and cried.

"I'll get you some food," her mother said. "You'll feel better."

When she returned, Bao ate five sesame seed cakes and drank three bottles of orange juice. Then she lay down and cried some more. After a while Doctor Li checked on her. She had stopped bleeding, and the cramping was almost gone. He gave her antibiotics and told her mother about aftercare. Bao was so tired she dozed off.

Her mother woke Bao when Grandpa arrived with the wheelbarrow. Bao put on a sweater and a pair of jeans. She wobbled as her mother helped her outside. Grandpa was white as a ghost. His arms shook as he lifted Bao into the wheelbarrow. He kept saying, "Make her comfortable," and covered her with a quilt printed with red peonies. The wheelbarrow didn't jolt when he pushed it home.

Bao closed her eyes and wore her sunglasses like a blind woman.

Chapter 7

LYING IN THE WHEELBARROW, Bao greeted her grandma. Her mother whispered a few words. The old woman's eyes reddened before she turned her face aside. She folded the quilt around Bao's legs while Grandpa carried her into the house. Passing the kitchen, Bao smelt cooking grease, sweet blood, and a raw odor of plucked chicken feathers. She wanted to throw up, but the morning sickness was a bygone privilege of motherhood.

"If a woman catches a chill after giving birth, she'll have lower back pain." Grandma tucked Bao up in bed like making an egg roll.

"But I didn't—"

"Doesn't matter." She draped a second quilt around Bao's waist. "Your body can't tell the difference."

Grandma was wrong, but Bao didn't feel like arguing. She fell quickly asleep. She was hungry when she woke up. She wanted only a bowl of rice with string beans. Meat and seafood reminded her of the bloody collection jar that had become Soybean. She wanted to forget—what was the use of remembering? She slept the rest of the day and most of the next day, waking only to take her meals, use the night pot, wash, and change her panties.

On the third day, Bao awoke to hear a rooster crowing. She sat up and glanced about her. The bedroom looked gloomy in the light let in by the small windows. A tall walnut armoire stood in the corner. An alarm clock and transistor radio rested on a red chest carved with two mandarin ducks. A picture of her mother wearing braids hung on the wall beside a framed collage of black and white baby photos: Little Bao slouching inside a wooden barrel, stark naked; Little Bao in Grandma's arms, both grinning; Little Bao sitting on Grandpa's shoulders and holding his stubbly cheeks.

She stretched her arms behind her back. All her exhaustion was gone, and she felt strong again. Her mother was sound asleep, her face buried in a pillow embroidered with goldfish and lotus flowers. Bao got up and dressed herself. When she opened the door, something caught her foot and she almost tripped.

"Be careful." Grandma looked out from behind the brick stove. "No doorsteps at your house, are there?"

Bao shook her head. Grandma folded straw into the stove. It seemed to be a primitive and tedious way of cooking. Up until a few years ago her family had used stoves that burnt coal cakes. After moving into their new apartment, her parents gradually modernized their kitchen.

"We use a gas stove," Bao said.

"Your mom told me. You wash clothes in a machine, too. It makes me wonder, can a machine cook?"

"There's a new appliance called a microwave. We don't have one yet."

"Doesn't sound like you need it." Grandma pumped the bellows to make the fire bigger.

On the wall above the stove, blackened by soot, hung a kettle suspended from a hook. A poster featured a fat baby boy riding a thrashing carp on bellowing waves. On another wall hung a feather duster, a curved knife, and a long-stemmed pipe with a brass bowl. A lone light bulb hung above the square dining table. Bao pulled the light switch, and it turned on. She let out the breath she'd been holding. The small house on the hillside had electricity, at least.

"Why do you waste electricity during the day?"

Bao switched it off.

In the fleeting yellow light, she had caught a glimpse of Grandma's shrewd, elephant-like eyes. Now Grandma wouldn't spare electricity on Bao. Did she love Bao less? When Bao was little, Grandma had cooked a snack for her every afternoon: a poached egg in jujube dessert soup, salted peanuts, water chestnuts, and roasted yams. Years later, Bao learned that being peasants, her grandparents had lived on the meager food production of their field. Her parents had more money because they earned salaries by working for the government. Yet she always ate better food at her grandparents' house.

"It's too soon for you to be up and about. A woman who had a miscarriage should be in confinement, like her first month after childbirth."

"I didn't have a miscarriage, Grandma."

"Your body can't tell the difference. Put on a coat or you'll catch a chill." She pressed down the burning straw with a fire poker.

Bao rubbed her elbows. Her arms felt sore. No use to make Grandma repeat the order, so she returned to the bedroom.

Her mother stirred on the bed. "You up already?" She pulled back the quilt to let Bao sit down.

"I feel fine." Bao put on her denim jacket and zipped it halfway. Better than she thought she would feel.

"I'm glad to hear it." Her mother sat up to put on her blouse.

Bao hadn't seen her mother change her clothes in years. The sight of her cotton bra and sparse armpit hair made her feel at once uneasy and close to her mother. She'd gotten the loose skin on her belly from giving birth to Bao eighteen years before. This badge of motherhood made Bao feel both guilty and envious of her mother. She had to look away to keep herself from touching her mother's belly.

"I'll leave tomorrow morning. Will you be okay here?"

Bao wrapped her arm around the bedpost. "Can you stay a few more days?"

"I have to go back to work, you know that." She ran a comb through her hair. "You're in good hands. Your grandparents are so happy to have you live with them for a month."

"Grandma said I have to be in confinement."

"She's trying to look after you. You need to rest and eat." She picked off a few hairs from her comb.

Bao looked out of the windows, caked with dry mud. The village was surrounded by rolling hills. In the distance, ragged ridges floated on oceans of cloud, and rounded hills surfaced like whales. Over the ridge two hawks slipped sideways, screaming in the wind, their voices thin. She envied them their freedom. She wanted to hike into the woods alone.

"I can climb onto that hilltop." She pointed outside.

"Don't be dumb and ruin your health. You'll regret it." Her mother patted Bao's shoulder. "I'll tell them not to restrict you too much, but you should stay indoors for a few days at least. Promise me?"

"Can I go home?"

Her mother bent down to fasten her shoelaces. Bao couldn't see her face.

"We won't let you return to an empty dorm, you know that. Besides, your father would keep a close eye on you just like your grandparents."

Bao remembered her father's tears. How could she spend two months under his wounded eyes? Perhaps the simple, humdrum life of the mountain village would be a nice vacation. She could learn to live her life without Tong. A month later she would return to the dorm when the other girls came back. The busy schoolwork and loss of privacy would help keep her mind off Tong. This was the purpose of the abortion.

"Would you tell Grandma not to treat me like a postpartum woman? I can't stand it."

Her mother folded the quilt into a rectangular block and laid the pillow on the top. "I'll talk to her right now."

The room décor looked gaudy in the morning light. Bright red drapery, embroidered with mandarin ducks, hung above the apple-green mosquito net. The quilt featured crimson peonies and songbirds with orange and purple feathers. The riotous colors made Bao feel claustrophobic. She walked out of the back door.

The brick house was surrounded by tiny plots of potato, cabbage, lettuce, corn, wheat, cucumber, onion, peas, and beans. On each side of the door, shaded by walnut trees, were pig and goat pens. Beside the house, on a cleanly swept area, grain was drying on straw mats. The old chicken coop was still there. Caged beneath an upturned basket was a mother hen, the basket raised just enough to allow her downy chicks, but not the hen, to wander in and out. A bony dog skulked around the corner as if ready to dodge a stone.

Goats bleating sounded like children crying. In the pen, three goats were tied to wooden stumps by leashes. A kid knelt on the ground to suckle. She let go of her mother's nipple, when Bao got near. She looked meek with round eyes, stubby nose, and droopy ears. Her soft bleating melted Bao's heart. A large buck with stiff horns stepped up protectively. If she tried to pet the kid, the old buck might attack Bao with his horns.

"Breakfast is ready, Bao," her mother said.

Bao returned to the house. Bowls of corn porridge, steamed buns, and pickles were laid on the dining table.

"How old is the kid?" Bao said.

"Six days old," Grandma said.

Bao bit into a bun and tasted sugar filling. How did her grandparents stay thin eating sugar buns? They might have fast metabolisms.

"Mom, can you eat my sugar filling?"

"Brown sugar is good for you." Her mother's voice trailed off as Bao glared at her.

Bao knew that countrywomen ate brown sugar after they gave birth. It was a custom from the old days when food had been lacking; people considered brown sugar a tonic that nourished one's blood. But Bao hadn't given birth. It was insulting to pamper her like a lactating mother.

"All right, I'll eat it for you." Her mother took the sugar bun.

"I saw the kid suckle." Bao tried to resume the conversation. "She's sweet."

"We teach children to watch a kid suckle," Grandpa said. "You can learn a lesson of filial piety. A kid doesn't stand but kneels to suckle. It's humble when it takes milk from its mother."

Bao pouted. Why did everything have some bearing on her situation? She would have to be a saint to forbear unsolicited advice. Her mother raised her eyebrows slightly, as if warning Bao not to be overly sensitive.

"The corn porridge is delicious," her mother said. "What's in it?"

"Guess." Grandpa rubbed his palms together.

"Is it honey?"

"This isn't ordinary honey." Grandpa went to fetch a glass jar, filled with amber-colored honey. "I learned the technique from the Baima people."

"Will you teach Bao how to keep bees?"

"If you like." He winked at Bao.

"Say yes." Her mother nudged Bao. "Before he changes his mind."

Bao didn't need to keep bees. She could buy honey at a store. Unlike dancing and playing tennis, beekeeping wasn't a skill that could attract potential suitors. Oh, she mustn't think about boyfriends so soon after the abortion! Bao had no friends here and didn't intend to befriend farmers. And yet, the bees were harmless. They wouldn't patronize her.

"All right," she said.

Grandpa burst into a smile. "It'll be fun."

His eyes curved into two half moons. His gray hair seemed to shine, and his wrinkled skin glowed pink. Bao looked away, a little unsettled that her answer made him so happy.

After breakfast Bao entered the bedroom. Her mother folded her shirts and placed them inside the duffle bag. Bao clasped her hands around a cup of warm water sweetened with honey.

"Will Dad ever forgive me?"

Her mother zipped the duffle bag. "Your father doesn't blame you for it, baby." She sat on the bed and patted the space beside her.

Bao remained sitting on a stool five feet away from her. But he did blame me, without a harsh word, she wanted to say.

"Bao, you're a big girl. I want to tell you a story about your father."

Bao sipped the water, sweet and fragrant.

"You may not remember much about the Cultural

Revolution." Her mother dusted her knee, like a peasant. "If not for the Cultural Revolution, your father and I would never have met."

Bao looked at the colorful bedding with contrition, because she forgot where she'd come from. Both her mother and she had grown up in Crystal Village.

"When your father worked on a labor farm in Songpan, he was one of the few people who'd studied at a university. The high school principal asked him to teach Chinese, but he refused. You know what he did?" She gave an encouraging smile, but Bao made no guess. "He pretended to stutter. They all said what a pity, he was like a teapot full of dumplings. The spout was too small for him to pour out the knowledge inside his belly, you know?"

"I've never heard him stutter. Was he a good actor?"

"He could act when he needed to. With that 'disability' he got a job as an accountant, distributing workers' salaries, buying groceries for the canteen, that sort of thing. So he relieved himself of the job of teaching children to worship Chairman Mao."

"Did he stutter for ten years?"

"No. After a year or so, people noticed he didn't stutter at all. He said to the county magistrate, 'Thank you for your help to reeducate me.' The flattery worked like a charm. By then he'd made a name for himself, fixing transistor radios and painting portraits of Chairman Mao. Did I ever tell you how we met?"

Bao shook her head.

"The first time I saw him, he was standing on a ladder and

painting Chairman Mao's ear." Her mother stretched out her long legs. The shirt rode up her waist, showing a bit of her pale, lax belly skin. "When someone called my name, he turned his head. He had the genteel look of a bookworm, his big eyes so full of warmth they seemed to talk. We had an instant connection."

Bao heard goats bleating outside, Grandma calling the chickens to feed. Inside, the sunlight shaded by the pink curtains was warm, inviting, and secretive.

"You were like me, Mom. We both have an eye for beautiful men." Bao lowered her voice. "Did you taste the forbidden fruit?"

Her mother's body stiffened. She tucked her shirttail into the elastic waistband.

"We didn't in those days."

Bao's face burnt with shame. She raised the honey water to her mouth, but the drink was cold. It tasted gooey, so she put it on the floor.

"In a way, our long-distance courtship taught us to be kind to each other." Her mother's voice was consoling, but Bao wasn't comforted. "When we saw each other, either in Nanping or Songpan, once a month or so, we bought groceries and cooked meals together. I washed his clothes, while he moved coal cakes, rice, and other heavy things for me. After a meal, we told each other stories about work and took long walks."

Bao felt like stepping outside for fresh air. The kid's bleating beckoned to her. Only the thought that her mother would leave the next day kept Bao in her seat.

"You know, PLA men were posted near the labor farm. They were hot shots from proletariat families. Many soldiers didn't finish middle school. Some university girls married them in order to leave the labor farm." Her mother drew up her legs and hugged her shins. "Your father once introduced me to a pretty girl, his former classmate. A soldier got her pregnant. Doctor Li, a medical student who'd been sent for reeducation, gave her an herbal remedy to abort the fetus. She couldn't get enough medicine to complete the abortion, so I helped her get more. In the end, she had a miscarriage that left her bedridden for a month."

Bao felt a familiar cramp in her belly. She breathed deeply to relax her muscles. The misery of another woman was strangely comforting. She no longer wanted to go outside.

"What happened to her?"

"The soldier helped her find a job and move to Chengdu, but he didn't marry her. After the Cultural Revolution we came to Nanjing University. The woman kept in touch with your father. A few years ago she asked for his help looking for a job at the university. It took him a while to find her a position in the library."

Her mother picked at her fingernails. She didn't look at Bao.

"Several years ago when we moved to the new apartment, I came across some old letters. Your father had once declared to the girl that she was his first love, although his letter was returned unopened." She sighed. "Forgive your father for being prejudiced against soldiers. He wanted to protect you above all else."

This caused Bao more pain than a slap in the face. A soldier had taken her father's first love. Like the other PLA man, Tong had gotten Bao pregnant. Like the other woman, Bao had an abortion performed by Doctor Li. It was dreadful how history repeated itself.

"So you knew Doctor Li way back." Bao tried to blink away her tears.

"He was a second-year medical student, one of the youngest in the labor camp." Her mother's face lit up. "Li came from a family of prestigious doctors. Both his parents were renowned obstetricians."

"How did he become an abortion doctor?"

"It was the Cultural Revolution, when good decent people suffered and were broken like animals in a circus, and mean ignorant people flourished like warlords." Her mother stroked the gray hair on her temple. "Doctor Li married a peasant. In 1976 your father encouraged him to take the graduate school entrance exams, but the earthquake caused a fire at his house. All his books were burned, so he couldn't review his lessons. Doctor Li never complained about his bad luck, he's made peace with life."

Bao thought of his gentle hands, his firm and confident voice.

"Doctor Li wastes his talent on a petty job. He could be a real doctor."

"He *is* a real doctor." Her mother scooted up to a sitting position. "Here in the country, barefoot doctors have ruined many lives. Men become impotent after vasectomies. Strong rosy-cheeked women become semi-disabled after having their tubes tied."

Bao had heard of barefoot doctors, farmers who received basic medical training for about six months and then practiced their techniques on people. Many of them still farmed and worked barefoot in the rice paddies.

"Why sterilization?" she said.

"By 1976, couples with more than one child were encouraged to be sterilized." Her mother didn't seem to mind the adult subject. Evidently Bao had become a woman in her eyes. "The Nanping county headsman set an example. He volunteered to have a vasectomy done by a barefoot doctor. Less than a year later his wife began to have affairs. When people asked her why, she said, 'He isn't a man anymore!' Over the years millions of peasants have been sterilized." She stared at the Mandarin ducks on the quilt. "As the old saying has it, 'Every trade has its master.' Doctor Li makes the procedure as safe and painless as it can be."

Bao wondered what her mother used for birth control. Suddenly the door opened. Grandma came in, wiping her hands on the apron.

"What do you want for lunch?"

Bao peered at her watch. It was only ten o'clock.

"Stewed hen? Boiled shrimps? Eggs fried with mushrooms?"

"They all sound fine, Mom. Do you need my help?"

"No, sit yourself down and talk to your daughter." Grandma closed the door with a loud bang. "She'll miss you bad!"

Bao made a face at her mother. They giggled quietly.

"Grandma is funny."

"She raised you and loves you like her own daughter." Her mother stroked the goldfish embroidered on the pillowcase. "When we were reunited, your father and I tried to make up for the lost years. On the surface we were a happy family. You were a bright, well-behaved girl. But who knew what we had lost? We didn't see your first step or hear your first words. You came to us, a big girl with your own thoughts."

Bao read desolation in her mother's face. She felt that she was robbed of those years when Bao had grown up in the countryside. In hindsight she had done her best—at least she raised a daughter who could sympathize with her heartache. Bao thought of Soybean, whom she could never know. Her first steps, her first words would remain her crushed dreams. If they were to meet in Heaven, could Bao ask for her forgiveness?

"Don't beat yourself up, Mom. I didn't confide in you, not because I didn't trust you, but because that's who I am." Bao remembered that snowy winter morning more than a decade ago, when Cauliflower Tail had died, and she had worried about disasters that might befall her family. "Now I can tell you a story."

Her mother smiled with tears in her eyes. "A story? About your grandparents?"

"About a pair of pandas." Bao crawled into the bed to sit beside her mother. She proceeded to tell her encounter with the pandas. She recalled every detail, the snoring of her grandfather, the screeching of the panda cub, and the tearing sound of Cauliflower Tail's flesh. When she said, "Long live

Chairman Mao!" from a bygone era, she felt the hair stand up on her neck.

Her mother stared at Bao in disbelief. "Did you make any of this up?"

"Nope. I let Cauliflower Tail die, because a panda is a national treasure. All these years I've kept it a secret. You're the first person I told."

"Why?"

Bao knelt on the bed to look at the hills yonder. There were remnants of the 1976 earthquake that had shaken this region. The slopes carried the wounds of reddish earth as if slices had been carved off. Below, valleys were partially dammed by a chaos of boulders, soil, and splintered trees. The mountain slope had ugly bald spots where trees had been logged. There didn't seem to be any wildlife there now. The vivid scene of her childhood had been a ghostly dream. Yet she recalled it without sadness or nostalgia. If the panda mother had risked her life to eat a hen and nurse her cub, why couldn't people survive earthquakes, the turmoil of the Cultural Revolution, and the massacre in the streets of Beijing? Like the ordeals that the whole country had endured, her loss of Soybean seemed to be Bao's destiny. It was her first real test in life, and difficult choices could make or break a person.

"I gave up Soybean, not because I didn't love her. You let me live with my grandparents, since that was the best you could do back then. I couldn't ask for more, then or now." She bit her trembling lip. "Especially after what I did."

"My dearest girl." Her mother stroked Bao's hair. "One day you'll have a baby. Remember an old saying that it's far easier for a person to carry a load of ten thousand pounds than hold a suckling in her arms. It's true. The joy, fatigue, and responsibilities of a mother will heal you and make you strong. Take heart, sweetie. Nothing else will be quite as difficult as what you just went through."

Her gentle whisper brought tears to Bao's eyes. She cried with relief, without bitterness. For a long while, neither of them moved or said a word. While Bao felt that she grew older and wiser, perhaps her mother grew younger in her presence.

"Tell the story to Dad. It's the deepest secret of my childhood."

Chapter 8

BAO WOKE UP AND HEARD the goats bleating. Beside her the bed was empty. Her mother was on a train returning to Nanjing. Bao wrapped the quilt tightly about her and tried to go back to sleep. Gradually she began to distinguish the kid's high-pitched cries from the goats' throaty bleating. The dog started to bark, and the chickens clucked as they fed. Her grandparents talked in the kitchen. Bao didn't want to lie in bed like an invalid. She got up, dressed, and combed her hair.

In the kitchen, Grandma pumped the bellows at an even pace. "Your grandpa is waiting for you."

Bao found him squatting outside the doorstep. He appraised her stonewashed denim jacket.

"This light blue won't disturb the bees. If you wear dark colors, they might think you're a bear. Bright colors make you look like a flower."

He put a white cloth hat on Bao. Its long veil hung about her face and fit snugly around her neck. As the veil blurred her vision, the sights and sounds around her were soothing.

He led the way to the backyard. "I just brought my bees

back from the jujube orchard. The owner was so gracious he lent me a tricycle to transport the hives."

"Why were they at the orchard?" Bao said.

"By pollinating the flowering trees, the bees raise the jujube production. My girls turn everything they touch into treasure. Honey and royal jelly are tonics. Beeswax, propolis, and bee venom are age-old medicines."

He showed Bao the hive, a rectangular wooden box. The opening at the bottom extended out in front like a porch. Inside the box were frames where the bees built their combs.

"The bees raise the brood—eggs, larvae, and pupae—in these combs."

A second box, called a super, about half a foot high, sat above the main hive. A plastic divider with many holes lay between the hive body and the super. The holes were small enough to keep the larger queen bee from passing through it to lay eggs in the super. The worker bees, smaller than the queen, passed through these holes to make honey.

"We keep the queen and her brood in the hive box. Only honey is stored in the super. At harvest time I take away the super, the bees in the hive box are not disturbed."

Bao lifted the cloth curtain as Grandpa moved the supers inside the old earthquake shed, now a clean, spacious workroom. Its four corners were propped up with wooden beams, four sides made of wooden boards, and the roof covered with tar paper. If there were an earthquake they could stay warm and comfortable in the new shed.

Grandpa opened the super with a small knife. There were nine frames inside. He pried a frame loose before removing it.

He showed her the neat honeycombs, like golden buttons. The bees sealed each cell containing honey with a cap made of wax. Bao handed Grandpa the serrated knife, which he had steeped in hot water. He sliced through the caps with the knife.

"Do the bees miss the honey you take?" she said.

"No." He installed the frame inside the spinner and started to turn a handle. As the spinner worked up speed, honey was extracted from the frame and collected in the barrel. "A hive needs about twenty pounds of honey to survive an average winter. The bees are capable, when I provide them the space, of making a lot more." He retrieved the wet frame and returned it to the super. "I leave this for my girls to clean up. I'm not as greedy as some people. They feed the bees sugar water, even artificial sweetener."

Bao recited a poem. "Be there plains or mountains, they forage all the fields. They gather honey from hundreds of flowers. For whom do they toil and make it so sweet?"

"You said it so prettily." Grandpa lifted another frame from the super. "During the honey season, they fly out to collect nectar from 3 a.m. until dark. A worker bee typically dies of exhaustion in a half month. So the queen must keep her colony going."

"They aren't all girls, then."

"The drones are raised and fed for one purpose—to mate with the queen. A drone dies after mating! The ones who get to live, because they haven't mated, are thrown out of the colony before the winter, because they eat too much." He sliced through the wax caps to expose the luscious, honey-filled cells.

"Some tough girls you have." She blushed.

"They teach you to live a useful life. No work, no food. Will you uncap the next frame?" He began to work the spinner.

She hesitated. Some bees swarmed about her. Her head felt as if it were inside a mini-cyclone. She reached inside the super and lifted a frame. Several bees crawled onto the back of her hand. She brushed them off gently. When she held up the capping knife, a bee flew into the opening of her sleeve. She tried to shake it out, but the bee crawled higher onto her forearm.

"Put down the knife and pull up your sleeve."

It was too late. Bao was stung. In her shock, she flung both the knife and frame to the floor. Suddenly more bees swarmed to attack her. She swatted at them and shouted, "Go away!" Although she wore a veil, she felt no protection whatsoever.

Grandpa said, "Stay calm!"

But she couldn't keep the bees at bay. When more bees flew at her, she cried "Help!" and dashed for the house.

Grandma raised her head when the front door slammed. "Finished so soon?" Panting, Bao waved her sticky hands. Grandma burst into laughter. "It's no good to run away. See how your grandpa does it."

Bao watched through the kitchen windows. Thick smoke came out of the shed.

"He burns cow dung," Grandma said. "The smoke calms the bees down."

"I got stung."

A red bump rose on Bao's forearm, two more on her wrist and hand. She was afraid to touch them. Grandma took her forearm and scraped at the red bump with her nail. She took out a stinger and showed it to Bao.

"A bee dies after stinging you."

"But I didn't mean it any harm."

"Never swat at bees." She lifted the veiled hat from Bao's head. "You must have good manners around them."

Bao blinked after her vision regained clarity. Beekeeping was harder than she'd thought and also more interesting. Grandpa waved at her from the shed. The bees must have calmed down, but she was afraid to return to the battle so soon after her injuries.

"I won't go out there without long gloves." She flexed her hand tentatively, and it hurt.

"We don't wear gloves. If you're clumsy, you may upset the bees even more." Grandma scraped out the stinger from Bao's wrist. "Bee stings are no cause for alarm. Few beekeepers get cancer, you know why? Bee venom prevents and cures illnesses."

"I'll leave the other stinger in then." She'd treat it as a reward.

Grandma smeared a little honey on her red bump. The spot on her hand hurt a little, but not much. Bao was becoming a veteran.

"I'll go help Grandpa now." She put on the veiled hat.

"Wait." Grandma took out a white coat and matching pants. "Change your clothes. The bees left an alarm scent. Others may attack you when they smell it."

The clothes could fit someone twice Bao's size.

"Why are they so big?"

"If you wear tight clothing, bees can sting through the fabric." She helped Bao put on the bee suit with elastic cuffs at the wrists and ankles and the zippers at the collar and torso.

Bao marched toward the earthquake shed.

For two days Bao loitered about the shed. Grandpa gathered the caps to drain into a clean bucket. The honey from the caps was the sweetest, he said. Bao helped him melt the beeswax and filter it. Grandma braided cotton wicks for candles. The golden-colored beeswax candle burned slowly with a bright flame, exuding a faint fragrance of honey, pollen, and flower nectar.

That night the transistor radio droned the local news. "This year, one-child policy workers have achieved significant success in the countryside."

There was no mention of the riots or arrests of activists. Two months of student demonstrations seemed to be a distant memory. Sitting in the kitchen with her grandparents, Bao wondered if the school boycott had left any impact except for the deaths, arrests, and fear of more punishment. She was a thousand miles away from Tong, and their passion was a thing from another world.

Grandma had a special recipe. She melted beeswax with sweet almond oil, added warm water, and blended them well until she had a thick cream. The hand cream was smooth and not too oily, with a delicate fragrance of honey and pollen. Bao wanted to bring home two large jars—one for her and one for her mother. Grandma beamed with pride at her acceptance of the gift.

While Bao spoke little to her grandparents, she planned for a secret excursion. Today she retired to her bedroom after lunch, pretending that she'd take a nap. Grandma ground corn in the courtyard. Grandpa fixed trellises in the cucumber field. Bao slipped out of the back door, took a small spade, and headed for the woods.

The hill ascended gently as she left the village behind. The trail was awful, dried mud churned by hooves; livestock had been driven up through the forest to graze on alpine pastures. She passed dogwood in bloom, and white-bellied pigeons flapped noisily away. Once in a while, she looked back at the village houses that shrank into squat shacks amidst green fields. Even if her grandparents were looking for her, she would not turn back.

The woods were dark, and sunlight spotted the trail. Wild peonies bloomed orange, maroon, pink, and purple. She walked up the mountainside, the murmur of a stream on one side, her tread so silent on the carpet of conifer needles that when a twig snapped underfoot the piercing sound startled white-tailed warblers from nearby willows. Further up the hill, she passed under the umbrella-shaped ficus virens trees that locals called yellow-rafters. They thrived on poor soil; like willow, a twig cutting could grow into a vigorous tree. Finally she was huffing and puffing and couldn't go any further.

When she turned to look behind her, her heart was filled with elation. The trail plunged into the valley she'd climbed out of and along the banks of a stream among massive yellow-rafters, their trunks encrusted with moss, their leafy canopies closing over a hundred feet above her head. She had arrived at the source of the creek. White water rushed over large, smooth boulders. She reached into the water and cupped a handful to drink. It slid down her throat, cool and refreshing.

She sat on a boulder and surveyed the site. Wild flowers flourished: primula, touch-me-not, trillium, mint, and buttercup. She recognized jack-in-the-pulpit, which started its life as a male and then solved its midlife crisis by continuing as a female. Tragopan chicks had hatched, a mother pheasant clucking as she led tiny puffs of down through thickets. Small dragon-children scurried away into the bush. The air was still and waterlogged, and cicadas screeched.

"You won't be lonely here, Soybean."

She began to dig with her spade. After a breeze, wild cherry petals drifted down like belated snowflakes. She took out a pair of panties from her pocket. She had worn them on the night when Soybean was conceived. On the white cotton, yellow daisies displayed their small, neat petals. She folded her panties to stuff into the hole and covered it with fresh petals. A snake, as thick as her thumb, handsomely speckled in yellow, brown, and green, slid into a cleft between the mossy rocks. She piled up the dirt into a small mound. Finally she draped the dome with a white handkerchief. She pushed twigs into the corners of the hanky to nail it to the ground. It was a mourning flag for the tomb.

"Rest in peace, Soybean." She bowed three times and

started to weep. "If you came to me a few years later, I would've carried you gladly. I was weak, baby, I don't deserve you."

Alone in the deep woods, she cried with abandon, like a countrywoman at her child's funeral.

"You were a love child, but I put you to death. I don't expect you to forgive me. But I beg you, Soybean, do not hate me, because hatred is poison."

A small voice said, "Hey, you."

"You're an angel, a hundred times better than me. Promise me you'll find peace and joy in heaven."

"What're you doing?"

This time Bao heard the voice, which had addressed her. She looked up and saw a disheveled woman wearing a hefty skirt. Her face was puffy and caked with dust. Her small hands cupped underneath her protruding belly, as if it were in danger of dropping to the ground. She looked anywhere between age twenty-five and thirty-five, but her almond-shaped eyes seemed much younger. They were timid, yet vigilant and antagonistic.

"I asked, just what do you think you're doing here?"

"Who are *you*?" Bao glared at the woman who was about her height.

"You shouldn't mourn dead people here, Little Sister."

"Is this your mountain?"

"Your bad luck may jinx my little one." The woman stooped to point at the white kerchief. Bao reached out a hand but found it unnecessary to stop her. The woman couldn't bend down all the way to touch the kerchief. As the swollen belly weighed her down, she grabbed her knees to maintain an upright stance. She looked pathetic and helpless to be on her own.

"How many months are you?"

"Just over eight months." A shy smile crept up her face. "He's on the big side."

Most peasants preferred boys to girls, because the families needed men to work in the fields. Bao had to disagree with her. "I would've liked a girl," she said.

The woman eyed the knoll covered with the white kerchief. "Is she here?"

"Soybean was never born."

"Oh, did you lose it?"

"I had an abortion." The candid words gave Bao a sense of relief. She couldn't say it to Grandma, but she told a stranger.

"You poor thing." She came forward to touch Bao's elbow. "Did they force you?"

"Who?" Bao frowned.

"The one-child policy workers, who else?"

Bao suddenly understood the situation. Evidently the woman was attempting to have a child outside her quota. She was hiding from the one-child policy workers. Bao had read stories in *Liberation Daily* about "guerrillas" who hid out to have extra babies. They were mostly countrywomen who were under pressure to have sons. Some guerrillas hid in their relatives' homes until they gave birth. The idea of knowing someone who risked her life to have a baby in the woods!

"Won't you go to the hospital for delivery? You may have complications." Bao wanted to add, "You may die here," but checked herself.

"My aunt will tend to me when it's time. She was a midwife."

"Is your first a girl?"

"She's about this tall." She raised her hand to her hip. "My girl will make a fine sister."

"What if . . . it's a girl again?"

The woman grinned so broadly she showed her bright red gums and jagged teeth. "I know it's a boy. My mother-in-law said so, too. He kicks like a stallion!"

Bao stared at her belly. The frail dirty-looking woman had the courage to defy the authority. What a triumphant story she would tell her future son!

"Ouch!" The woman pressed both hands to her skirt. "You can't crawl out from my ribs. Be a good boy!"

"Is he kicking?"

"He sure is, jumping up and down, more like."

"Can I touch him?" Bao was surprised to hear her own request.

"All right, Little Sister." Her cheeks brightened with a blush.

Bao put her hand on the woman's belly. Hard as rock! She had thought a pregnant woman's belly was soft like a balloon. When the baby was born, the air would be let out of the balloon. Oh! She felt a movement—swift gliding.

"Is . . . is it an arm or leg?"

"Probably an elbow." The woman smiled. "He hiccups, too. It tickles, a very funny feeling."

Bao tried to trace the movement, but it had ceased. Was it

playing hide and seek? The cunning baby!

"Can I listen to him?"

The woman complied. She sat on a boulder with her hands propped behind her. Bao crouched down to put her ear to the woman's belly. She heard grumbling, ruffling, and swishing sounds.

"Boy, is he busy!" Bao patted the belly. "Is he comfortable?"

"I'm sure he is." The woman stroked Bao's hair. The intimate gesture made her shiver. None of her friends, not even Lily, had touched Bao so boldly. "Don't worry, Little Sister, you'll have other children."

Bao didn't like to be pitied, especially by a guerrilla who valued boys more than girls. The woman might have lived in Crystal Village all her life. She'd never been to Nanjing or any other metropolitan city—she might not even know what a university was. She had the gall to predict that Bao would have other children! What about the one-child policy? Bao wouldn't hide in the woods to be a guerrilla. What was more, she abhorred the treatment of females as inferior to males.

Bao stood up and dusted her hands. "I wasn't forced by the one-child policy workers."

The woman gazed at her face, as if studying a puzzle. "Why did you have an abortion?"

"I'm not married." Telling the truth was easier than Bao had thought. "I'm a university student. I don't want to have a child yet."

"But where's your fellow, Little Sister?"

"We broke up."

"How could he, after what you went through?"

The look of pity on her face vexed Bao. "We loved each other, but we weren't ready to settle down."

"Why not?"

It would hurt Bao too much to explain. She walked behind an enormous yellow-rafter until she reached the edge of a precipice. In the distance, cliffs wore jagged scars where huge chunks had seemingly been wrenched off from the surrounding rock. Clouds descended and filled the valley, cool like a glacier, a river of light so smooth it seemed she could skate over it. She felt like standing on the pivot of the earth. Everywhere she looked, the world was vast and alive. Limestone cliffs thrust into the blue sky like the teeth of a saw. Wisps of birch bark, thin as a snake's skin, quivered in the breeze.

"Little Sister, you're so young." A hand landed on her shoulder to pull her back. "Don't take things too hard."

"I'm not going to jump." Bao would never admit that the thought had crossed her mind.

They returned to the creek side together.

"Rest in peace, little one." The woman picked a wild peony to place on the grave. "Your mama grieves for you."

"I didn't bury Soybean here. It was just a memento." The woman didn't seem to understand her meaning, so Bao explained, "I buried my panties here."

"Why did you . . ." The woman burst into a knowing smile.

"I don't want you to worry that it may jinx your little one."

The woman nodded her head slowly. "If you take out the white mourning flag, I suppose it'd be okay."

"How will I find it next time?"

"I'll mark the place for you: just south of Rooster Peak."

Bao glanced around, half expecting to see a prominent sign in calligraphy, popular landmarks in a public park.

"Look at that tree, isn't it like a rooster?"

The gigantic yellow-rafter seemed to grow out of the cliff. Digging into the rock clefts, its gnarled root protruded like a dozen chicken feet. Thick branches held up a lush crown, while the leaves hung beside the cliff like a rooster's tail.

"Do you live around here?"

"Why do you ask?"

Bao tried not to alarm her. "Will I see you again?"

"If we meet again, it's all right." The woman shook her head. "If we don't, that's fine with me."

Why was she so secretive? Bao wouldn't reveal her hiding place to anyone.

"I won't take off the mourning flag—it marks Soybean's grave."

Her lips quivered. "Do as you like."

"Bye." Bao picked up the spade and wiped its tip on the grass.

Before she walked far, the woman called behind her. "You won't tell anyone, will you?"

"I won't, if you don't touch Soybean's tomb." Bao turned around, and the woman stood frozen. "I promise you on the grave of Soybean."

Nodding eagerly, the woman dropped her shoulders and grinned. Bao knew she'd return to the spot and find Soybean's tomb intact. She would meet the woman again and hear her talk about her unborn son. This gave her hope. She descended in a cloud, the sun casting shafts of pale light. Fern fronds pushed up through the mat of sodden leaves, imparting a soft, green sheen to the slope downhill. A musk deer stood silent as fog, screened by a shrub, its miniature tusks gleaming. She watched so intently that her hand loosened its grip on the spade. The deer bounded away and vanished in the dusk.

Chapter 9

BAO EXPLAINED THE BENEFIT of taking a walk in the woods, but Grandma shook her head.

"Too soon," she said. "You need to rest more."

"Next time, do tell us where you're going and when you'll be back." Grandpa knocked his pipe against the table. "Then we won't be worried sick."

"There's nothing to worry about."

"Your parents entrusted you to our care." He took a deep drag of his pipe, but it didn't seem to give him any pleasure.

"Sorry I'm such a burden to you."

"What're you talking about, Little Bao?" Grandma put away the broom after sweeping the floor.

"I'm not little anymore. I had an abortion, not a miscarriage. I was feeling numb, now I want to mourn my loss." She started to cry.

Grandma held Bao to her chest. "Let it out, child."

"Grandma, you don't know how horrible it was—"

"It wasn't our place to intervene." Grandpa pulled his chair closer to her. "I wanted us to talk about it, because we could have raised your child. We raised you and your mother. Have we done a shabby job?"

"But Dad doesn't like Tong."

"I don't blame him." He coughed and cleared his throat. "How could you like someone who did this to your daughter?"

"We should've talked about it," Grandma said, "but your mother was in such a hurry she didn't even get home."

"Doctor Li was leaving, and he'd be gone for a month. We had no time."

"You won't get yourself into this sort of trouble again." Grandpa put down his pipe and cupped her cheeks in both hands. Bao felt the thick calluses on his palms. "But if you have difficulties, anything at all, you come to tell your grandparents. We'll help you however we can—we won't stand by and watch you suffer."

Bao took a deep breath. Her tears stopped easily when she felt loved and protected.

"I'll tell you next time when I take a walk."

"Good girl." When Grandma pinched her earlobe, Bao bit her lip and smiled.

"Did you see a man?" Grandpa said. "In a faded army uniform and a wrinkly cap with a red star."

"A PLA man in the mountains?"

"They were donated clothes. He's a madman."

Bao had known a madman, the janitor at her elementary school. He hadn't talked to anyone but smiled at girls like an old uncle. Some children threw rocks at the madman. Bao peered at him and walked away. One day the madman touched her cheek with his warm, calloused hand. Her friends said the madman had wiped the toilets with his bare hands. This made her nauseated.

"Does he touch people?" Bao said.

"No, he's harmless. If you give him some food, he'll eat and not bother you."

"I'll bring some next time." Bao picked up her chopsticks.

For two days Bao had stayed home, only stepped out of the house to feed the goats and watch the kid nurse. She was devising a plan to make friends with the guerrilla woman. She wanted to tend to the birth of her baby. This desire, so sudden and unreasonable, yet so powerful, consumed her heart and mind.

She had repeated dreams about a birth in the woods. In one dream she assisted a midwife with bound feet. Another time she alone helped the woman who lay on a bed of straw fashioned like a bird's nest. When the baby's head appeared, Bao fainted at the sight of blood. She couldn't see the baby but heard its hoarse cry, before she woke up in a cold sweat.

The next day Bao told her grandparents that she'd take a walk and come home for supper. She collected a bottle of honey and a jar of hand cream. Her mother could afford to buy Ponds cold cream. The beeswax cream would be useful to the guerrilla woman. It could keep her hands smooth and help with her stretch marks. Later she could use the cream on the baby's bottom. Bao stashed her gifts in a nylon handbag.

She hiked up the mountain. Wild azalea leaves glistened, their buds swollen and pink, ready to burst into flower. The red bark of birch trees caught the sun's slanting rays, and lichens drooped in luminous strands from their boughs. She sweated from exertion. Never in her life had she imagined fawning over a peasant who tried to circumvent the one-child policy. Bao was a university student, the elite of Chinese youth, and a law student at that! Puffing and huffing, she noted with some comfort that the woman wouldn't be able to move on a steep mountain—it wasn't safe or easy.

She heard a shrill cry and looked up. A blue-nosed golden monkey hung from the mossy fir branch. Two large monkeys followed. They chased each other and flew through the trees. Bao stared. She'd only read about these beautiful creatures in books. The monkey family melted into the woods as suddenly as they had appeared. The air vibrated with their cries, and the trees seethed and rocked as in a storm. Bao went on her way and soon found the white handkerchief on the ground.

Soybean's grave was intact. The handkerchief wasn't hers but another one embroidered with a pink lotus flower. Should she take offense at this sleight of hand? The lotus, a noble flower that rose unsullied from the mud, was a fitting metaphor for Soybean. The guerrilla woman must've put some thought into it when she changed the white handkerchief.

Bao cupped her hands around her mouth. "Where are you?"

Her voice resounded in the valley.

"I'm back." The echo lingered, growing gentle and insistent.

"I'm your friend!" Bao said.

She leapt a little as if to send her declaration across the hills. There was no answer. Holding the nylon bag over her head, she turned around slowly to speak to every direction.

"I brought you gifts."

She repeated her greetings, time and again. Several birds scolded, but there was no sign of the woman.

Half an hour later, Bao was hoarse and weary. If the woman had moved away, she wouldn't have bothered to replace the white mourning flag. Bao studied the creek, trees, and boulders. Only rabbits, frogs, snakes, and lizards could hide in the cracks of stones and rotting logs. Where could a woman with a huge belly live?

Bao walked toward the cliff, where age-old vines sprawled and clung to the rocks. The valley was invisible underneath a sea of clouds. Could the guerrilla woman hide in a tunnel dug in the earth, like a groundhog?

Then a thought chilled Bao to the bone. Could the woman have given birth? A premature baby might die in the woods.

"Is your baby alive?" Her voice trembled. "What do you need? I'll help you."

The echo grew dull and died away. She no longer expected an answer, her heart full of despair. A rustling noise came from behind. Feeling the wind, she hugged her shoulders.

"Little Sister," a voice said. Bao turned around and saw no one. She might've heard it in her own head. "I'm behind you."

Bao recognized the voice. "You're alive!" She wiped her tears.

"Do me a favor—leave the cliff, please." Bao waited for the woman to continue. "I won't come out until you're in safety."

"Where are you?" Bao glanced about her, left and right, up

and down, front and back.

"You make me dizzy, Little Sister." The vines shook gently. To Bao's amazement, a small fence pushed out the vines to open up a hole the size of a trap door for dogs. The door opened onto the narrow path along the side of the cliff. "Now you see me. Get off the cliff, so I can come outside."

Bao went to the creek side. A moment later the guerrilla woman appeared. Her face was flushed and her hair disheveled. She appeared to be panting in agitation.

"I brought these for you." Bao gave her the gifts as a peace offering.

The woman took out the honey and hand cream. Bao told her about their backyard beehive, when a man emerged from the cliff and stood beside the woman. A blunt crew cut accentuated his prominent brow ridges. He looked guarded with small eyes darting here and there. Skin peeled from the wings of his nose, and his lips were chapped. He was fastening the rope belt of his baggy pants. He must be her husband! They might have been having sex while she had shouted outside their cave.

If only Bao could disappear into a hole in the ground! Years ago she had seen a movie, *Red Sorghum*, by director Zhang Yimou. In a controversial scene, actress Gong Li lay down in the sorghum field and offered her body to her lover. Critics coined the term 'copulating in the field.' Many argued that it degraded Chinese peasants; for sure, even the poorest peasants had the decency to make love in the privacy of their bedrooms, instead of humping in the field like dogs. Never had Bao expected to run into such a spectacle. And yet, what was wrong with them having sex in the cave? They were married with a child. Perhaps the lust of the flesh, as well as the need for posterity, motivated them to have another baby.

"My old man Candor brought me food," the woman said. "When did you get here, Little Sister?"

"A while ago."

The woman was flushed with afterglow. Bao could feel the heat in her own face.

"Little Sister brought me gifts."

Thank goodness for the change of subject. "My grandpa and I harvested honey and made the beeswax cream together. I thought you might like it."

"Is your grandpa Cao Zidong?" Candor said.

Bao nodded. "You know him?"

The woman exchanged a glance with her husband.

"Who doesn't know Bee-tamer Cao?" she said. "Your grandparents came to our wedding. They gave us a pair of thermos bottles printed with swans that we use every day."

"Your grandparents are good folks." Candor smiled, crowfeet rippling from the corners of his heavy lids. "Old Cao learned beekeeping from the Baima people. His honey nourishes the body and makes one strong. You must thank him for us."

"Grandpa didn't know I took it." Bao looked the woman in the eye, as if to assure her: You see, I haven't mentioned you to anyone—I'm trustworthy.

Candor wrinkled up his forehead.

"I'm Gu Bao." She offered her hand, which Candor

automatically shook. "I'm glad to meet you, Candor."

Fear flashed in the woman's eyes. She hadn't meant to disclose her husband's name. She must've felt tenderness stronger than reason toward Bao. What else could have induced her to answer Bao not once, but twice? Candor peered at his wife, as if asking, "Who is she? Why did you make friends with her?" The woman averted her eyes. She opened the bottle and dipped a finger in honey. She tasted it and put her finger in Candor's mouth. He wrapped his dry lips around her finger and sucked with relish.

"You keep it." He pushed away the bottle. "If I take it home, Daisy will lap it up in two days."

"Let her, she doesn't get a treat every day." She put the honey bottle in his pocket. "I'll keep the cream. It's so smooth." She smeared a dab on his chapped lips.

Candor rubbed his lips together. "I'd buy it for you, Orchid, if I find it in the store."

"It fixes up your face pretty good." She dabbed more cream on his nose, cheeks, chin, and forehead. He had to run his palm over his entire face to smooth out the cream. He grinned at his mischievous wife.

Bao was mesmerized. She often heard that countrywomen were pressured to have sons; those who bore daughters were mistreated, even beaten and starved. This couple seemed to be genuinely fond of each other. Bao heard a loud bang, clear yet muffled, resound in the valley.

"It's on the south slope," Orchid said.

"Let's get inside," Candor said. "Someone may come here."

"What's that?" Bao said.

"A gunshot. Some poacher may be hunting down a musk deer. The musk pod from a stag is valuable medicine." Candor held up a makeshift fence as Orchid crawled into the cave. "You coming?"

Bao stole a glance at the shadowy woods. "Yes." She got down on her hands and knees.

The crude fence, made of twigs and tree branches, kept the cave opening covered and left small holes for air to circulate. Camouflaged by the vines, the fence gave one a handle to raise the vines without damaging them. Little wonder she'd never suspected it to be a hiding place.

Orchid lit an oil lamp. The cave was about four meters long. Bao could only stoop. A large oilskin was spread on the ground, covered with a black bearskin and several quilts. The top quilt was twisted like a pretzel before Orchid straightened it. There was a kerosene stove, a thermos bottle, several pots and bowls contained in a washbasin. Orchid threw a pair of half-finished sweater pants onto the bed, trailing a roll of woolen yarns.

"Have a seat." She offered Bao a bamboo stool, while she and Candor sat on the bedding.

"Are you knitting?" Bao's voice sounded muffled.

She heard a dripping sound and looked up. The ceiling was damp and covered with moss. Orchid opened a canvas blanket to cover the top quilt.

"Woolen pants for my son." Orchid tugged at the unfinished leg. There was a small opening in the crotch.

"He'll be born in August. Won't they be too warm for

him?"

Orchid studied the knitting with a frown. "I've been here for a month. It feels like winter all the time."

She endured her life in the cave. At the end of her ordeal was the hardship of having an "extra" child. The baby would bring his parents fines and other material punishments. Orchid still looked forward to his birth. Bao had sacrificed Soybean in order to pursue her career. How could she criticize Orchid for preferring a boy to girl? She hung her head in shame.

"Candor is being both Mom and Dad to Daisy. He works in the fields and delivers provisions for panda researchers. I should be of more use, instead of playing with this." Orchid threw the knitting on the pillow.

"You have your hands full." Bao reached out to pat her knee. "Take care of yourself and have the baby: you're doing enough for the family." How did these words get into her mouth? Bao used to think the one-child policy liberated women, but now she comforted Orchid like a country sister. "If you need things, anything at all, tell me and I'll do my best."

"How old are you, Little Sister?"

"Eighteen. I'll turn nineteen in two months."

"You city people look after yourselves." There was jealousy in her eyes. "Candor is twenty, and I'm twenty-one. We look like old hags beside you."

How could they be younger than Tong? They were dressed in baggy clothes like people in the Cultural Revolution. Their somber eyes spoke of the burdens in their lives.

"You can help me, Little Sister." Orchid rubbed her lower

back with a fist. "Daisy likes to play with young women, when Candor works in the field. She'll be fond of a nice-looking girl like you."

"I'd love to go and meet her," Bao said.

Another gunshot crackled. This time it sounded nearer.

"The hunters should be punished by barrenness!" Orchid laid her head on Candor's shoulder and moaned. "Make them go away."

He stroked her matted hair. "They're after a musk deer, you know that."

His words didn't soothe Orchid. She stared at the ceiling, her eyes glazed. Her hands tugged at the woolen yarn hanging from the unfinished pants.

"Imagine the happy day." Candor stroked her cheek with the back of his hand. "We'll have a fat baby boy in our arms."

"Yes, but it hasn't been easy. I had two abortions." She fixed her eyes upon Bao. "After having Daisy, I got pregnant again. The one-child policy worker team caught me twice and forced me to have abortions. They warned me about the third strike. If they catch me again, they'll tie my tubes for good."

"Hush!" Candor clasped his hand over her mouth. "Don't say such unlucky things."

Bao had read in *People's Daily* that women from poor mountain regions volunteered to be sterilized, because they couldn't afford other methods of birth control. Were they lies to cover up the crime that healthy women like Orchid were sterilized by force? The silence was eerie, after the gunshots stopped.

"You won't be caught," Bao said. "We'll see to it that you

aren't."

"Listen to Miss Gu." Candor stood up and raised a large basket onto his shoulders. "You mustn't get upset. Look after yourself while I'm gone. I have to go home and cook supper."

"Won't you stay a bit longer? Your seat is barely warm."

"Daisy will cry if I'm late." Averting his eyes from her face, he straightened the basket on his back. "Miss Gu can keep you company."

Orchid smiled at Bao. "You'd better go home, before your grandparents start grilling you about where you've been."

"I can help you with things like fetching water—"

"Come another time, now you know where I live."

Bao became her friend. "I'll go see Daisy and bring you news about her." Bao patted her shoulder, and Orchid answered her with eager nods. When Candor lifted the fence, Bao got down on her knees to crawl outside.

"Don't fret about things at home. You stay warm and get some sleep." He crawled outside after Bao. "I'll come and see you in three days." He began to cover the cave opening, but Orchid stopped him.

"Let me watch the sunset." Propping a twig behind the fence, she arranged the leaves on the vine to make a peephole. "I'm a day closer to having my son in my arms."

Candor led the way downhill. The basket on his back bobbed behind trees. Bao could barely keep up with him. He was a native of the Min Mountains and a professional porter. She slowed down as she approached a precipitous slope. A slippery, almost sheer patch of hard-packed gravel lay under her feet. She calculated her distance to the nearest yellow-rafter, where she could grab hold of the trunk.

"Don't be afraid." Candor turned back and stood at the bend. "If you walk zigzag, you won't come down too fast." His advice sounded sensible, but she didn't know how to practice it. He walked up the slope in a zigzag line to meet her halfway. "Take my hand."

Bao glanced at his raised face. An hour ago he had made love to Orchid in a cave. He wasn't much older than the boys she had danced with at the university, but Candor was a family man. She dashed down the slope in timid small steps.

"Zigzag!" He waved his arm. To avoid running into him, she took a long stride and turned sideways, which effectively slowed her down. "Good! You made it." Candor slapped his thigh with a laugh. "I've taught university students the ways of mountain people before, but you're a natural, Miss Gu."

Candor seemed to stop worrying about Orchid for a moment. His white teeth gleamed when he smiled. If he had a good haircut and wore some fitted clothes, he could stride down the University Avenue attracting girls' glances.

"Do you know a lot of university students?" she said.

The creek grew narrow around the bend, while the resonance of gurgling and splashing deepened.

"Twice a week I deliver meat and fresh vegetables for the researchers." The basket rattled as he skipped over the creek. "I've seen a few students coming and going. They don't like working here. You can hardly blame them. They live in tents, can't have a hot meal every day. Many have rheumatism, and some have female problems."

He descended a steep slope in a zigzag line. She followed his example and walked down the slope easily.

"Even Orchid lives better than these university girls," he said.

A typical peasant, he compared his life to those less fortunate.

"The researchers devote their lives to safeguard our national treasure," she said.

"This national treasure business is going to an extreme, if you ask me." His face turned red as spittle flew from the corner of his mouth. "At the breeding center, researchers grab a female panda and give her a shot of male panda's seed. You tell me that's not rape."

A rabbit hopped out of the shrub. It perched on a tree stump to look behind. Bao heard a man's slurred words. "You run too fast, son. Daddy is old. My legs are stiff." A man in a faded army uniform stumbled out from behind a yellow-rafter. As he lunged forward, the rabbit dashed into the bush where agitated stems briefly traced its progress.

Candor waved his hand at the man. "How are you doing, Brother Liao? Did you have supper?" He took out two steamed buns from his basket to put on the tree stump. "I made them, a bit dry and chewy. Eat slowly so you don't hurt your teeth."

The man peered up from under his matted long hair. Candor gestured for Bao to follow him. As she walked away, she stole a backward glance over her shoulder. The man squatted beside the tree stump and gnawed at a bun.

"So that's the madman."

Candor remained silent until they were out of earshot of the man. "He's better off mad. Otherwise he'd have to commit murder."

"Why?"

"They had two daughters. When his wife got pregnant again, the one-child policy worker team ordered her to have an abortion. She refused. If they were like the others, the worker team would've caught her and done it." He picked up a tree branch and whipped at the thicket. "But Brother Liao was a butcher. The worker team was afraid to use force."

Bao looked behind her. The meek madman was out of sight.

"This lasted until the worker team got a new head, we call him Childless Du. He gave Brother Liao an assignment to deliver the provisions for the panda reserve. Brother Liao needed money to pay fines. One day after he left for the mountain, the worker team caught his wife. Childless Du had a barefoot doctor induce her at eight months." Candor threw away the tree branch and dusted his hands. "Brother Liao got back and found his wife in the hospital, their baby son dead. His wife died a day later from hemorrhage."

Bao felt so weakened she stopped to lean against a poplar. Its small leaves caught the setting sun and shone like a constellation of golden stars strewn against the evening sky. Could a homeless peasant find comfort wandering on the mountain slopes?

"Brother Liao stayed beside his wife's empty sickbed for three days. On the fourth day he came to the woods, he'd gone mad." Candor waited for her to catch up. "People take pity on him, we give him food and clothes. The girls went to live with their grandparents."

They were already at the outskirts of the village. Bao could see her grandparents' goat pen and broad bean field.

"See that yellow-rafter up north?" He pointed. "That's our front yard. I'll get Daisy from our neighbor's house. Goodbye, Miss Gu."

"I'll visit you someday. You may drop off Daisy at my grandparents' house. We live at—"

"I know where they live." He walked backward a few steps. "But I won't bother them."

Candor observed the proprieties. In the real world outside the college campus, this habit was an admirable personal trait. She waited until he was far away, then strolled out of the woods, leaving the shade and entering the bright sunshine. Against her better judgment she admired the peasant couple who defied authority and protected each other. She wanted to have a share of their courage. Then one day she would be reunited with Tong.

Bao managed to stay quiet during supper. Afterwards she put away the leftover food and wiped the table, while Grandma washed the dishes. There weren't many chores to do that night. Grandma poured a large cup of roasted peanuts on the table and asked Bao to chat with them. Never before had she found the invitation so welcome.

Grandpa shelled a peanut. "Did you have a good walk?"

"Not bad." Bao tried to sound casual. "I ran into a villager who you may know."

"The madman?" Grandma said.

"We saw him too, but I met Candor first. He has a daughter named Daisy."

"I haven't seen his wife Orchid for some time. Did he say how she is?" Grandma cupped her chin in her palm.

"His wife? We didn't talk about her." Bao used both hands to shell a peanut. "Candor delivers provisions for researchers in the panda reserve. It was pretty interesting." She felt sweat on her upper lip. When had she become a terrible liar? She chewed vigorously. Her mouth was so dry the peanut tasted burnt.

"Candor is honest and hard-working," Grandpa said. "Their family has had some hard times."

"Orchid is unlucky. When she was born, a fortuneteller read the signs of her birthday and said she'd have a hard life." Grandma rattled on. Normally Bao would think her gossipy, but tonight she listened with great interest. "Her brother was a bachelor at age thirty-five. Being an older man, he couldn't find a wife unless he had some money, so he took up a job as a tour guide. Two years ago he fell down a cliff and died. Orchid borrowed money to give him a decent burial and kept a three-day vigil."

"There wasn't a dry eye when the villagers attended his funeral." Grandpa rubbed the red skins off the peanuts and then put them in his mouth.

"After his death, Orchid vowed to have a son. She wanted her boy to take his uncle's family name. Candor didn't mind it—he's a generous man." Grandma put a spoon of honey in her cup and stirred the warm water. "They already had Daisy.

When Childless Du got the news, his worker team kept a close watch on Orchid. She got pregnant twice and was quickly taken to have abortions. After the second time, she said she gave up."

"Is this legal?" Bao said. "How could they force anyone to have an abortion? In Nanjing, Orchid would pay a fine if she had an extra child."

"Who can argue with the one-child policy worker team?" Grandma said. "They work for the government. We're peasants."

"Peasants have civil rights, too." Bao clenched her fist. "The thugs should be prosecuted!"

"Easier said than done." Grandpa sat back with a sigh. "Childless Du's team tied many women's tubes, some only with one child. How dare they do this without powerful backing?"

"That still doesn't make it right."

Her grandparents exchanged a worried glance.

"Did Candor say anything about his wife being in trouble?" Grandpa said.

"No, not at all." Bao looked down to shell a peanut. "I don't know Orchid."

"But you know her brother, he's been to our house." Grandma shelled the last few peanuts for Bao. "He used to be the militia leader. After the earthquake he found two dead bears in the mountain."

"Yes I remember he gave us a bear heart, that tasted like chicken gizzard." The black bearskin in Orchid's cave must have been a memento from the great earthquake. "I didn't know he had a sister."

"She was much younger. Their parents died young, so he raised his sister. He didn't marry during the Cultural Revolution, fearing that his wife might mistreat Orchid. Back then it was hard to feed an extra mouth." Grandma collected peanut shells into a small mound.

"He was a bit hot-tempered, but a very good, decent man." Grandpa yawned.

Grandma swept the peanut shells into a bamboo dustpan. Bao was not at all sleepy, but her grandparents had been toiling since daybreak. She said goodnight and returned to her bedroom.

The events of the day whirled in her mind; people's faces, their stories and voices were mixed up to form a chorus. Was Orchid afraid in the dark cave? At least she had the company of her kicking baby. Pressing down her belly, Bao felt only firm muscle. She pinched her skin and pulled it sideways. How did it feel when a baby kicked inside?

She took out a pen and paper and started to write.

> How are you, Tong? I'm writing you from my grandparents' house in Pingwu, Sichuan. I had an abortion.

Her fountain pen pressed down on the word "abortion" and left a dark blue smudge. She thought of Orchid, her forced abortions, her dead brother, and her determination to have a son. Countrywomen like her had sorrow deeper than Bao's, but they lived with hope, not despair. Taking a deep breath, she began to write faster and with determination.

> I shouldn't make excuses for myself. I'm used to letting others run my life: the university and my parents. I didn't stand up for you, for us, because we had little power. What could we have done, really? Could you put yourself in my position? But enough about us. I want to tell you about my new friend.
>
> She has so little, not even a roof over her head or a bed to sleep in, but she is courageous. I wish I were more like her. Perhaps I will be, if I learn to take charge of my own life. You were right about one thing: where there's a will, there is a way.
>
> We ought to put what happened behind us. This is not being cowardly. We have serious tasks ahead of us: to forgive and heal. I still love you, Tong. I need you. I want you to come and take me into your arms. I'm still your girlfriend. Even after we break up, I'm your girlfriend. I'm not making any sense, am I? But you know what I mean.

She put down her pen and wiped away tears.

> My parents don't understand us. They just focus on the "damage" that you did to me. But we've shared so much: love, desire, and Soybean. I can't let her go until you mourn her with me.
>
> Yours,
> Bao

She folded up the letter without giving it another glance. She would mail it in the morning. If Tong didn't answer, she would know they had parted ways for good. But she hoped he would come here and comfort her. As the old saying had it, "Let him who tied the bell on the tiger take it off." Whoever started the trouble should end it. His love would help her heal, if they could start anew as a couple.

Chapter 10

AFTER BREAKFAST Bao set out to visit Daisy. She passed plots of peppers, eggplants, and beans. Smoke rose from the chimneys of peasants' houses. Clusters of red peppers hung under the eaves. Old people sat on doorsteps chatting, and children skipped and raced around. Just beyond the road, dark ridges crisscrossed one another. Beneath a large fig tree she stopped to look over the murky river flowing past the village. Several boys ambled home carrying bamboo poles and strings of the small, pink fish they had caught.

She found Candor's hut, shaded by a flowering yellow-rafter. The wind rustled the glossy oval leaves. The walls of the house were made of vertical wooden boards, soaked white by summer rain, and the roof was covered with tarpaper. Pigs grunted in their pen. A girl in a red overcoat picked up the small ruby-like fruits raining down from the yellow-rafter.

"Hello." Bao waved. "Are you Daisy?"

When the girl raised her head, Bao recognized Orchid's almond eyes and Candor's prominent brow ridge. She was a dainty girl. Her eyes, though not big, were like two coal cakes inside a porcelain face. A dimple on her pointed chin made her look sweet and intelligent. As she stood up and backed away, a handful of fruits fell and rolled in the dirt.

"Let me help you." After collecting the fruits, Bao chose the shapely, ripe ones to offer the girl. "Here you go."

The girl ran into the house and slammed the door. A moment later Candor appeared.

"What wind has blown you here, Miss Gu?" His brown face burst into a warm smile.

"I came to see Daisy." Bao eyed the girl hiding behind Candor. "She doesn't like my offering." She opened her palm to show the red fruits.

"Don't worry, she'll warm up to you."

Bao sat on the doorstep, dusted off a deep red fruit, and popped it into her mouth. Sweet and puckery. When she was little, she used to carry yellow-rafter fruits in her pocket and relish them one after another like raisins.

She held up a large fruit. "Want it?"

The girl peered at her from behind Candor's leg.

"Go play with Auntie Gu." Candor tried to free his leg from her grasp. "I'm going to the potato field." He patted her shoulder but she didn't budge. "If you come along, we have to watch out for the yellow dog at Old Wang's house."

The threat worked. She let go of Candor's leg and squatted on her small, sturdy legs.

"I'll comb your hair and make you pretty." Bao stroked her tangled hair. "My name is Gu Bao. Will you be my friend?" She held the girl's small hand in her palm.

Daisy seemed to be startled by her touch. She leapt up and ran into the bedroom.

"She likes you," Candor said.

A moment later Daisy returned with a wooden stool.

"For me?" Bao sat down and stretched out her legs. "Thanks a lot, Daisy."

"I'm going to the field." Candor pointed to a plot toward the south. "Shout if you need me, I'll hear you."

Bao gave him a bottle of honey. "For Orchid."

"Did you—"

"I'm not a snitch."

Daisy touched her hand. "Where's Mama?" she asked.

"Your mama is at your auntie's house." Candor sounded as if he'd answered the question twenty times before.

Daisy pouted, tears welling in her almond eyes. Bao remembered how Orchid had looked when Candor rose to leave the cave. She lifted Daisy onto her lap and combed her loose hair behind her ears.

"Your mother will come home soon. You want to look pretty for her, don't you?" Bao took out a rubber band strung with two pink plastic balls.

"Pretty." Daisy plucked at the rubber band to make the pink balls bounce.

"Be good and play with Auntie Gu. I'll be back in an hour." Candor swung a hoe onto his shoulder.

Daisy nodded, her hair brushing Bao's cheek.

"Say goodbye to Daddy." Bao held up her small hand and waved.

The touch of her soft flesh made Bao tremble with strange pleasure. If she hadn't had an abortion, would she give birth to a girl as lovely as Daisy? She fondled the girl's plump forearm and delicate elbow. Daisy giggled and rubbed her forehead against her chin.

"Darling." Bao kissed her temple.

Pursing her lips, Daisy pecked Bao's cheek. "Auntie, you're pretty, like a fairy."

"You little flatterer."

Bao combed her fine hair and divided it into three equal parts. She tied up the middle strand with the rubber band. The hair stood up on her head like a goat's horn. Her face appeared rounder and her eyes brighter. Bao picked her up and carried her into the kitchen.

"Let's make you even prettier."

Bao found a large water urn covered with a wooden lid. She filled a bowl with water, wet her hanky, and scrubbed Daisy's cheeks, forehead, neck, and the back of her ears. The bowl of water was muddy when she finished.

"Do you have a mirror?"

"By Mama's bed." Daisy wriggled down from her lap.

Bao followed her. Unlike her grandparents' house, the bedroom appeared rather empty with only a medium-sized bed and a narrow cot. A stool, covered with musk deer hide, stood before a wooden chest. Even the maroon and purple beddings didn't give a homey touch to the plain furniture. Daisy handed Bao a small mirror, its rim bound by red plastic tape.

Bao led her to sit on the doorstep. "Let's have a look at you." What a drab coat she had on! Daisy would look adorable in a seersucker dress with a jewel neckline and puffed short sleeves.

"My face is pale." Daisy stared into the mirror, as if seeing a stranger. Then she gazed at Bao. "Even whiter than yours, Auntie."

Surprised, Bao flushed in exasperation. "A girl is pretty when she's little, but you'll grow up, sooner than you think."

"I want to be like you." She leaned on Bao.

She knew nothing of Bao's disgrace; Daisy was innocent of the ways of the world. When she grew up, her body would become the vessel to carry a man's offspring. Would she still want to be like Bao?

"No, you don't." Bao stood up abruptly.

In the yard, a hen pecked rice from the ground. Her feathers jiggled as her neck stretched out and then drew back. With each strike she picked up a grain of rice. She looked like Cauliflower Tail, who had filled the belly of a panda mother years ago.

"Were you feeding the hens?" Bao said.

Daisy nodded.

"Why don't you carry on?"

Daisy shook her head. She seemed to be holding back tears.

"What's wrong?"

Daisy folded her hands in her lap and crouched forward as if nursing a bellyache. How could Bao be so callous? She had lashed out at Daisy when she least expected. A young heart was defenseless against her volatility; the hurt was deepened by the sense of betrayal.

"Let's feed the chickens together," Bao said softly.

Daisy cast her a doubtful glance.

Bao retrieved the rice basket from the yard. "Will you teach me how to feed the chickens?"

Smiling with tears in her eyes, Daisy grabbed a handful of grains. "*Go-go-go.*" She tossed unhusked grains on the ground.

"*Go-go-go.*" Bao flicked her wrist to spread the grains farther away.

Grains showered on a hen that kept on pecking. Suddenly a hen leapt out of a rattan crate and made *go-go-go* calls. Daisy went to dig into the crate. She held up an egg with both hands.

"Mottled Tail lays an egg every day."

"Mottled Tail is a pretty name. Did you name her?"

"I named them all." Daisy pointed at the hens one by one. "Red Face, Stocky Neck, Hump Back, Black Beak. Lemon Feather and White Head are digging up worms in the field."

"What a bright girl you are!" Bao lifted her chin. "Do you want to learn a nursery rhyme?"

Daisy put a finger to her nostril. "What's a nursery rhyme?"

Bao gently took hold of her hand.

"It's a song children your age learn to sing." Bao started to sing, "*I'm looking for a friend, a good friend.*" She clapped her hands. "*I've looked everywhere. Finally I find a little friend.*" She tapped her feet and wagged her head. "*I take a bow and smile at her. We shake hands and become friends.*" She shook the girl's hand. "*Now you're my good friend.*" She hugged Daisy to her chest.

"Teach me, Auntie!"

"*I'm looking for a friend, a good friend.*" Bao clapped her hands, and Daisy followed her example. "*I've looked everywhere.*" Daisy glanced about her as if searching for someone. "*Finally I find a little friend.*" Daisy nodded with a grin. "*I take a bow and smile at her.*" They bowed at each other like a pair of scholars from the old days. "*We shake hands and become friends. Now you're my good friend.*" Clasping each other's hands, they whirled in the yard and kicked up the dust.

After a few rounds Bao was out of breath and couldn't stop giggling. Daisy let go of her hand and danced in the yard. The hens scattered and clucked in panic, which made them laugh so hard they had to stop dancing for a little while. When they started up again, Bao felt her body grow lighter, as if she were the young girl dancing for her grandparents more than a decade ago. For a moment she saw herself inside the earthquake shack covered by plastic and felted sheets. She tapped her feet, clapped her hands and sang, her heart brimming over with joy and hope.

For four days Bao made daily pilgrimages to Candor's house. Grandma asked Bao to bring roasted peanuts and boiled water chestnuts. While Daisy gobbled down the treats, Bao's bosom swelled with warmth. She could imagine the precious little tugs on Orchid's breast when baby Daisy suckled. It must've been heavenly to hold the tiny wiggly bundle and kiss her wet mouth with intoxicating milk breath.

A letter from Tong was waiting, when she came home for lunch on the fourth day. "My sweet little flower," it began. Her heart almost stopped in fright. She took the letter to her room to read.

My sweet little flower: How I dreaded that I may never see you again! I told my parents about you, and they already love you. I'll wait for you to graduate and marry you, if you will have me.

Since you left, I've been thinking about all the wrongs I

have done you. The abortion was my fault, not yours. I requested a leave, so I can come to visit you. I'll ask for your forgiveness in person. I should never have let you go there by yourself—I was a coward.

Your father doesn't think highly of me; he's entitled to his opinion. I'm grateful that you give me a second chance, sweetheart. You're not alone in this suffering. I'll remain by your side where I belong.

Yours,
Tong

His words echoed in her head as she ate lunch. She felt warm, flushed with desire. Would she cry if they made love again? Did the abortion leave a scar, a tender spot inside her? Tong wanted to ask her for forgiveness, but she couldn't give him any—he needed to ask Soybean.

She pushed away her rice bowl. "I'm going to see Daisy."

"Aren't you going to take a nap?" Grandma said.

Usually Bao visited Daisy in the morning and stayed home after lunch, but Candor would deliver provisions for the reserve this afternoon. She had volunteered to babysit.

"I feel fine." Bao put a hand on her hip. "Not tired at all."

"You ought to rest—"

"I promised Candor I'd look after Daisy. They're expecting me."

Bao left home without waiting for an approval. She wanted to spend the whole afternoon with Daisy, so Candor could stay with Orchid a while longer. She walked with a springy step, humming a new nursery rhyme she had for a surprise.

Candor returned home late, his face glowing with

contentment. Bao was glad he had enjoyed his time with Orchid. She said goodbye to Daisy. The girl sucked her thumb, her face drawn as if she'd cry. Bao skipped a few steps on the ridge, turned and waved again.

"I'll come tomorrow. We'll play 'Finding a Friend!'"

Daisy nodded, the pink plastic balls glowing in her hair like rubies. She wasn't a spoiled girl. Although her parents were fond of her, they were expecting a son. Soon Daisy would have the responsibilities of an elder sister.

"*I'm looking for a friend, a good friend,*" Bao hummed when she entered the house. On the stove, Grandma was stir-frying eggplant. Bao grabbed an ear of corn from a bowl. "*I've looked everywhere. Finally I find a little friend.*" She bit into the cob.

"It's already dark," Grandpa said. "Where have you been?"

"I went to see Daisy."

Grandma laid the eggplant with pork on the table. "What did you do with a four-year-old till this late?"

"I told you already: Candor delivered the provisions for the reserve today, so I went to babysit." Bao chewed a neat ring around the cob. The corn was hard and gritty. "I taught Daisy nursery rhymes, and she's a fast learner."

"We can talk while we eat." Grandpa pulled out the bench for Bao. Evidently he had more serious matters on his mind than food.

Bao put down the corncob. She would eat after her grandparents finished their interrogation.

"I can't figure out why Orchid left home without taking her daughter. It's so unlike her." Grandma put a piece of eggplant in Bao's bowl. "Did Candor say where Orchid was?"

Bao averted her eyes. She didn't have to answer. However, her refusal to explain would arouse their suspicion. Her grandparents might think she was fooling around with Candor.

"He said Orchid was visiting her relatives," Bao said.

"Her cousin in Mianyang?" Grandma said.

"Probably."

"Bao, you're young and inexperienced." Grandpa knocked his pipe on the dining table. The brass bowl made a dull clucking sound. "You mustn't spend too much time at Candor's house when Orchid isn't home. Villagers may gossip. You may not mind them, but we live here. They'll think badly of us if we don't teach you manners."

Bao picked at the corncob. How unfair he sounded! Never in a million years would she commit adultery with Candor.

"I just went to see Daisy! Is that a crime? She's so sweet . . ." Her voice broke.

"Don't cry." Grandma stroked Bao's cheek. "One day you'll be married with a baby of your own." She put a piece of fried eggs in Bao's bowl, as if this could comfort her.

Bao bit her lip. "She needs me now. I make her laugh, and she's so lonely."

"You're a big girl, Bao." Grandpa patted her bench. "Please understand that we and your parents want to protect you as best as we can, and the only way we know how." He cast her a wary glance. His bushy eyebrows came together like a pair of swords. "Pound for pound, we've eaten more salt than you've eaten rice. Trust us, we never want to lay any undeserved blame on you. If you tell us what you did, and why you did it, we would understand and won't suspect you of wrongdoing."

"I shouldn't have raised my voice." Bao peered at her grandparents' bowls, their food untouched. "I won't make any trouble, I promise. I want to play with Daisy, because she makes me happy."

"We understand. Make sure you don't go there every day, only play with her for a short while and come home before dark." Grandpa put out his pipe and picked up his chopsticks. "I know Candor, I don't doubt his decency. I just want you to be careful."

Bao started to eat dinner. There was a large pork chop in her bowl, which she was obliged to eat for nutrition. Tearing a piece of lean meat to chew, she wondered how she could invite Tong to visit her when her grandparents were so protective. Where would he stay? When Tong showed up, Grandpa might take out his gun—Tong would be shot before he touched her sleeve. She had to hide him from her grandparents.

"Where is the nearest hotel?" Bao said. Her grandparents looked puzzled. "Lily, my best friend, may come to visit me. Crystal Village is on the way to the panda reserve." Her heart raced as she attempted to offer the whole story. Grandpa wasn't an easy person to fool, but she was determined to see Tong.

"Did you mention your . . ." Grandpa paused, as if for her to fill in the missing word 'abortion.' "To anyone?" Bao shook her head so hard it made her dizzy. "Good. You mustn't risk your reputation with anyone. Confide in no one, except for your family."

"I said I'm here visiting my grandparents."

"If your friend wants to visit the panda reserve, she should go to Jiuzhaigou in the northwest. Pingwu is rural and has nothing interesting—"

"It's the best place in all Sichuan." Grandma patted Bao's cheek. "We raised you and your mother here. It's our home."

"Are there any . . . hotels near here?"

"The nearest hotel is in town, fifteen kilometers away," Grandpa said. "I heard it isn't cheap or clean."

"How will she get to the village?" Bao could hardly sit still as her plan began to take shape.

"We have the tricycle. Your grandpa can pick her up at the train station." Grandma held Bao's shoulder. "Why don't you invite her to stay at our house? You two can share a bed."

Bao nearly burst into laughter. She took a savage bite of the pork chop to chew.

"What's wrong?" Grandma said. "Isn't our house good enough?"

"It is, Grandma." Bao smacked a loud kiss and rubbed pork grease on her cheek. "Lily would love to make a trip out here, but most likely she won't."

"Why?" Grandma said.

"She was grounded by her parents." This reason came to Bao quickly. It was the half-truth, which she uttered with confidence. Or was she getting better at lying?

"What did she do to get herself in trouble?" Grandpa said.

"It wasn't her trouble alone but the trouble with all of China." Bao was excited to talk about the student unrest, a taboo subject at home and at university. "Her boyfriend was killed on June 4th when PLA men forced their way to clear Tiananmen Square. He was only taking pictures, and for this he was shot in the head."

"How sad." Grandma sounded incredulous and confused.

"I heard the news on the radio," Grandpa said. "There were some riots and looting. Nobody died in Tiananmen Square."

"You heard the official story. It was a lie."

Grandpa raised his voice. "Were you in Tiananmen Square on June 4th?"

Bao shook her head. "Lily told me what happened to Hongzhi. The troops opened fire on unarmed civilians."

"So you believe your friend rather than the Central Broadcasting Station." His face reddened as a blue vein stood out in the middle of his wide brow.

Grandma's face was pale and taut. Her eyes darted left and right between her husband and granddaughter, as if watching a ping-pong game.

"Of course I believe Lily. I met Hongzhi before it happened. He was a nerd, so smart but naïve. Who dared to take pictures of PLA men killing the civilians? Why didn't he run for his life?" Bao bit off the cartilage from the pork chop and chewed it with effort. "The Central Broadcasting Station lied to the Chinese people, but we're not surprised. One of the main goals of the student movement was the freedom of the press. Ironic how it ended up!"

To her amazement, Grandpa leapt to his feet and bolted the door.

"No wonder your mother asked us to watch over you." He folded his hands behind his back, his shoulders stooped. He seemed to have shrunk in an instant. "You grew up in the

Cultural Revolution, but you were too young to understand what life was like for ordinary people. If the Red Guards caught a word of what you just said, you would've been locked up in a prison and probably never released! Do you have any idea what a serious offense it is to talk like that?"

Bao opened her mouth to argue, but no words came to her. Her grandparents were from a different era. They had no television, no newspaper, only a transistor radio that couldn't receive shortwave stations such as the Voice of America and BBC. How could they know what went on outside the lush mountains and pastoral fields of Pingwu?

"Don't worry, Bao." His voice softened. "We're your family, and we'll never turn you in to the authorities."

"What authorities? It's 1989, Grandpa. The Red Guards are dead and gone."

"Some things never change!" Grandma's voice startled them both. "You think the Red Guards were stupid and mean. Guess what? If young people today were given the power, wouldn't they turn into the same monsters?"

"What's so monstrous about wanting a little personal freedom—"

"Let me tell you a story about the Red Guards," Grandma said. "Once they dug up some old corpses that they called revolutionary martyrs. They wrote stories to educate us peasants, and we held mass meetings to worship the martyrs. In the end we found it was all a lie. How dared they take us for fools! We grew the grains they lived on, but they acted like our liberators."

"But we're not Red Guards—"

"Young people always want to change China—they think it's so easy. What can they do: bring back another Cultural Revolution?"

"Let's eat in peace." Grandpa picked up a bok choy heart to place in Bao's bowl. "Politics isn't for grass people like you and me."

"But it is! The students fought to make everyone's opinion count."

"Some count more than the others." Grandma's face was contorted with loathing. "Childless Du decides who'll have her tubes tied. She can hide or run. When she comes home, his team will hunt her down. You know what they say, 'An arm cannot fight a strong leg that kicks.'"

Who was this Childless Du? How did he come to represent the government? If Grandma was a duped peasant, Crystal Village was no haven from injustice.

"We can't resign ourselves to tyranny." Bao put her arms around Grandma's back and squeezed her gently. "How can we be happy?"

"When you're as old as me, child, you'll know the answer."

Bao shook her head with a smile. She would invite Tong to visit her in the village. He was of her generation and spoke the same language. Enough of this sheltered life! She wanted to face Tong, as a woman to a man, both carrying the burden of shared loss. Together they would learn—from their past and from her villager friends, whose future was surely dismal.

Chapter 11

Bao hiked up the trail, treading upon dewy grass and occasionally making her way through knee-deep ferns and thorny shrubs. She heard footsteps and looked around. It was the madman, Brother Liao, who clasped his hands around a low branch of the yellow-rafter. She took out a steamed bun with red bean paste filling, still warm. She left the bun on the gnarly root of the tree and walked away. After a while she glanced over her shoulder. The bun was gone.

The tender leaves of the yellow-rafter stood upright, shining in the sunlight. A breeze made the leaves sway like little penguins. Yellow-rafters were peculiar because their life cycles were defined by the seasons when they were planted. A tree planted in the winter would sprout new leaves in the winter and drop its leaves in the spring.

From a distance she saw the gigantic yellow-rafter at Rooster Peak. A beehive the size of a small bucket perched at the top. Hundreds of sparrows, larks, and crows chirped in the branches. She walked toward the precipice, where leaves hung above the cliff like a rooster's tail.

"You'll have a boy this time, because you live in the

rooster's belly."

"You're nice, Little Sister." The leaves shook as the fence door was pushed up.

Bao crawled inside. "Is the baby kicking?"

"Night and day, I can get no sleep." Orchid tucked the skirt around her barrel belly, as if wrapping up a fragile parcel.

"Is the time near?"

"It won't be for a while yet, I hope." Orchid knitted a sweater in the dim light. After finishing a row, she used the spare needle to scratch her scalp. "You know what they say, 'A son is a treasure if he's overdue, but a daughter is grass if she's born late.'"

Bao had been born two weeks late. She shrugged.

"When will your midwife come?"

"In about ten days. My aunt has arthritis. The long hike will be hard on her."

"I can fetch water or run errands."

"Labor isn't fitting for an unmarried woman to watch."

"Why ever not?" Bao grabbed the ball of yarn to roll up the loose thread.

"You haven't shared a bed with a man."

"But I have, you remember Soybean."

"That was different." Orchid tugged to let out more yarn.

"I did what married people do. What else don't I know?"

"Have you heard a woman howl in pain for hours on end?" Orchid put down her knitting. "After seeing her blood, cuts, and bruises, you may never want to have a baby."

"Giving birth isn't worse than having an abortion, is it?"

Orchid froze, her eyes darkened with grief. "You'd better

leave, Little Sister."

Orchid was so superstitious she was afraid a white kerchief might jinx her baby. How could Bao remind her of the forced abortions that were worse than rape? No apology could undo her offense. Water dripped in the cave. Outside, mountain wind rushed toward the cliff. Before it approached the cave opening, the gust of wind retreated and resounded in the deep valley.

"I came to ask you a favor," Bao said.

"Candor told me, your fellow is coming to visit." Orchid wrapped the yarn around her pinky as she hoisted the needles on her hands.

"Could Tong stay at your house for a few days?"

"Why can't he stay at your grandparents' house?"

"I don't want to ask them."

"Should I keep a secret for you, Little Sister?"

"But I did for you. I have to, I feel like your sister." Bao reached out a hand to touch Orchid. "You care for me, too. You came out to talk to me when I was crying. I didn't want anyone to hear me, but I'm glad you did."

Orchid jabbed a needle into a loop to lift the yarn onto the other needle. "I told Candor your fellow can stay at our house as a guest, but listen up, we have Daisy. You two mustn't do anything unfit to be seen by a young girl."

"I don't plan to . . . to . . . What do you take us for, farm animals?"

"I'm a mother." Orchid raised her head. "I ought to protect my baby, oughtn't I?"

"You have my word: Tong and I will behave respectably in

your house." Bao thought the matter over and grinned. "You sleep in the same room as Daisy. Did you conceive this one while she was sleeping?"

"I don't know for sure." Orchid burst into a fit of giggles.

"Where else could you do it?"

"In the kitchen, for one."

Bao remembered the greasy stove blackened by soot. "Yuck."

"Sitting on a stool, of course. He was bursting to take off my pants—I had to cut the rope belt with scissors!"

"And?"

"In the goat pen."

"Did the buck threaten you with his horns?"

"He watched, like anything!" Orchid laughed so hard she wiped her eyes. "How did you get into trouble?"

"In my bed." Bao blushed. "It was my first time."

Orchid cast her a curious glance. She put down her knitting and took Bao's hand.

"Did you want to do it?"

Bao smiled with tears in her eyes.

"You can tell me."

"I wasn't . . . prepared." Bao slid a hand between her thighs.

"Hadn't your mama told you what could happen to a woman?"

Bao shook her head. "I hid my boyfriend from my parents for as long as I could."

"You sly girl." Orchid tapped Bao's nose. "Now you have to take care of yourself."

Bao took out a sheet of paper from her pocket. "This is from Daisy." On it sprawled a large word "Mama" and a pencil sketch of a daisy with five petals.

"Let me see." Orchid snatched the paper and waddled to the cave opening. "My daughter learned to do things I haven't taught her." She traced the word with her fingertip, her eyes brimming with tears.

"Please don't cry, it isn't good for the baby."

"Don't I know it?" Orchid wiped her cheek with her palm. "I miss Daisy."

"She's doing fine, and she's so bright. She must be taking after her parents."

"Candor says she sings like a canary. Her favorite song is—"

"'Finding a Friend,' and she sings every note perfectly." Bao got tingles up and down her spine, as if she were bragging about her own daughter.

Orchid brushed the paper against her closed eyelids. "In a few weeks, I'll go home with my son. Our family will never be apart again."

Bao would also return to Nanjing in about two weeks. That could be the end of their friendship.

"I promised my grandparents to help them with supper." Bao stood up.

"Come again, Little Sister." Orchid tugged Bao's sleeve. "Bring me the news of Daisy."

"I will."

"If you want to, you may help me when I'm in labor."

The invitation was so sudden Bao felt her heart flutter.

"Really? Oh, thank you!"

Orchid shaded her eyes with the drawing, although it was dark inside the cave. "Be careful when you see your fellow again."

Sunlight blinded Bao when she crawled outside. Returning to the creek side, she skipped a few times and leapt in the air. She'd be the best helper Orchid could ever want! She would not only give Orchid comfort but also protect her from harm. Oh, if only she could share her mission with another person! Tong might help her if he came to visit. Then she caught sight of the lotus kerchief on the ground.

"Soybean, my angel." She knelt to smooth out the corner of the tattered kerchief. "I have no right to ask you for a favor, but if you're in heaven, you may hear me." She wiped away a tear with the swift brush of her hand. "Please, bless Orchid's baby. He'll soon make his way into the world. Let it be a safe journey, and ask him to be gentle to his mama."

She bent down to kiss the kerchief and smelt the damp earth. Inside the shallow grave, her panties might have become moldy. She pulled a few weeds and knocked off the dirt from their roots. Then she looked up and saw the majestic yellow-rafter.

As a little girl she once had a high fever that had lasted for days. In desperation her grandparents had prayed to the spirit of the yellow-rafter. Fortunately the Red Guards hadn't learned of their 'superstitious practice,' or her grandparents would've been denounced. After Bao healed, the yellow-rafter became her godfather. Her grandparents always gave offerings to the yellow-rafter on the festivals.

Bao prayed to the yellow-rafter to bless Orchid's baby. Kneeling on the ground, she kowtowed three times, then stood up and bowed three times, each time lower than the one before it.

"May the yellow-rafter god bless you, too, Soybean."

The yellow-rafter god had blessed many children, according to the villagers. Surely Bao could appeal to the higher power. She kowtowed at Soybean's grave, again and again, her forehead touching the hard ground. The grating pain reassured her, because she wanted to believe. Like a pious village woman, Bao headed home feeling solaced and blessed.

Bao lived through two days of euphoria. She had erotic dreams about Tong, making love in the woods, by the stream, and in the cornfield. During the day, she fantasized about helping Orchid with her delivery. It was the daydream that gave her the most pleasure. In Nanjing hospitals, men were barred from their wives' delivery rooms. Bao earned a rare opportunity to witness a birth. She hoped Orchid would start labor soon.

One morning Bao was awakened by loud chatter in the kitchen.

"It's outrageous!" Grandpa said. "A beast robbed me in my own backyard. Why should I hush it up? I'm a farmer, not a zookeeper!"

"We didn't see the panda," Grandma said. "No one will believe you."

"Its droppings have bamboo fiber. What more proof do I need? Do you remember the news from last year?" Bao got up to pull on her jeans as she listened to Grandpa. "One night a beekeeper found a panda strolling in his pigpen. He couldn't harm the panda, so he locked the door. The next morning he found two buckets of honey and some ham missing from the shed, his hives strewn far and wide. He complained to the reserve but didn't get reimbursed until the honey season was over."

"Did we wake you?" Grandma scooped a bowl of porridge for Bao.

"Grandpa may be right." Bao thought of Cauliflower Tail, the star egg-layer who had filled the belly of a starving panda. "Candor may know if the droppings were from a panda."

"I don't mind it taking my honey, but look what it did."

Bao followed Grandpa to the backyard. Several supers were smashed to pieces, frames scattered in the potato and broad bean fields.

"Where are the bees?" Last time the panda mother had been nursing. What was this panda's excuse?

"It had several helpings of the bees. Fortunately the beast didn't smash the hive." Grandpa entered the shed and pointed to the hive laid on a low table. "The queen is alive and well. You can help me fix the supers later. Go have breakfast now."

Bao returned to the kitchen. She ate the porridge with a steamed bun. Tong would arrive today. She would meet him outside the village and take him to Candor's house. So far her plan seemed feasible. Her grandparents were too busy today to watch her closely.

Something peculiar happened in the backyard. A black cloud poured out of the shed and rose in a cone-shaped spiral.

Was the shed on fire? She stood up. The black cloud drifted toward the east like a cyclone. There wasn't flame or smoke. Some villagers yelled in nearby fields, while footsteps pattered on the ridge.

The front door swung open. "Our bees swarmed," Grandma said. "I'll help your grandpa catch them."

Several villagers jogged past the vegetable plots. Grandma carried two bee-snares and joined the crowd running toward the orange grove.

"Bees, thousands of bees!" a boy yelped.

Bao gulped down her porridge. Then she left the house and ran along with the crowd.

When she arrived at the grove, there were about a hundred villagers, most of whom she didn't know. Men, women, old people, and children chattered loudly in the old cemetery. Their voices startled the sparrows and warblers nested in the orange trees and bamboo grove.

The cluster of bees landed on an old orange tree in a ball the size of a watermelon, squirming with a loud buzzing sound. Grandpa had once described the phenomenon of swarming bees. When rapeseed plants flowered in the spring, they provided an abundant nectar source for the bees. As the bees multiplied, their hive became overly crowded. A group of bees would leave the hive with a new queen to look for another place to live. Grandpa didn't mention that a bear robbing the hive could cause the bees to swarm—perhaps he hadn't expected this. Swarming bees was an omen that a beekeeper's fortune would be ruined.

A toddler girl cried and mumbled words that Bao didn't understand. Her mother picked her up and rocked her in her arms. "It's okay, baby. Bee-tamer Cao will catch the swarm, and then all the bees will come home. That's right, your grandma will have royal jelly to help treat her rheumatism."

"Are they flying away?" The girl pointed at the mountain slopes in the distance.

"Don't you want honey in your porridge?" The mother cupped the girl's hand inside hers to make a fist. "Then quit pointing and help."

Bao's Grandpa climbed onto the low branch of the orange tree. Grandma stood beside a clump of bamboos. Both lifted their snares toward the cluster of bees.

"Queen bee, enter the snare!" They sounded like chastising a child. "Queen bee, enter the snare!"

The two-foot snare, shaped like a bullhorn, was woven with thin bamboo strips. Its bottom protruded like the core of a flower, dappled with honey and pollen. Grandpa raised his snare to cover the ball of bees. Grandma shook her snare to lure the bees inside. For half an hour, they called the queen bee and jiggled their snares. But instead of entering the snares, the bees started to fly away. When Grandma waved her snare, irritated bees flew to sting her head and hand.

"Stay calm," Grandpa said. "Don't swat at the bees."

It was too late. Grandma dropped the snare and ran away. A dozen bees chased her, and the crowd of villagers parted to allow her to retreat. Grandpa slid down the orange tree and examined the cluster of bees. Loosening at the edge, the bees bunched tightly in the middle.

"Go home," he said. "Fetch our hats and suits. The bees will remain for an hour."

Several boys volunteered for the task and raced off. Grandma sat on a boulder and moaned, while a young woman scraped bee stingers from her neck. As soon as the boys returned Grandpa suited up, leaving only his eyes exposed.

Bao took Grandma's place. After suiting up, she climbed onto the orange tree. The crowd below stared up with admiration. Candor lifted Daisy onto his shoulders. Bao felt bashful in the gaze of young men, some of whom were handsome. Did she look fat high up in the air? She lifted the snare, some thirty bees circling about her head. She forgot what to do.

"Move your snare toward the front," Grandpa said. "Don't be afraid. Bees can't get through your veil. I put my snare behind yours, that's it. Now let's call them: queen bee, enter the snare!"

"Queen bee, enter the snare!" Bao's voice sounded muffled inside the veil.

The chanting swelled as young people and children joined the chorus. "Queen bee, enter the snare! Queen bee, enter the snare!"

Bao had been away for more than six years. Few villagers recognized the university girl who had once donned pigtails. Their fervent chanting was a warm welcome to Bao, who had grown up in the village but became a stranger over the years. Now perching on a tree with the bee-snare, she felt sensual and confident wearing the beekeeper suit.

Half an hour later, some bees moved toward Grandpa's snare. After a pause they crawled inside. Bao thrust her snare toward the bees.

"Don't scare them," Grandpa said. "If they fly away, you'll never catch them."

Before he finished, the cluster of bees rose like a black cloud. The crowd gasped as the bees droned overhead. Bao thought she'd failed. Holding the snare in one hand she began to slide down the orange tree.

"Don't move!" Grandpa said.

Bao stopped with a shudder. Grandpa took off his veiled hat. He circled the orange tree to examine the cluster of bees. Then he shaded his eyes with a hand to look toward the east. The bees flew toward a towering tree with a lush crown. He nodded with a smile.

"What do you think?" he said.

"The queen is still here," Grandma said.

"Right!" He returned to the orange tree. "Continue to call the bees."

Puzzled, Bao said nothing.

"The bees are gone," a young man said. "You waste your breath calling after them. Why don't you give the young miss a break?" His long head topped with greasy hair, he stood with his legs apart and his hands on his hips.

"You aren't old enough to grow a beard." Grandpa waved his hand. "What do you know about bees?"

The crowd fell silent. Even the babies were hushed.

"The queen is still here." His voice softened. "The bees will return."

Grandpa was the expert beekeeper. Bao jiggled the snare and called, "Queen bee, enter the snare!"

Following her lead, young people and children chanted with renewed enthusiasm. At last, the queen bee crawled into Bao's snare, followed by a bowl-sized cluster of bees.

A cheer rose from the crowd.

"Honey!" several boys shouted in unison, "We want honey!" before they were hushed by their parents.

"It's a happy day for a beekeeper," Grandpa said. "We welcome all of you to our house for a honey drink."

Bao covered the snare with a piece of blue cloth. She slid down the orange tree and ran toward the house. Nearing the goats' pen, she took off her veiled hat. A crowd followed as if Bao were a returning heroine. Celebratory firecrackers sounded in a nearby yard. Dogs barked and people chattered.

Bao gave the snare to Grandpa. He took it to the shed and restored the bees into the hive.

"You did a fine job for your grandma." A toothless old woman patted Bao's cheek.

"Teach us a few bee tricks." A young man clasped his hands as if bowing to a kung fu master.

A man with a chubby belly laughed. "Watch out, he's a honey thief."

"Whoever steals honey is a black bear!"

Bao turned away with a smile. When Daisy tugged her sleeve, she picked up the girl and walked toward the shed. Candor studied the droppings in the nearby field.

"These are from a panda, no doubt." Candor threw away a

twig and dusted his hands. "If you file a complaint, the reserve should reimburse you for your loss."

"More important, my bees are back," Grandpa said. "You know the saying, 'As long as the green mountain remains, there won't be a lack of firewood.'"

Daisy got down and held Candor's hand. They returned to the house, where honey drinks were being served. Candor thanked Grandma for a bowl of warm honey water.

Bao laid the bowls on the table, scooped two spoons of honey into each one, added warm water, and let Daisy stir the drinks.

"How I miss those days when you shadowed me in the kitchen!" Grandma winked at Bao. "Now you have a little helper."

"She's a fun one." Bao patted Daisy's head.

Serving the refreshments, Bao was surrounded by young men who waited for their turn. After a group left, Grandma washed their bowls to serve the next round of guests.

The air thickened with the smells of cigarettes, warm rice wine, burnt firecrackers, sour sweat, and sweet honey. Voices vibrated in the air, and laughter crackled and boiled over in a wave of happy sounds. When the villagers were satiated with honey drinks, more bees returned like a black cloud and flew into the hive.

Empty bowls were stacked on the dining table. Finally the crowd left the house. Grandma washed a basket of rice to cook lunch. Grandpa was fixing the frames on the porch. A boy wearing open-slit training pants picked wood splinters in the field. Tired and elated, Bao remembered she was supposed to meet Tong half an hour ago.

Bao hurried toward the outskirts of the village. She found Tong sitting on the dirt road that led to the orange grove in the cemetery. He wore an olive-green uniform and rubber-soled shoes. His head was bare. She wanted to shout his name but decided against it. As she approached him, her heart pounded and her throat felt tight. What if he leapt up and took her into his arms? Such behavior would draw attention.

"Hi," she said.

To her disappointment, Tong sat with his head bent, having a doze. She shook him awake. He was dazed, and for a second he didn't seem to recognize her.

"Hey you." She managed to smile.

"Bao, is it you?" He squinted his eyes. "What're you wearing?"

She still had on Grandma's oversized bee-suit. It was so comfortable she'd forgotten to change.

"I was busy working this morning." She blushed. "I would've changed my clothes, had I not been in a hurry to meet you."

He lifted her chin, as if seeing her for the very first time.

"You're tanned like the locals. What have you been doing?"

"Beekeeping, among other things."

He burst into a smile. His teeth were pearly white, and his breath was minty. She hadn't seen anyone so handsome and well groomed since she left Nanjing. The young men who had flattered her this morning paled in comparison.

"It sure is good to see you," he said, "even in these

clothes."

She undid the elastic cuffs and zippers and slipped out of the white coat and pants. Somehow she wanted to take off more than she had on.

"The beekeeper suit is supposed to be big. If I wear tight-fitting clothes, the bees can sting through the fabric." She headed for the orange grove, and he followed. "I caught a swarm of bees this morning."

"Now I know you're brave."

She leaned against the orange tree that she'd climbed earlier. She had fantasized about the moment of reunion: they would fall into a pile of hay and melt into each other's arms, reconnecting passionately as if they'd never been apart. Instead, they gazed at each other like strangers.

"How was your trip?" For the first time she spotted several tombstones scattered in the orange grove, some half-buried in the weeds. Not a villager was in sight. "Did you have trouble finding the village?"

"The train ride took forever. I wished I had wings." He yawned. "I took the first bus out of Mianyang. For hours I sat on a sack of dried beans in the aisle. I got lucky in Pingwu and hitched a ride in a jeep."

She reached a hand toward his short hair. Then a glance from Tong caused her to lower her hand and pat his collar instead. "A jeep?"

"Like I said, I was lucky." He sat on his duffle bag and took out a pack of cigarettes. He didn't drag her onto his lap, as he had often done in the past. "A few cadres were on their way to the hospital. They overheard me bargaining with the pedicab man, so they offered me a ride. I sat next to a plump lady who wore heavy perfume." He wrinkled up his nose.

Bao bit her lower lip. "Was she pretty?"

"She must be twenty years older than you." Tong lit a cigarette. "I guess she likes to see a man in uniform."

"This is Pingwu. No one heard of what PLA men did in Beijing. In fact, my grandparents still believe the army can do no wrong."

"Not all PLA men are the same." He flicked off the ashes.

Tong never used to smoke. How quickly a man could change!

"I didn't get to write and tell you." She cleared her throat. "I arranged the lodging for you, I hope you don't mind."

"Why should I mind?" He blew out broken smoke rings.

"I'm staying with my grandparents, but you can't." She looked at the ground. "I didn't tell them you're coming."

There was a moment of silence.

"Will you tell them?"

"I'd better not. Grandpa has a gun."

"I could've stayed at the hospital. It's only a fifty-minute walk."

"Really?" She turned toward Tong. "Is there a guest house at the hospital?"

"The cadres will stay there for the night. The hospital has plenty of clean beds, you know."

"What will the cadres do there?"

"Their official assignment is to oversee the one-child policy work. Of course that's their excuse to take a field trip and enjoy the local scenery. They came from Jiuzhaigou Park, and tomorrow they'll tour the panda reserve. Local cadres kiss up in order to get raises, you know how it is."

Tong sounded like a different man now. He spoke lightly of widespread corruption; moreover, he was willing to befriend corrupt officials.

"You should've stayed at the hospital," she said.

"Are you turning me away?" He put out his cigarette and stood up. "I spent thirty-six hours traveling thousands of miles. I was afraid I wouldn't find you. Can you give a guy a break?"

"You have no idea." She held his hand between her palms. "How much I missed you."

He shivered, and his eyelids grew red. He must've been waiting for her to give him a sign.

She put her head on his shoulder as he held her tightly. His stubble prickled her cheek. She pressed every inch of her body against him and sniffed the dusty scent of his hair. A bat flitted through the air in the deserted cemetery. When he pulled away, she felt breathless as if she'd run a long distance.

"I arranged for you to stay at a villager's house. They have a four-year-old daughter. I promised her mother we won't do anything . . . inappropriate there."

He watched her mouth with a smile. "Would it be inappropriate for me to kiss you?"

"Help yourself." She pressed her lips to his mouth. She smelt his cigarette breath, which made her even greedier. She licked his teeth and sucked his lips. He moaned softly as she rubbed her breasts against his chest.

"That's enough." He plucked her hand from his belt buckle.

"What's wrong?"

"We won't do that until you're completely healed." He backed away as if he were afraid of her. "I asked a doctor. She said we can't do this for at least a month. You may feel okay, but your body needs time to heal. There're scars inside you—"

"You can help me heal, fill me up again."

"No! How could you?" He snapped off a dead twig from the orange tree. "You're being irrational. It's partly the hormones. It takes a while for them to be flushed out of your system."

"You think I'm crazy?"

"Listen." His eyes were somber. "I promised your father I'll take better care of you. I will keep my word."

She knew better than to beg. She walked south to a small dock, shaded by an enormous yellow-rafter. Clumps of weeds grew under the tree. A boat with a bamboo awning rocked gently in the river. There was no one on the boat. A fishing rod and bamboo trap lay in the water. A drizzle started to fall, dimpling the surface of the river. Sparrows flapped their wings to dive under the lush canopy of the yellow-rafter.

"Do you resent me?" she said. "Soybean was yours, too."

"It wasn't your fault." He rubbed his palm on his pants. "I should've been there and held your hand. Will we ever forgive ourselves?"

"I don't know."

Yet she began to feel the hollow inside, it wasn't entirely empty. At the core was a flesh wound, starting to scab over.

She held his hand and stroked his fingernails. "I want us to be a couple again."

"Sweetheart." He caressed her face, earlobes, and the sensitive skin in her nape. "I ought to do better to deserve you."

The rain stopped as suddenly as it had started. Within ten minutes, the sky was blue, dabbled with white clouds. Splashing noises broke the silence. A fisherman paddled a bamboo raft. He might be from the village upstream. After collecting his rod and bamboo trap, he turned to smile at Tong and Bao, as if in greeting. Then he left the way he had come.

Chapter 12

BAO SLEPT FITFULLY THAT NIGHT. For the first time since her arrival, she realized that daylight came about an hour and a half later in Pingwu. Some western countries like the United States had several time zones, but all of China used Beijing standard time. This inflexible clock tormented her.

She rose at seven o'clock, when there was just a glimmer of light in the windows. After getting dressed, she opened the bedroom door and listened for sounds from the kitchen. There were none. She longed to see Tong, but it was too early. A door squeaked, and dim light poured into the house. Grandpa sat on the doorstep to have his smoke.

Bao approached him, combing her hair with her fingers. "Morning, Grandpa." Covering her mouth, she faked a yawn.

"You're up early today." Grandpa smiled. "Are you like me, can't sleep thinking about how to fix the hive?"

Her heart sank. Yesterday she had returned promptly after taking Tong to Candor's house. Grandpa had been fixing a super and told Bao to measure the frames. She worked while thinking about Tong's touches, smiling to herself now and then. She made several mistakes in half an hour. Instead of dismissing her, Grandpa lectured her about how to make a super. She had to submit like a dutiful apprentice.

Bao walked to the old mill, which had been in the family for generations. The millstone was thin with constant use, its surface dented and cracked. There was a cleft in the spout, like an old woman's mouth with missing front teeth. Soybeans were soaking in a basin of water. In the afternoon Grandma would grind soybeans to make bean curd jelly, so silky, buttery, and delicious that it melted in your mouth. This local specialty would have been a treat for Tong, if only he could enter the house.

Grandma came out of the bedroom and pulled up her over-sleeves. "You two are up early. Is the queen bee laying eggs?" She went to the stove to light the firewood.

"Didn't we fix the bee super yesterday?" Bao said. "I was planning to see Daisy today."

"Not yet." Grandpa cast Bao a sidelong glance. "Our work is not done."

"But I want to visit Daisy." She picked up a few soybeans, soft and plump. She rubbed off their skins with her fingers. "I have two weeks left before going back to Nanjing. I can't learn much more about the bees."

"You did fine yesterday."

"But I'm not a beekeeper." She tossed the skinned soybeans in the basin and wiped her hand on her jeans. "Back in Nanjing I probably won't see a honeybee."

"There're cockscombs, daisies, and chrysanthemums blooming everywhere." Grandpa knocked his pipe on the doorstep and made a dull sound. "How could you not see honeybees? You only have to look."

"Don't be so hard on her." Grandma prodded brushwood with a fire poker. Twigs and dry leaves caught fire, crackled and burned. "You saw how Daisy clung to her like an elder sister."

"You're right." Grandpa coughed and spat in the front yard. "Candor asked me to thank Bao. Their family needs all the help they can get. Go and play with Daisy. Her mother will be grateful."

Her grandparents looked serene and innocent. They seemed to understand Candor's family situation even better than Bao. Maybe they knew Orchid's whereabouts but didn't say anything in order to protect her family. All the better, their knowledge saved her the trouble of making up excuses for going to Candor's house.

"Bye now."

"What about breakfast?" Grandma said.

"I'm not hungry." Patting her belly, Bao walked backwards a few steps. "I'll be home for lunch, so save me a bowl of bean curd jelly."

The sun reddened the clouds on the horizon. As fog lifted from the loamy field, traces of moist air flickered like white smoke. She passed a large front yard, where a piglet with a curly tail poked at a bok choy heart with its snout. Three roosters fought over an earthworm wiggling in the mud. A toddler wearing a greasy bib sat on a doorstep and played with rocks. Seeing Bao, he sucked his muddy finger. The rural scene was idyllic because she didn't have to live here. Soon she would return to Nanjing, resume her studies, and continue her love affair in secret. Years later, she and Tong would reminisce about their vacation in Pingwu as the new beginning of their relationship.

She knocked on the door and heard Candor's voice.

"Who's there?"

"It's me, Gu Bao."

"Good morning, Miss Gu." The door opened. "Please come in."

She stepped over the tall doorstep. It took her eyes a moment to adjust to the dim light. Two benches and three chairs, padded with quilts, stood in the middle of the kitchen. Tong wasn't there.

"He's outside washing up." Candor pointed at the back door.

She found Tong wearing a red tank top and brushing his teeth.

"Did you sleep well?" she said.

Tong nodded, his mouth full of white foam. She reached out to feel his bicep. Under the warm skin, his muscles yielded to her touch. Shuddering, he let out a sharp laugh. Of course he was ticklish. He rinsed hurriedly and spat foamy water on the dirt.

"Why are you so naughty?" he said.

"I'm . . . happy to see you."

He lifted her face and kissed her cheek. "I missed you, too." They stood watching each other. He broke the gaze first. "Brush your teeth, Daisy."

Daisy came outside with her mug. A blob of pale green

toothpaste disappeared inside her mouth. Tong soaked a towel in a basin of water. He washed his face and scrubbed his neck and behind his ears.

"They ran out of toothpaste, so I let them use mine." His face, red and raw, gradually recovered its pale complexion. "Grownups can brush their teeth with salt and water, but a little girl needs toothpaste."

Bao had brushed her teeth with salt when she was a girl. Her grandparents couldn't afford toothpaste, and they hadn't asked her mother for money. Bao had hated the grainy salt on her gums and tongue, and at times she refused to brush. Seeing Tong give Daisy such a thoughtful gift, she felt a bit jealous of their closeness.

"Did you bring me a gift?"

"I left in such a hurry I didn't have time to go shopping." He wiped her forehead with the wet towel. "I can't give you toothpaste, not even a new tube of the finest kind."

"Put this on before you catch a chill." She threw him the uniform.

"I'm going to the fields." Candor appeared in the doorway. "Breakfast is on the table. When you're done, Daisy will wash your dishes."

"Please don't trouble her." Bao rubbed Daisy's shoulder. Her prominent collarbones and shoulder blades resembled a young chicken's. "Who do you take us for, making Daisy wait on us?"

"You're guests." Candor patted Daisy's uncombed head. "And she's used to helping around the house."

"Where's her mother?" Tong said. Bao elbowed him hard

and made him grimace.

"She's visiting her folks in Mianyang." Candor folded his pant legs to his knees and swung a hoe onto his shoulder. "Daisy, you be good at home. Uncle Tong and Auntie Bao will play with you."

Daisy followed him to the front yard. After Candor was gone, she went to the kitchen and filled a small basket with rice. She squatted on her heels and called the chickens. The hens hovered around her, flapping their wings as they fought over morsels of rice.

"Come have breakfast," Bao said.

Daisy glanced at her blankly and then resumed calling *go-go-go* to the hens. Bao left her and returned to the kitchen. Tong grinned at her.

"What're we going to do today?" he said.

"You heard Candor: we'll play with Daisy."

"That's all?"

"Why, do you have something else in mind?" Bao sat on his lap.

"Don't tempt me." He rocked her gently. "I want you so much I can't stand it."

"I may be . . . healed."

He pushed her away. "I won't be so irresponsible again."

Daisy came inside, took her rice bowl, and sat on the doorstep. Tong bit into a steamed bun and chewed for a while. He peered at Daisy, whose back was turned.

"I'm risking my career, you know. To request a leave, I said my grandparents were sick."

"What if they find out you're here?"

"I'd lose my job if they knew what I did to you. But I'm sick of politics. I can't stand them saying it was right to kill the mobs."

Bao grew teary as she remembered Hongzhi. Tong must have thought of him, too.

"After you left, I began to read history." He gulped down porridge. "No Chinese government has killed students like ours did. In 1919 warlords succumbed to students' pressure, and they refused to sign the treaties with foreign powers. Even the Gang of Four didn't kill protestors, although they hired thugs to beat up people. Of course the students thought the worst that could happen was to be beaten up—"

"When are we going to play?" Daisy turned her head.

"How about now?" Bao stood up. "I'll wash the dishes. If you get a stool for Uncle Tong, we'll play 'Finding a Friend.'"

"I don't know if I want to go back." Tong watched her wash dishes in a pail of well water. "Better desert than be forced to murder."

"So you aren't risking your career for me."

"But I need a job. In order to marry you, I have to earn a good living. A man is nothing without a job."

Bao dried the bowls with a dishrag and then washed her hands. She combed Daisy's hair into a goat-horn.

"Let's teach Uncle Tong the song," she said.

The girl's head bobbed up and down at the invitation.

"*I'm looking for a friend, a good friend.*" Daisy clapped her hands, and so did Bao. "*I've looked everywhere.*" Daisy glanced about her archly, and Bao laughed. "*Finally I find a little friend. I take a bow and smile at her.*" Bao bowed deeply until she heard a

slight click in her hip joints. "*We shake hands and become friends.*"
They clasped each other's hands. "*Now you're my good friend.*"
Bao hugged Daisy to her chest.

"Bravo." Tong clapped.

"Join us." Bao dragged him to form a circle.

"*I'm looking for a friend, a good friend.*" Bao clapped her hands
and prompted Tong to do the same. "*I've looked everywhere.
Finally I find a little friend. I take a bow and smile at her. We shake
hands and become friends.*" Tong stood aside with a forlorn
expression on his face. "*Now you're my good friend.*" Daisy
marched over to hold Tong's hand.

"Once more!" Daisy giggled.

"I'll have a rest." Bao sat on the doorstep.

Daisy sang, clapped her hands, and kicked her heels, while
her goat-horn bobbed merrily. At first Tong stood watching
her. Then he joined her by humming the simple tune and
followed her heels like a waddling goose. After a few rounds,
his face glowed pink, sweat beads glistening on his upper lip.
He sang so loudly that the hens stopped pecking rice and
watched him with alert eyes. Bao laughed so hard tears came
into her eyes.

Grandpa was late for lunch. As Bao scooped spicy bean
curd jelly into her mouth, her heart melted with contentment.
She downed two bowls of bean curd jelly before pulling out a
hanky to wipe the sweat off her forehead.

"Why didn't you teach Mom to make bean curd jelly?" she
said.

"She doesn't have time to grind soybeans with a mill, like

an old woman." Grandma replenished the sauce, made of red peppers, bean paste, and green onion. "She has a job and family. Besides, she earns enough money to buy you all the bean curd jelly you can eat."

Bao licked the rim of her empty bowl. "Our bean curd jelly tastes nothing like this." She'd eat more if her stomach had room for it. "Maybe you can teach me how to make it."

Grandma could barely suppress a smile. "You don't mind doing the chores?"

"Grandma, I can't always travel for two days to come here and eat your bean curd jelly." Tong would also love the bean curd jelly, but Bao couldn't say it. Then she heard a tune, sung by Grandpa's gruff voice.

"A young boy carrying a schoolbag. Rain or shine, I go to school every day. My teacher cannot call me lazy." He stomped into the house. *"If I fail in my studies, I cannot face my parents."*

"I thought Bao was chipper today," Grandma said. "What's up with you?"

"My fine ladies." With a chuckle he reached into his breast pocket and kept his hand there.

"Silly old man." Grandma's eyes widened, as he took out a wad of cash.

"Count this."

"Eighty yuan." Grandma recounted the money. "Where did you get it?"

"First things first." He sank into a chair. "Let me get some food in my belly."

Bao scooped rice and bean curd jelly in two bowls and brought them to Grandpa.

"I went to the Panda Reserve Office to file a complaint." Grandpa gulped down a spoonful of bean curd jelly. "I ran into Candor, and he went with me as the witness. The reserve workers reimbursed me right there."

"Without an investigation?" Grandma added sauce to his bean curd jelly.

"Thanks to Candor, he talked about the bamboo fiber in panda droppings like a scientist, and he's friends with the reserve workers. Without him, I'd file a report and wait for months. But now Candor has a tough job." He turned to Bao. "Candor will set off for the mountain this afternoon. After lunch you go to look after Daisy, bring her here if you need Grandma's help."

"What happened?" Bao said.

"Some cadres from Chengdu were touring the panda reserve. There's a woman among them, who wanted to lose a few pounds, so she hiked high up on the mountain. She got herself into such a tight spot she couldn't climb back down. They have to hire someone to carry her downhill."

"Who's the cadre?"

"Some high-ranking cadre from the Chengdu Family Planning Office."

Candor was too sensible to slave away for his enemy.

"She offers to pay five hundred yuan. Candor can use the money."

"For five hundred yuan, Candor will risk his life for some stupid cadre?" Bao said.

"Candor is the best climber in the village," Grandma said. "He knows the mountain like the back of his hand. If Buddha keeps score on the good deeds one does, his family may benefit from his heroism."

Bao couldn't argue with her reasoning. "I'll go see Daisy."

"Bring her here," Grandma said. "I'll make her honey biscuits."

Bao hurried down the road, because she wanted to dissuade Candor from going. What if Orchid went into labor while he was gone? Money drove a man to do things against his will. In a way Tong was the same, stuck in a career he grew to detest.

No one was at the house. She checked the dining table and makeshift bed but didn't find a note. Where had Tong taken Daisy?

She left the house and walked down the ridge. Seeing a crowd, she entered a shady bamboo grove, a spacious area. There were food stands and peddlers selling assorted handicrafts. Three dining tables stood side by side, upon which three stoves were boiling food. Several people sat at the tables and ate with relish, Tong and Daisy amongst them.

"How did you get here?"

"As we all know: Food is heaven." Tong handed her a kebab with boiled turnip, cabbage, and potato doused in spicy sauce. Bao wasn't hungry, so she gave the kebab to Daisy. "Candor packed a few steamed buns and left for the mountain. There was no lunch, so I took Daisy out to eat." He tapped her hand. "How is it?"

Warm vapor rose from Daisy's head. Her cheeks and lips were bright red, her eyes dark and shining. "Yum," she said with her mouth full.

Bao sat down and watched Daisy eat. She doused a kebab in plenty of hot sauce and ate it with her mouth open, slurping through her teeth. Bao used to eat spicy food when she'd lived at her grandparents' house. After she moved to Nanjing, she no longer had the palate for authentic spicy food. Now Grandma cooked food with spice on the side. Bao took a kebab from Tong's bowl. It was so spicy that her tongue and throat burned.

"Ouch."

"You can't be a local." Tong gazed at Daisy with frank admiration. "She can take more spice than we."

Bao tugged his sleeve. "I need to talk to you." She eyed a tree ten steps away from the crowd.

Tong got up and patted Daisy's head. "Eat slowly."

Licking her greasy lips, Daisy reached for a kebab strung with oyster mushrooms and lettuce.

Bao stood with her back to the crowd. "Candor shouldn't have gone to the mountain."

"Why?" Tong gave her a piece of plum candy. "It soothes your throat after you eat spicy food."

She pushed away his hand. "Why did Candor leave his daughter with a stranger?"

"You're so worried, because I'm not trustworthy."

Bao paced a few steps. She opened her mouth but closed it again.

Tong folded his arms on his chest. "Will you tell me the truth, or should I ask Daisy what the matter was?"

"No, please, don't breathe a word to Daisy." Bao took the piece of plum candy, unwrapped and then put it in her mouth.

"His wife is in hiding."

Tong glanced at the diners, none of whom paid them any attention, and led Bao behind a tree. "Does she need help?"

"Not yet, I hope." The sweet and sour candy soothed her throat and also made her salivate. "She hides in a cave and may go into labor anytime."

At the hot pot stand, a man pounded the table with his fist. "Go away, stinky madman."

Brother Liao stood aside and bowed at the diners, his face red with longing.

"Come with me," Bao said. "Please buy a few kebabs for a hungry man." She dipped several kebabs in hot sauce and gave them to Brother Liao. He bowed at her, turned, and jogged away. His dirty green uniform disappeared in the bamboo grove.

"Is he a veteran?" Tong paid the bill after Daisy rose.

"Just some nut whose wife died," a man said and cleaned his teeth with a toothpick.

"He's an unlucky bastard." A stocky man with bristling hair wiped sweat from his pockmarked face. "Other women with two children all had their tubes tied. The one-child policy team was already lenient with them. His wife had an abortion but didn't make it. Their ancestors hadn't burnt incense to ask for Guanyin's blessing."

Bao was appalled to hear Brother Liao's tragedy being discussed in front of Daisy. She led the girl away to the snack food stands. A peddler held up a straw mat, upon which displayed dozens of sugared haws on sticks, glowing like abacus beads.

"Ready for dessert?" Bao said.

Daisy moaned and twisted her waist. "I can't eat another bite."

Several grocery stands sold household goods, clothes, hairpins, brushes, and medicine clay pots. Tong took Daisy's free hand.

"Do you like this?" he said. "How about that? Okay, take your pick."

Daisy pulled free, slipping into and out of the crowd like a kitten. Some people stared at them, but Bao wasn't worried. It was fun to be with Tong, and she felt guileless. Daisy squatted in front of a stand selling sunhats made of bright-colored polyester. She stroked the purple lace of a pink sunhat, the gaudiest hat Bao had ever seen.

"What a pretty hat." Tong reached into his pocket for the wallet. "How much?"

The peddler stared at his black leather wallet. "Five yuan." He rose with an eager smile, when Tong pulled out a ten-yuan bill.

"How much is this?" Tong picked up an embroidered tiger hat.

Red threads outlined the tiger's fierce eyes, while yellow threads formed the word King in the middle of its forehead. Stuffed brown cloth made its stout back and short legs. Mighty and childlike, a tiger hat symbolized the force protecting babies, especially boys.

"If you buy them as a set, I'll give you a discount." The peddler held up a pair of shoes with the matching tiger patterns. "Three items for fifteen yuan."

"Ten." Tong made a fist around the bill.

"I'll be honest with you, mister. We hardly make any money as it is." The peddler licked his chapped lips. "My wife and I live on a tight budget, and we have a teenage son to support."

Behind the stand, a middle-aged woman threaded palm fibers into a bamboo slat punctured with holes. She finished a brush, laid it on a low table, and went on to make a new one.

"What's the brush for?" Bao said.

"You can use it to wash clothes and shoes." The woman handed a brush to Bao. "Buy one, Little Sister, my brush will last you for years."

Bao always brought her laundry home to use the washing machine, but she liked the brush. It was plain and sturdy.

"Fifteen yuan total." She handed Tong five yuan. "Or we won't buy a thing."

The peddler pursed his lower lip until it covered his upper one. Although he acted exasperated, Bao knew he was relieved.

"You two drive a hard bargain." He handed the goods to Tong. "My tiger hat and shoes were made by the best local hands. Your baby will look like a king wearing them."

Tong placed the baby shoes inside the tiger hat and handed them to Daisy.

"I don't want them." Daisy tied the pink ribbon of the sunhat under her chin. "They're for boys."

"Keep them for me. They're a gift."

"Can I use them to play house? I won't get them dirty."

"Sure." Tong clasped his hands behind his back and stretched his arms like a gymnast. "Have fun with them."

Unfortunately Candor didn't come home by dark, so Bao had to take Daisy to her grandparents' house for supper. She managed to dissuade Daisy from wearing her new sunhat, which would arouse suspicion. She made Daisy promise not to mention Uncle Tong at Grandma's house. They said goodnight to him and left him cooking instant noodles. Bao boasted about the delicious food Grandma had prepared: spicy bean curd jelly, eggplant stewed with pork, red bean rice dumplings, and honey biscuits, the last of which persuaded Daisy to go.

Sitting at Grandma's dining table, Bao began to miss Tong. If only he could enjoy the tasty dishes! She tried to get Daisy to eat a scoop from a bowl of bean curd jelly, but the girl wrinkled her nose with distaste.

"I'm not hungry." Daisy let out a loud belch.

Grandma touched the girl's forehead, as if measuring her temperature.

"What did your dad feed you, fatty pork with rinds?"

"I ate a whole lot of hot pot today."

"I took her out because Candor didn't cook lunch." Bao fought back the desire to cover Daisy's mouth with her hand. "Try Grandma's bean curd jelly, you'll love it." She held up the spoon to the little red mouth.

"Too spicy, my tummy hurts." Daisy turned her face away. "I want some honey biscuits."

Grandpa pushed a basket of biscuits toward the girl. "They're special, made with the honey harvested in our own backyard."

Daisy took two biscuits, one in each hand. She nibbled them alternately.

Bao breathed a sigh of relief. After supper, she wanted to take Daisy home and be relieved of her duty. Tomorrow she hoped to spend more time with Tong. They might even have a chance to rekindle their passion.

"If Candor comes home late, Daisy should sleep here tonight." Grandma combed hair back from Daisy's forehead. "Would you like to sleep with Grandma?"

Daisy licked off the cookie crumbs from her lips. "Can I sleep with Auntie?"

Bao choked on a mouthful of bean curd jelly and coughed. "Why . . . me?"

Daisy smiled at her hopefully.

"Why not?" Grandpa winked at Bao. "You're so eager to run to their house all the time."

Bao didn't want to be a surrogate mother tonight. She wished to be a lover. Since she couldn't sleep with Tong, she wanted to be alone and dream about him.

"Your dad will come home in a little while." She was almost glad to see Daisy's disappointed eyes.

"Suppose that he doesn't," Grandma said. "I'll make the bed for both of you."

Daisy studied the two biscuit halves and laid them side-by-side to make a whole. She gripped Bao's arm, her eyes glowing.

"If we ask Uncle Tong to come here, will you sleep with me?"

Bao felt cold.

"Who is Uncle Tong?" Grandpa said.

Bao felt her scalp smarting, her tongue numb in her mouth.

"Uncle Tong took me to eat hot pot and bought me the

prettiest sunhat, but Auntie Bao wouldn't let me wear it."
Daisy covered her mouth with a hand. "Oh, I'm not supposed
to . . ."

A loud buzzing filled Bao's ears. She didn't hear the rest of
Daisy's words.

"Are you friends with this man? Bao, do you hear me?"
Grandpa's stern voice was unreal.

"Yes." Bao was suddenly angry, angry with herself for lying,
angry at Daisy for betraying her, and angry with Tong for
making her life difficult.

"Who is he?" Grandma said.

"Who else?" Bao smiled with tears in her eyes. "The only
man I care about. Serves me right, don't you think?"

Her grandparents looked at each other in confusion, before
Grandpa's eyes popped with astonishment.

"Did he come from Nanjing?" he said. "Why is he staying
at Candor's house?"

"Don't blame Candor. He did me a favor." Bao held her
forehead in both hands. "You wouldn't let Tong stay here.
You'd report him to my parents and tell them what a slut I
am."

"That's a bad word, Auntie Bao." Daisy's whisper startled
everybody.

No one replied. The embarrassment was palpable.

After a long silence, Grandma reached out a hand to rub
Bao's back. "You didn't do anything with him, did you?"

"Oh, we had lots of fun with Uncle Tong! We played
'Finding a Friend.' Auntie Bao and I ate hot pot with him.
Then we bought a few things together."

"You heard her." Bao laughed in spite of her misery. "We were never alone but with Daisy all the time."

"That's good." Grandpa looked upon the girl with gratitude. "Bao, you should've told us about this man. How could you not trust us, your own grandparents?"

Grandma held Bao's hand. "If anything happened to you, what should we tell your parents?"

"Tell them I'm almost nineteen years old. By law, I'm an adult."

"But you're always our Little Bao." Grandpa's lips trembled as if he were holding back tears. "This man Tong, is he even sorry for what he did?"

"He didn't do it." Bao slid to the edge of her seat. "We did, and I love him."

"Oh child." Grandma touched her cheek. "Did your mother not see you like this? We would've raised your baby."

"Uncle Tong let me use his toothpaste and bought me gifts. He called Auntie Bao his sweetheart." Daisy swung her legs as she rattled on.

The glitter in Grandpa's eyes dimmed, and slowly his face relaxed into a frown.

"We should keep our friends close and enemies closer." He pondered the words. "Chairman Mao said that, good strategy."

"You're wrong." Bao surprised herself by correcting him, "Sun Tzu said it in *The Art of War*. Mao quoted it and applied the principle in his war strategies."

They gazed at each other's face for a while. Finally Bao burst into a smile, and Grandpa beamed, too.

"Let's pay Tong a visit," he said.

"What're we going to do?" Grandma wrung her hands. "We can't invite him to stay at our house."

"Don't worry about that yet. He can stay at Candor's house. We just need to keep an eye on him."

"Will you tell Mom and Dad?" Bao heard her trembling voice and cleared her throat.

"Do you want us to?" Grandpa said.

Averting her eyes, Bao ate a spoonful of bean curd jelly. It left a burning sensation in her throat that made her woozy.

"Not to worry, child." He patted her head. "You'll go home in a little more than a week. We just want to keep you safe and sound."

"Let's eat, the food is getting cold." Grandma picked up a poached egg to put in Daisy's bowl. "After supper we'll get going."

"Auntie Bao," Daisy whispered into her ear. "Can I sleep with you tonight?"

"I toss and turn all night long." Bao glared at her. "You won't get a wink of sleep."

Daisy pulled back, her small body tensing up with surprise.

"You can sleep with me, baby." Grandma cuddled Daisy in her arms. "Tell me, what sort of a man Uncle Tong is."

Chapter 13

BAO POINTED A FLASHLIGHT at the dark ridge as she led the way to Candor's house. Grandma held Daisy's hand, while her small heels pattered in mud now and then. Grandpa carried a cotton thermos bucket that kept the food warm. Inside there was rice, bean curd jelly, eggplant stewed with pork, and stir-fried pea leaves with tomato. Approaching the house, Bao shot a beam of light at the front door.

Stepping onto the porch, Daisy yawned and rubbed her eyes.

"Maybe Dad isn't home."

Grandma squatted down and patted her shoulder. "If he isn't, you can come and sleep with me tonight, I promise."

Bao heard Candor's voice inside the house.

"Hurry up and knock," she said. "Your dad is home."

Daisy turned and bumped into Bao.

"Don't you miss your father?" Bao raised a hand to knock on the door. "Candor, your daughter is home."

When Tong opened the door, Bao was surprised to find several strangers inside. Two middle-aged men and a woman sat on the benches and chairs that had been Tong's makeshift bed. Her grandparents and Daisy filed into the house. Tong paid no attention to them, as he spoke to the others in a loud and clear voice.

"Candor needs a hundred yuan to buy medicinal plasters to treat his knee. Plasters of tiger bones and musk are best, but they're expensive. Candor also needs to see an acupuncturist. On top of it all, he has no insurance against lost productivity." Tong peered at Daisy. "He needs to look after his daughter. With an injured knee, Candor can't work in the fields for at least a week."

Grandma approached Candor, who sat in a chair with his legs stretched out. "How badly are you hurt?"

Candor pushed himself up on his fists, his face grimacing with pain and effort. "My knee . . ." He sniffed and blinked hard. "It gave out." He drew up his right leg, while the left leg remained limp.

A woman's voice made their heads turn. "I owe you for your help." Her plump body filled a sturdy walnut armchair. She wore a beige vest with coin-sized prints and a blue and white pleated skirt. Bao had seen her high-top Nike shoes in a department store, priced at six hundred yuan. "I cannot say my thanks to you well enough." Her pancake-shaped face softened with a smile. She looked flirty with long narrow eyes slanting toward her temples. Her double chin was drawn back to give her a moony face.

"Comrade Fang has expressed her thanks over and again." A man in a blue Mao suit stood up, a gray peaked cap shading his eyes. He was almost a head taller than Tong but had a bashful expression on his smooth hairless face. "Let me remind you, Candor, you had agreed to help Comrade Fang for five hundred yuan. You carried her downhill for less than an hour. Isn't it more than fair that she pays you six hundred yuan? It's more than four months of my salary, which you earned in an hour." He pointed a finger at Candor, his hand showing blackened stumps of nails. "How could you ask for seven hundred? People in my village aren't known for being greedy."

"Being our village chief, you ought to be fair," Grandpa said. "Candor isn't asking for more money out of greed. Like Mr. Tong said earlier, Candor needs to buy medicine and see a doctor."

Tong raised his head. He seemed surprised to hear his name being called by a stranger. He looked at Bao's face, as if asking, "Who is he?"

A thin man walked to the center of the room. His hair was gray, and he wore glasses.

"Old Du has a few words," the village chief said.

Du looked like a professor at first glance. Bao was amazed to hear his deep voice boom inside the house.

"Candor was injured during his service. Nobody denies this fact. On the contrary, we commend him for having made a sacrifice." He moved to his tiptoe and appeared a few inches taller. His slim fingers groped beside his ear, as if trying to catch a butterfly. He put down his heels as swiftly as he had raised them. "Comrade Fang works for the Family Planning Office in Chengdu. I work in the village, a grass roots unit. Bear with me when I use a military analogy."

He blinked rapidly as if he had dust in his eyes.

"Upholding the one-child policy is like a war, consisting of many battles. If Comrade Fang is a company commander, we grass roots cadres are soldiers under her command." His flat lenses cast a cold reflection of light. "We didn't desert you, Candor, after you were wounded. Despite the danger and her fatigue, Comrade Fang walked the rest of the way. The village chief and I carried you for a stretch. We were comrades-in-arms on the mountain. How could you haggle for every—"

"I wouldn't call Candor my 'comrade-in-arms' if I were you." Tong frowned at him with poorly concealed disdain. "I would *not* rob Candor of his rightful earning."

"Young man, you aren't a veteran like me." Old Du smiled, his eyes growing smaller but gentler. The corners of his mouth pulled upward and revealed his strong white teeth, slightly crooked. "You wouldn't be so cocky if you'd been in a war."

"Candor didn't have supper yet." Grandma laid the thermos bucket on the dining table. "We brought him food."

"We came here to settle a simple matter. We'll leave when it's finished."

"Rightly said, Old Du." The village chief walked to Comrade Fang's chair and rested his hands upon the high back. "Comrade Fang, I invite you to my house afterwards. My wife has prepared a simple dinner. She makes the best spicy chicken in the village."

No doubt he would host a banquet with at least ten courses.

"Please don't tempt me with rich food." Comrade Fang writhed in her chair. "It raises my cholesterol level."

Everyone seemed to relax as food became the topic. The village chief straightened his peaked cap as he got ready to leave. Old Du patted Candor's shoulder and slid a cigarette into his mouth.

"We all had a long day, Candor. Let's not drag this into the middle of the night. Comrade Fang made you a good offer." He lit Candor's cigarette with a match. "When her life was endangered, it was our responsibility as citizens to help her. You did a fine job, Candor, and money isn't your only reward. If you insist upon two hundred yuan, you may sour our work relationship with Comrade Fang. Ask yourself: is this worth it?"

"Don't bully an honest farmer who risked his life." Tong looked down at Old Du, who stood below his shoulder. "Candor ruined his knee. He could've died! Why didn't *you* carry Comrade Fang down the hill? Were you afraid of falling off the cliff? Why, I thought you're a veteran!"

"I know you want to be helpful, Tong." The woman turned to her colleagues. "I gave him a ride in my jeep yesterday, so we sort of know each other."

She showed Tong such an evocative smile it made Bao jealous.

"It isn't that I'm unwilling to pay the price—a man's good work deserves the pay, but my salary isn't high. We have to pay high fees for our son to have a private tutor. He has to get accepted by a key high school next year, or he won't be able to enter a university. For him we save every penny and rarely buy new clothes. His father has a heart condition that requires long-term use of red ginseng from Heilongjiang. The bottom line is that I didn't budget for an expensive expedition."

"It was my fault." Blushing deeply, the village chief scratched his scalp under the peaked cap. "I suggested that we visit the panda reserve. The tour has nothing to do with our work. We saw no pandas, and you had a good scare. You must pardon me by letting me pay some of the expense."

A faint grin flitted across the woman's broad face. She turned her slanting eyes toward the village chief, like a benevolent queen addressing an anxious eunuch.

"You were kind to introduce me to your local attractions. How could I blame you for my misfortune?"

The village chief cocked his head so eagerly his hat fell off, exposing a large bald spot on his crown. "A leader must take responsibility for his actions." He pulled out a few bills from his wallet and counted them twice. "I can go home and get more money." He replaced his hat with a trembling hand.

The chief's show of generosity sparked competition from Old Du, who puffed out his chest saying, "I'll pitch in." Old Du reached into his pocket and gave her eighty-three yuan.

"Well, you don't have to do this!" Comrade Fang added five hundred yuan and gave total six hundred and fifty-nine yuan to Candor. "I envy you for having such good, decent leaders."

Candor stuffed the bills in his pocket. "We're getting by." The cigarette fell to the ground as he opened his mouth. With his head hung low, he looked miserable as if he'd received an arrest warrant.

"Eat your supper, and you'll feel better." Grandma took out the dishes from the thermos bucket.

The bean curd jelly was buttery white, dabbled with orange-colored hot sauce and green onion bits. The eggplant stewed with pork was bright purple and dark maroon. The stir-fried pea leaves were deep green mixed with half-moon shaped tomato chunks. The steamed rice was still warm.

"It's late, Old Du. I shouldn't eat a big meal anyway." Comrade Fang leaned close to sniff the delicious aroma. "May I try some of this?"

"Help yourself." Grandma forced a smile. "We brought the food for Candor and Tong." This was all she could say to discourage the woman from eating their supper.

Tong backed away from the dining table. "I already ate."

"I'll pay, of course." The woman opened an alligator skin wallet and pulled out two yuan. "I eat like a bird, still I pack on weight."

She gave such a helpless smile that Bao was certain every man in the room was affected by it. Comrade Fang might have become a high-ranking cadre through her feminine charm and brazenness rather than her qualifications.

"You're in your prime, Comrade Fang," the village chief said. "You need proper nourishment after the strenuous hike. My wife has prepared . . ." His mouth hung open as he stopped in the middle of a sentence.

Bao turned around and saw Daisy sitting on the bedroom doorstep. Her sunhat cast a red halo around her head. The tiger hat and shoes glittered in her hands like brocade.

"What's that?" Candor said.

"Gifts from Uncle Tong." Daisy tied the satin ribbon under her chin, her cheeks glowing with pleasure.

"Is this your daughter?" Comrade Fang smiled at Daisy. "How old are you?"

"Four years and seven months old." Daisy strutted toward the guests, reveling in their attention. She was probably imitating Comrade Fang. The shy girl modeled herself on the femininity beyond her years.

Old Du stared at her hands. "Why, you have a tiger hat and shoes!"

Candor frowned in puzzlement. Suddenly his face turned ghostly white. His expression wasn't lost upon Old Du who stood nearby. Tong snatched the tiger hat and shoes from Daisy.

"I told you they're for my nephew. They aren't your toys." He thrust them into his duffle bag and zipped it up. "The sunhat looks good on you."

Old Du bent down to address the pouting girl. "Did he buy them for you?"

"Of course not." As Bao stepped forward to hold Tong's hand, every head turned toward her. Her heart pounded in her chest, and her mouth was dry. She was surprised to hear her own voice, calm and resolute. It gave her courage to continue. "I helped Tong choose the tiger hat and shoes. They were made by the best local hands. We can't find nice handmade crafts in Nanjing for a reasonable price."

"You don't live here," the village chief said, "but you look familiar."

"You remember our granddaughter. She's visiting us for the summer." Grandpa sat beside Daisy on the bedroom doorstep. "The last time you saw her, she was a little girl. Now she's a law student at Nanjing University."

"Do you know him?" Old Du tilted his head toward Tong.

"We're friends." Bao blushed, and her coyness announced their relationship to every adult present. "I invited him to visit me."

Old Du and the village chief looked at each other. They turned toward Candor.

"Why are you taking a lodger?" the village chief said. "Where's your wife?"

"Orchid is visiting her folks in Mianyang." Candor's voice shook a little.

Old Du knelt on one knee. "What a pretty hat!" He kneaded the lacy fringe of Daisy's sunhat. "Your mama will be happy to see you wear it. Do you miss her?"

Daisy nodded, her eyes glittering. Bao held her breath when Old Du retied the ribbon under the girl's chin. "Do you know when she'll come home?"

Daisy shook her head.

"Orchid would never leave her daughter unless she had to." Grandpa pulled Daisy to sit on his lap. "Her cousin has acute hepatitis, so she went to look after the patient. She didn't bring Daisy because the disease is contagious." His story stunned Bao, since she had never heard him tell a lie. "What sort of hepatitis was it?" he asked Candor. "You told me once before, but I forgot."

"The sort?" Candor seemed to wake from a dream. "The third type, maybe."

"Hepatitis C? It's very rare." Comrade Fang leapt to her feet with surprising agility. She thrust her hands into the vest pockets, as if protecting herself from the invisible virus. "If it's highly contagious, it must be hepatitis A. There was an outbreak in Shanghai after people ate raw river clams." She frowned upon the dishes. "It's late. We should get going."

"This way." The village chief opened the door.

"We hope to see your mother soon." Old Du grinned at Daisy.

Comrade Fang shook Candor's hand. "I can't thank you enough." Candor's lips moved without making a sound. She released his hand. "If your family comes to Chengdu, you're welcome to visit me anytime."

She left with her colleagues.

Everyone in the house remained silent until the footsteps faded on the ridge. Candor whimpered and slapped his forehead.

"What am I going to do?" He pounded his left knee. "I can't climb the mountain anymore, I'm a useless man."

"Don't worry," Grandpa said. "Get some rest. You'll be well in a few weeks at most."

"If I don't climb for a week, I'll lose money, and I . . ." He started sobbing like a little boy.

Bao suddenly understood his anguish. He had to bring Orchid food every three days.

"I'll help you. I promised her, too." Bao broke down, as hot tears welled in her eyes. Her sheltered life hadn't prepared her for this, and Candor's pain moved her so deeply that her heart felt as if it were trampled upon.

"We'll help you." Grandma rubbed his shoulder blade.

"Don't worry, Candor. You're hurt, but it isn't the end of the world."

"It sure feels like it." Candor wiped his eyes on his sleeve, but tears kept pouring down his cheeks. "I can't take many more days like this, living like an animal."

"Let me warm up your food." Grandma went to the stove. "You'll feel better after you eat."

"I'm not hungry." Candor rolled his head about and wailed like a madman. "I'm weary and broken. Is there no end to our suffering? Will our children live the same lives we do? Then why bother bringing them into the world?"

"Don't despair, Candor." Grandpa wiped the corner of his eye. "Remember the saying: Every child is a treasure, because he brings his own grain ration."

"Daddy, don't cry." Daisy wrapped her arms around his waist. "I'll make the bed for you to lie down."

"I know you will, baby." Candor covered his face with a sleeve as he wept.

Bao watched Tong across the room. He sat in a chair with legs apart and hands resting on his thighs. On the surface he seemed unaffected, but she knew he wept for the family in his heart. Otherwise, he wouldn't have put himself out to strike a hard bargain with Old Du. Yet, no one felt any better for the extra money that Candor had earned. No word was comforting and no action could help, when Candor lost his hope in the hour of trial.

Grandma brought bowls of food to the dining table. "Candor, eat your supper."

"But I'm not—"

"Nonsense!" She set a pair of chopsticks on the rice bowl.

"Young man." Grandpa waved Tong to his side. "You take his left arm and I take his right. Let's help him up."

Tong and Grandpa lifted Candor from his chair and took him to the dining table. Candor plied rice into his mouth. At first he was slow, as if he didn't have an appetite. After a few bites, he started to gulp down food. Wheezing between bites, he tried to swallow food faster than he could chew.

"Food is heaven." Tong watched Candor with relief and satisfaction.

Gazing at Tong, Grandpa nodded his head with a smile. "No one has ever gotten money out of Childless Du before, and few have dared to try."

Bao could hardly believe that Du was the consummate villain. The middle-aged man looked pedantic and ordinary, even a little frail.

"How sly you are, Grandma!" Bao stared at her. "You knew Orchid is in hiding."

Grandma threw steamed buns in a bamboo tray and then replenished the steamer with raw dough chunks. "Several women disappeared before and went to their relatives' houses to have babies. Some had girls and gave up trying. We haven't seen Orchid in a while." She added firewood and pumped the bellows. "We don't know where she is, and it's better this way. Childless Du has a way of finding out things."

Bao poured hot soup into a tin can and snapped on the lid. Grandma packed a lunchbox with stewed hen and mushrooms. She filled a medium-sized box with green chives and stir-fried eggs.

"Orchid needs to eat well," Grandma said. "Or she won't have the strength to deliver the baby. What has she been eating lately?"

"I don't know." Bao scooped rice into a large bowl. "Candor brought the food to her."

Grandma wrapped two dishrags on the handles to carry the hot wok from the stove. "Candor is a man. Like your grandpa, he can cook to feed himself." She scooped bean curd jelly into a deep tin can and added hot sauce and chopped cilantro. "I had your mother, and I looked after her when she had you. I know this much to be true—an expecting woman rarely enjoys her husband's cooking."

"What did you say about me?" Grandpa turned his head.

"Nothing." Clutching the end of a nylon rope in her teeth, Grandma tied up the lunchboxes together in a neat bundle. "This is heavy. You need help to carry it on the mountain."

Tong turned toward Grandpa, who sat beside him on the doorstep. "Let me go with Bao. I promise I'll look after her."

"I should bring the food to Orchid," Grandpa said, "but it may get her into trouble. Childless Du is a cunning man."

"He doesn't look like a one-child policy worker," Bao said. "How did he come up with that war analogy?"

"We should never have elected him." Grandma wiped her hands on the apron.

"It's a long story. Old folks like us know how he came to Crystal Village." Grandpa sniffed. "Is something burning?"

"No, I'm steaming the buns." Grandma returned to the stove.

"Sichuan Basin was flooded in the summer of 1955," Grandpa said. "That year farmers in many counties had almost nothing to harvest. They left their homes to beg and scrabble for a living. Childless Du was five or six years old then. His parents couldn't feed him, so they left him to an old childless couple here."

Grandma kneaded dough on a thick cutting board. "They were good folks, vegetarians and devout Buddhists."

"They gave the boy's parents a bag of rice, some soybeans, red beans, and dried broad beans. Everything filled a burlap fertilizer bag. When Childless Du was a teenager, he often said his parents had sold him for a bag of rice. His foster mother cried when she heard this. You know, they loved him like their own flesh and blood." Grandpa leaned against the doorframe and folded his arms on his chest. "At eighteen Childless Du joined the army. He didn't come home when his foster mother died. His foster father died several months later. By then, he was fighting USSR frontier soldiers on Zhenbao Island."

Tong groaned and shaded his eyes with a hand. Bao wondered if her boyfriend was unfit for combat.

"Childless Du came home in one piece," Grandpa said. "It was the Cultural Revolution. His uniform and sullen attitude made him a star among young women. He married a tailor's daughter, the prettiest girl in the village. For more than ten years they had no child. His wife wanted a divorce. It wasn't granted by the Women's Federation until the early eighties, when divorces became more common. By then, there was so much gossip even village children called him Childless Du." When a dog skulked behind the goat pen, Grandpa stood up and waved at the dog. "Go, keep a watch!"

"You can't be too careful." Grandma peered out from behind the stove.

"Our dog barks its head off when it sees Childless Du." Grandpa returned to sit on the doorstep. "We used to think a veteran valued lives more than some matron who envied young couples. It took us a while to find out how ruthless he was."

"He looks like a professor with those glasses," Bao said. "Isn't a soldier required to have perfect vision?"

"He has eagle eyes. Those glasses were a prop that helped him win the tailor's daughter. Like you said, she must've taken him for a veteran with intellectual abilities."

Grandma laughed aloud. "One day a lens fell off, but he didn't know and walked around wearing half a pair of glasses. Children chased after him, calling him Childless Du." She wiped tears from her eyes. "What a sorry sight he was!"

"Childless Du doesn't seem to have the strength to truss up a chicken," Grandpa said, "but he has stooges working for him."

Bao remembered the men eating the hot pot in the bamboo grove. "I saw some men bullying Brother Liao as if he were dirt."

"Childless Du is a hundred times more evil than those men with dirty mouths and pea brains." Grandpa spat on the ground and smudged it with his heel. "After destroying Brother Liao's family, he donated his old army uniform to the madman."

"Unbelievable." Tong dusted his sleeve.

"Childless Du forced women to have abortions and sterilized them afterwards." Grandma fetched the steamer to place on the counter. "He may take his revenge on women for his ex-wife's insult."

"There's no excuse for a man to do evil," Grandpa said.

"Childless Du's stooges may follow you on the mountain." Tong spoke up. "I'm a stranger in an army uniform. They won't suspect me, if I deliver the food to Orchid."

"Orchid will be frightened out of her wits, if she sees you." Bao reached for the backpack. "It's best that I go. She trusts me to be with Daisy."

"You two stay home." Grandma took off her apron. "I'll bring the food to her."

"If you hadn't berated his man for knocking down Mrs. Li last month, I would ask you to deliver the food." Grandpa put a hand on Grandma's shoulder and squeezed it. "Please, for Orchid's sake, I beg you not to go within a mile of her hiding place."

"What if something happens to Bao? There're poachers on the mountain."

"I'll go with her." Tong opened his duffle bag to take out a police baton. With a flick of his wrist it expanded to three times of its original length. "I couldn't bring a gun on the family leave, but this comes handy."

Bao touched its cool steel surface. "Have you used it before?"

"I was trained but never used it while maintaining order at the Drum Tower Square." Tong pushed it against the floor to collapse it. "No hooligan will lay a hand on you, when I carry this."

"Take good care of Bao." Grandpa gazed at Tong's Adam's apple. "Don't let us down, young man."

"I'd rather die than hurt a hair on her head."

Grandpa pounded Tong's chest. He stood firm and didn't flinch.

"I believe in you, because you wear a uniform." He slid the straps of a heavy backpack onto Tong's shoulders and made sure they were secure. "Go now and come home for supper."

Bao set off with Tong. They passed the goat pen. Kneeling on the ground, the kid nibbled on a tender leaf. Her droopy ears and snub nose made Bao smile.

"My grandparents like you."

"What makes you say that?"

"They didn't throw a cake at you."

"Lucky for me, your grandparents are old-fashioned. I don't trust every man who wears the uniform." The wide-eyed look softened his face. "But I trust me."

They met few villagers in the woods. Once they stopped to look at a gray-headed bullfinch perching on a willow, her feathers fluffed. On a side branch, a male tragopan raised a red-crested head to show off his crimson plumage, dotted with white spots bordered by black. Suddenly his blue facial skin expanded into two hanging lappets extending down both sides of the breast, marked with bright red patches, and two blue "horns" propped up from the top of his head. Not to be outdone, two other male tragopans expanded their facial skins simultaneously and surrounded the brown-feathered hen with their fantastic displays.

"The hen looks so dull," Bao said.

"Male birds are handsomer." Tong winked.

Bao knew in a few years her fresh looks would fade. She would use anti-wrinkle cream to moisturize her skin. In contrast, Tong would remain young into his thirties, while his beauty routine was a daily shave.

"You're vain," she said.

He snatched up a long tree branch. Hiking up a steep slope, he used it as a walking staff. Then on level ground he waved the long stick to whip the shrubs at the roadside. He mumbled an inaudible tune, like a boy riding a wooden horse into an imaginary battle.

"You can very well leave the shrubs alone." She straightened his backpack. "Don't spill the soup."

He raised the stick over his shoulder and flung it forward with all his might. A jackrabbit hopped out and dashed into the woods. He slapped his thigh.

"I have an idea! If your parents refuse to accept us, we can move here and look after your grandparents."

His plan had its charm, but she wasn't tempted.

"What about our careers?" she said.

"I'll be a hunter and you'll be a plant gatherer, like nature made us." When he reached for her hand, she backed away.

"I won't be a peasant and submit to Childless Du." Her shout echoed in the valley. "My child will have a proper place in this world!"

"You're proud like your father."

The sound of rushing water drowned out the rest of his

words. Tong quickened his steps toward the source of the water. Standing on two flat rocks, he cupped the water to drink.

"Does this place have a name?" he said.

"Rooster Peak." She pointed at the gnarly roots of the yellow-rafter. "Aren't they like a dozen chicken feet?"

He gazed upon the majestic yellow-rafter. "This tree has a soul."

"Let's go see her."

They walked to the cliff side. Bao tapped on the fence door.

"It's me, Little Sister." There was no answer. "Candor asked us to bring you food. Will you let us in?"

"Are you with someone?" Orchid's voice was muffled.

"It's my fellow from Nanjing, I told you about him before." Bao plucked a tender leaf from the vine. "He helped me carry the food here."

"You scared me to death," Orchid said.

The fence door lifted a bit, and Bao crawled inside. She tugged Tong's pant-leg. He crouched down and crept into the cave. Once inside, he knelt a while longer. Then he rose cautiously and reached out his hand to Orchid.

"How do you do? I'm Li Tong."

Orchid sat on her bed. "Where's Candor?" Her eyes darkened with worry and bewilderment.

"He made a little money yesterday." Tong slid off the backpack from his shoulders. "He did a good deed but paid a price."

Orchid's face turned white in the dim light.

Bao had to tell her the truth. "He hurt his knee. Don't

worry, he'll fully recover. He can't climb the mountain for a few days, so we came to bring you food."

Tong undid the strings that bound the lunchboxes and tin cans. "Help yourself, the soup is still warm."

Orchid opened the box and looked inside. Her face wrinkled up with fear.

"Your grandma made this. What happened to Candor? Can he not get out of the bed—is he dying?" Her hands shaking, she spilt soup on her skirt.

"No!" Bao and Tong said in one voice. As they stared at each other, even Tong looked nervous. Bao had to clarify. "He hurt his left knee, nothing more, honestly. It's best for him to stay home and look after Daisy, so he'll heal—"

"How did your grandparents know? Does everyone know? Does Ch . . ." Her lips quivered with the effort to speak, but no word came out.

"Nobody but my grandparents and we know about it, I promise you."

"Why didn't your grandpa bring me food? Why did they ask a stranger to come here? How did your fellow get mixed up in this?"

A truthful reply would surely bring up Childless Du. The odious name would frighten Orchid.

"Tong is here," Bao said with a flash of insight, "because he wants to meet you."

"Why?"

"Bao told me how determined you are to have your baby. You and Candor put us to shame." Tong wasn't usually a good liar, and yet he said it with such conviction that Bao felt tears in her eyes.

A weary smile brushed Orchid's face. It disappeared just as quickly.

"You're joking, Big Brother. You two are young and good-looking, you'll have many years of happiness ahead. How do we shame you?"

"I didn't fight for Soybean." Bao turned her teary eyes to the cave wall.

Tong massaged her back. "Bao and I would love to have a daughter like Daisy—"

"Stop it." Bao pulled away. "I have to go, Orchid. I promise you, Candor will be here in a week or two. Everything is fine at home, just take care of yourself and . . ." She stood there but couldn't finish her sentence.

She crouched down and crawled outside quickly. She heard Orchid call, "Little Sister" but didn't turn her head. She stumbled to kneel before Soybean's burial mound. Hot tears streamed down her cheeks. What a release it was!

After a long while, Tong came to stand beside her. "Why did you run out like that? We did a fine job of convincing Orchid—"

"I buried something here. Do you have any idea what it means to me?"

He stared at the kerchief. The pink lotus was dusty and brown.

"Soybean." She started to sob.

"Oh." He knelt to kiss the kerchief. "I'm so sorry that you were buried here, far away from your parents."

"Don't flatter yourself. We're no parents." For the first time since the abortion she wanted to punish Tong and make him hurt as much as she had. "Soybean was scraped out of me, put in a collection jar, and discarded like a piece of garbage."

"I hate that this happened to you, Bao. I'm so sorry."

"I had nothing to put in her tomb—I had no tomb—so I buried my panties from our first night together."

She sobbed with all her might. For a while she heard nothing but her loud wailing. When she quieted and raised her head, Tong sat on a boulder with his shoes and socks off. He was washing his feet in the mountain spring.

"You'll hate me forever."

"How could you put me at such risk? Were you so selfish?"

"I asked if you were safe."

"How was I supposed to know? Could I really be safe from this—my first time?" She pounded her thigh with a fist. "We weren't married."

"I want to marry you!" He threw a shoe in the stream and splattered water on her pants. "You didn't even talk to me—I was summoned to hear your decision. I had no say over my own baby." Tears welled up in his red eyes.

As she reached out a hand to touch him, he squatted down and held his head in his hands.

"If only I could take away your pain," he said. "I hate myself!"

She had never heard a man sob the way Tong did. She felt his pain, her pain, joining together and overlapping like waves. She breathed deeply through their pain, excruciating yet intoxicating. Ecstasy ensued like sexual pleasure. In this pain she felt Soybean, still growing in her womb, snug and happy. If she could do it over again, she would have carried their child, her belly growing so large her skin was taut. Then one day she would cry out in pain and happiness, being reborn into a mother.

"It was my fault, too." She wiped tears from her cheek.

"If I didn't love you so much, I'd never talk to you after your father threw me out!" He flung his other foot in the stream and made a great splash.

Wiping away water from her cheek, she was at a loss for words to comfort Tong. Then she remembered her consolation prize.

"When the time comes," she said, "I'm going to help Orchid with the delivery."

Tong stared at the stream, motionless.

She retrieved his shoe, stuck in the clefts of mossy rocks. After squeezing out the water, she laid it on the rock to dry.

The shade of trees elongated in the setting sun. Bao glimpsed the shadow of a man behind a beech tree. Wearing a faded army uniform and olive green hat, he darted like a squirrel.

"You scared away Brother Liao." She'd forgotten to save a morsel for the madman. "I've never seen him so high up in the mountain. There's no one to beg from. Poor guy lost his mind after his wife died."

Tong put on his wet shoes and slid the backpack onto his shoulders.

"Men are pathetic. We can't help those we love the most."

He dashed down a steep slope, raising a trail of dust.

She descended carefully in a zigzag line. As the distance between them widened, his head floated behind a clump of fir trees. Sunlight glazed the flattened needles, quivering in the crisp mountain air.

"Wait," she said. "Don't leave me here."

His wet shoes squished as he slowed down. "We won't stand a chance after we return to Nanjing. After quitting my job, I'll have to start over again." His shoulders drooped, and his face was downcast. "I shouldn't be so selfish. Your father was right: you deserve a better man."

She didn't know what to say or do, that would draw him back instead of pushing him away. Why did it hurt so much to love someone? She wiped her tears and kept walking.

The sound of rushing water faded. A Nightjar called from the top branch of an oak tree. She left the shadowy woods and walked on the broad level path. The setting sun painted the clouds crimson in the western sky. Rice plants swayed in the breeze, their tender stems shiny and bright green. A farmer held a cast iron plough, dragged by an ox through the loamy earth. Now and then he cracked a whip and scolded the slow animal, his voice breaking the silence.

Bao took a deep breath until her chest was full, and her mind was depleted of yearnings. The village houses were in sight, blue smoke rising from the chimneys.

Chapter 14

WHEN TONG DIDN'T JOIN THEM FOR DINNER, Bao told her grandparents he had been tired out by the hike. They didn't seem to believe her. With her eyes averted, she gulped down a bowl of bean curd jelly and then returned to her bedroom. She cut her bangs with a pair of foldable travel scissors without using a mirror. Who cared how she looked, now that Tong had turned his back on her?

She didn't come out for breakfast until both her grandparents were working in the yard. Grandpa was installing a new super into the beehive. A dozen bees circled his bare head and arms. Grandma swung a long-handled wooden scoop to water the lettuce field. In the goat pen, the kid knelt and chewed tender bean leaves. As the mother goat licked the kid's temple, her white hair grew sleek and shiny. The old dog sunned himself on the porch, scratching his belly with a paw.

"Quick, Bao!" Tong's voice startled her. He stood in the doorway, his face red and sweaty. "Orchid is in trouble."

Bao took a steamed bun and followed him outside. "Is she in labor?"

"The village chief visited Candor. He said Orchid is at the

clinic, she'll be 'taken care of.'"

"What happened?"

"I don't know." He jogged toward Candor's house. "Could someone find out where she was hiding?"

"If they did, Childless Du would kidnap her."

Bao slowed her steps, her legs feeling like lead. Orchid would be induced, her baby murdered, then her fallopian tubes would be tied. Maybe she would bleed to death. Then Candor would go mad like Brother Liao.

"Oh no." She squatted on the ridge.

"Are you okay?"

Her teeth chattered, while hot sweat broke out underneath her jacket. She was freezing and sweating at the same time.

"How could I be so stupid?" she said.

"What?"

"I was relieved that Brother Liao didn't come to beg for food, since I had nothing to give him. But I forgot the obvious: Brother Liao never hides his face. It must've been someone else on the hillside."

They stared at each other. Neither dared to utter the name: Childless Du.

Finally Tong broke the silence. "You said you were going to help Orchid with the delivery."

"You didn't keep quiet, either! You threw a shoe in the water."

"Look what we did!" Tong backed away clenching his fist. "Candor should never have trusted us."

"I wanted to go alone. Why did you follow me?"

"Grandpa gave me a second chance." His voice softened.

"*Our* second chance."

"And you blew it. Worse still, it wasn't about us. Orchid's life was at stake, and her little one. They could die, because we played some sick game: Go, prove yourselves."

Tong bit his lower lip hard. "Now we agree: It isn't worth trying anymore."

"Unless you help me save Orchid."

"Are you setting me up for another failure?" He turned away, so she couldn't see his face. "Don't bother."

Her temples pounded, and blood rushed to her face. She sprang to her feet and dashed for the woods. Tong didn't follow her this time. Fragments of his sentences rang in her ears, "Candor should never have trusted us." "It isn't worth trying anymore." "Are you setting me up for another failure?" Perhaps it wasn't the abortion or her parents but Bao herself who had caused the breakup. She began to cry. Her chest heaved so hard that it hurt to breathe. She slipped on the dirt path and nearly sprained her ankle, but she felt no pain. Nothing could hurt her anymore, now that her heart was numb.

Out of breath, she couldn't run any further and looked down the cliff. The valley was filled with spiky treetops and white clouds. If her death could save Orchid, she'd jump without hesitation. Candor would be moved by her sacrifice, but her parents and grandparents would be desolate for the rest of their lives. She wiped away tears and continued climbing.

The thickets bordering the beaten trail were hushed, her

steps muffled by sodden leaves. After a steep stretch, rushing water spilled over boulders and made bright white waves. The familiar sound comforted her. She glimpsed the majestic yellow-rafter and the kerchief on the ground. Little seemed to have changed. Walking toward the cliff, she had a glimmer of hope to find Orchid knitting inside the cave.

Then she saw the cave opening. The fence door had been ripped off, taking away some of the vines. She craned her neck to peer into the valley. There wasn't a trace of the fence door but a chaos of logs, fallen trees, and white clouds. Feeling dizzy, she turned around and crawled into the cave.

Mountain wind whistled outside. It felt like winter inside the cave. Orchid's abductors seemed to have cleared out all evidences that a pregnant woman had once lived here. Bao squatted to comb the ground with her hands. She found a piece of paper, on it sprawled a large word "Mama" and a pencil sketch of a daisy with five petals.

Bright sunshine made her squint when she stood outside. Perusing the paper, she found the word "Mama" smudged by a shoe print. Had Childless Du trampled on it? She scrubbed the paper with her fingernail and tore it in the middle. Holding it up against the light, she tried to mend the hole with her wet fingertip, before a cold draft took the paper. She chased after it, the paper drifting uphill like a white dove.

She stumbled upon rocks and tangled weeds. A strong wind lifted the paper higher and higher. She grabbed onto the tall grass to climb up. When the paper flew toward the cliff, she waited until the mountain wind returned it to her side. Finally she caught up with it, and the gust of wind stopped. The paper whirled down the slope and fell into the stream, flanked by pine trees. She stared at the water, spilling over the boulders in cascades, in splashing leaps, and in places it scurried over fallen trees. The stream carried Daisy's letter downhill.

"Bye," she said. "You're going home to see them."

The loss brought her serenity. She knew the awful truth—Orchid would be safe if she hadn't met Bao. It didn't matter that Bao had good intentions. She had inadvertently led Childless Du to Orchid's hiding place. If her unborn baby shared Soybean's fate, how could Bao ever forgive herself?

Bao continued her hike. Further up the hill the forest grew dark and damp with fog. A Spangled Drongo flew up from a field of wild peonies. She was hungry, her teeth chattering in the cold. She wanted to go far away, outrun her failure, and hide her shame. She bit her lip so hard she drew blood.

She heard a call, hooting and squealing and barking not far ahead. Her stomach growled with discontent. She settled under a spruce to eat the steamed bun she'd brought. She reclined in a shaft of sun, a log pillowing her head, and watched the flow of light and dark on the foliage.

Angry roars startled Bao. There was a fir ten meters away, its bark heavily clawed. Animal droppings littered the area. She glimpsed a furry bough amidst the green bushes. The glaring sunlight might be playing a trick on her. She squeezed her eyes tightly shut. When she reopened them, the black and white bough whipped through the air. A round head perked up from behind a clump of bush.

She covered her mouth to stifle a shout.

A giant panda raised its arms above its head, stretched, and yawned cavernously. As it rolled up from the ground, she stood in awe of its full figure. Its back was broad and muscular, the white of its coat striking in the somber forest. Its round head had an almost hypnotic effect as it lumbered closer and closer toward her. Suddenly it bellowed and raked the air with a paw. Before she could hide, the panda turned its head and fixed its small eyes upon her. The black goggles made its eyes look wistful and sad.

The panda gave agitated, bleating honks, a strangely vulnerable and timid sound from so large an animal. She noticed its foot caught in a coiled wire snare. Since the wire was taut, the panda couldn't touch her.

Bao drew closer. At first, the panda snorted mild threats. As she took a few more steps, it gave a peculiar chomping sound, teeth clicking and lips smacking in a show of anxiety. When this failed to deter her, the panda emitted a roar so explosive that Bao involuntarily turned to flee. In her haste, she bumped her shoulder against a tree trunk. Then she heard a gunshot, dull and loud like a firecracker, echoing in the valley. The pelt of a panda was worth a good deal of money to poachers.

As if sensing the danger, the panda charged Bao, its attack abruptly thwarted by the end of the snare cable. It bit large slivers of wood from the tree, roared, and swatted the air in frustration.

"Take it easy now, big guy."

She searched her pockets for a tool to cut the wire. She didn't bring her key ring, where she kept a small knife to peel fruits. In her pant pocket she found a pair of foldable travel scissors with which she'd cut her bangs the night before. She opened up the scissors and went to the other side of the fir. She began to cut the wire snare with her scissors. Her heart pounded and she was short of breath, but her hand didn't tremble. This could be the panda cub from her childhood. She wouldn't watch it suffer and be killed by poachers.

Slumping against the fir, the panda scratched and pawed flies off its face. She cut the old, rusted wire that wound around the tree. The scissors pinched her fingers until they were sore and numb. She bent the half-cut wire back and forth. The panda snorted to itself, its head bobbing up and down. Finally the wire broke open, and the panda was free.

Bao retreated behind a cypress. She expected the panda to bolt for freedom, but there was no response. For about twenty minutes the panda sat with its back to her. Its honks grew softer as its head sagged onto its chest. It seemed to have fallen asleep. Suddenly the panda barked and raked the air with a paw. As if recharged with energy, it rose from the ground and crawled up a slope, moving like a cloud shadow from thicket to thicket.

How many chances did a person get to save a national treasure? Bao decided to pursue the panda, a long-lost friend from her childhood. Its pelage gleamed softly in the somber darkness of cedar, spruce, and fir. When a five-foot gap—over a ravine—halted her advance, she took a deep breath, leapt and gained the other side. Above, the fat white panda tail moved in the thickets, like a candle flame drifting in the woods.

Bao threaded her way upward through a clump of trees and

mangled undergrowth. Finally she reached a crest. There was a fir tree with a hollow base and an entrance fifteen inches in diameter.

The panda crouched inside the hole and fondled a small black and white creature with its forepaws. Was she telling the cub how she'd escaped the poacher's snare? The cub opened its mouth and pawed her face, while she nuzzled its head and chest. A strip of broken coil wire dangled outside her den.

From uphill came the sound of a gunshot, echoing in the valley. The panda listened and turned away, hugging her cub tightly.

"You're home."

Few villagers had ever seen a panda in the wild. Bao felt touched by fate that two mother pandas had come across her path when she was most vulnerable in her life. Surely it was her destiny to save the national treasures. Human lives were as valuable as the pandas. If Bao had once failed to protect Orchid, she was now the chosen one to save her baby. Feeling uplifted by a sense of purpose, she wanted to shout a message to the hawks that soared in the air, their screeches piercing in the wind.

"Give me the power, and I'll do it right this time. I swear I will!"

The forest was dark, when she hiked downhill. Every once in a while, a shaft of sun slipped through layers of leaves and penetrated the twilight. The feathers of a Sunbird were brilliant in scarlet and yellow. She walked on the level ground for a stretch. Approaching a steep decline where the nearest handhold was a thorny rosebush, she remembered Candor's advice and descended in a zigzag line.

Bao went to Candor's house and banged on the front door.

"Come outside, Tong! I have something to ask you."

After a long time, an old woman opened the door. Strands of gray hair were stuck to her tear-stained face. Her eyes were red and swollen like skinned peaches.

"You must be Orchid's auntie."

"My poor, poor niece." She took off a shoe and slapped it against the dirt floor. "She doesn't deserve so much suffering. Let Heaven take my life, for I'm old and useless."

"Auntie." Bao knelt on one knee and patted her shoulder. "I'm looking for a young man who stayed here last night."

"Gone."

"To where?"

As she tried to shut the door, Bao pushed with her forearm to keep it ajar. The old woman wavered. "What do you want from us?"

"I want . . ." There was so much Bao wanted to say, but words swarmed in the back of her throat like angry bees. "I have to . . ." Her voice quivered despite her resolve to stay calm. "I have a plan to rescue Orchid."

The door was closing in her face for a second time. Bao elbowed it open, leaned her weight against the door, and made the old woman stumble back.

"Let me talk to Candor, he'll believe me."

The old woman said a few words to someone inside the house. "Candor says you should leave. You city people ruined Orchid, now leave us alone." She released the door for Daisy to come outside.

"Uncle Tong went home. He was walking."

"Don't talk to her," Candor said. "She's a broom comet!"

Country folk saw a comet as an omen that brought death and destruction. A broom comet was an insult meant to double the bad luck. Daisy started to cry.

"Don't yell at the baby, Candor." The old woman cuddled Daisy in her lap.

The door shut with a thud. Bao gazed at the red couplets that had been pasted on the door during the Spring Festival. The paper that read, "The country flourishes, and people live in peace," was peeled at the corners, and parts of the words were missing. Standing on the rundown porch in the midst of broad bean fields, she determined to stop at nothing to rescue Orchid. Chairman Mao had once described young people as the flowers of China, who had a shining future like the rising sun. But Orchid didn't have a future; the abortion and sterilization would endanger her life and break her spirit. Bao deserved to trade places with her less fortunate country sister.

Bao went home and found no one there. Her grandparents must have gone out to look for her. In the backyard she found the tricycle and loaded it with three bottles of fresh honey. She put on Grandma's oversized bee suit, tied an apron around her waist, and covered her hair with a blue-checked handkerchief.

She examined herself in the mirror. Her cheeks were too rosy for a village woman. She dug up a handful of dirt and rubbed it onto her cheeks, nose, and forehead. Then she grabbed a pillow to stuff underneath her bee suit. Her parents wouldn't recognize Bao if they saw her now. The slender, fresh-faced university girl was gone, and in her place stood a country beekeeper in her third trimester. Bao swallowed a laugh, her voice raspy.

She mounted the tricycle and pedaled toward the main road. A single beaten path led to the county clinic and train station. Dark green and mustard-colored vegetable fields lined the path. Every once in a while, a dog leapt onto the ridge and barked at the tricycle. She hunched her back to pedal at full speed.

She remembered the revolution stories she had heard as a young girl. The Communist Party had won the war against the Nationalist Army with guerrilla attacks. Many women had fought alongside their husbands and lovers. In the battles, some mothers suffocated their crying infants to prevent them from exposing the fighters lying in ambush. Those women wept in silence. During the Long March, mothers gave their newborns to local peasants so they could keep on marching with the Red Army. Few of these women found their children after the war. Bao peered at the three bottles of honey in the cart. She imagined herself as a young guerrilla, transporting weapons for the Communist Party troops.

The tricycle jolted as its front wheel ran over a stick. Bao pushed up the headpiece that fell upon her eyes. The road swerved around a pond where a water buffalo drank from it. A man walked down the bank to immerse a bamboo crab trap in the water. On the opposite side of the pond, Tong sat on a duffle bag and fanned his face with a hat.

She let the tricycle glide a stretch before applying the brake. Now was the time to test her plan.

"Big Brother," she said in the local dialect. "You need a ride or something?" Even her intonation sounded like Orchid's.

Tong cast her a glance. As if disappointed by what he saw, he quickly turned away.

"Do you know how far the train station is?"

"Far enough, you have to walk ten li or more." She took off the headpiece to fan her face with it. "Come on, I'll give you a ride."

His eyes widened. "Bao? What happened to you?" He leapt up and dropped his hat.

She put her arms around her swollen belly and enjoyed its new girth. "Why, don't the clothes fit me well, Big Brother?"

"Quit talking like a bumpkin!" He dashed down the grassy slope to grab his hat. "What're you up to?"

She strutted toward Tong. "Hop onto the tricycle and pedal away, Big Brother. I'll tell you by and by."

"Stop calling me Big Brother!" He kicked his duffle bag.

"All right," she said in Nanjing dialect. "Here's my plan: we'll go to the abortion clinic together. I'll switch places with Orchid by putting on her clothes. You take her to my grandparents' house. They'll help you find a place to hide Orchid."

"What?"

She saw a bicycle approach them. "Will you pedal while I explain the rest to you?"

A middle-aged man passed them by, carrying a basket filled

with skinned frogs.

Tong threw his duffle bag in the back of the tricycle. "Sit low, don't fall off the wagon." His bottom shifted on the seat as he began to pedal.

"I was practicing my act, you know." She patted his haunch. "We'll act as a married couple: I'm Orchid's sister, and you're my husband. We go in to give Orchid the honey. I'll tell the guard that fresh honey heals scars, have pity on my sister, her full-term baby will be aborted, her tubes tied, so on and so forth. If he doesn't let me see Orchid, I'll kneel and beg him, cry all night and wipe my snot on his pants, until he gives in. When I get inside, I'll switch places with Orchid."

"You're crazy. Besides, aren't you too late?"

"I hope not. Doctor Li, the resident abortion doctor, is on vacation visiting his newborn grandson in Chengdu. He'll return in three days."

"How about other abortion doctors?"

"None, because Doctor Li is overqualified. I saw a certificate of merit when I was in his office last time. They don't need to hire another abortion doctor."

"We have time, then. You need to sleep on it and think it through."

"Don't stop!" She pushed the metal spring underneath his seat. "Childless Du has stooges. A barefoot doctor induced Brother Liao's wife and ended up killing her."

"Isn't the barefoot doctor system abolished?"

"Not here." She remembered her mother's stories. "They still perform botched sterilizations. Men become impotent, and women are disabled after the procedures."

The chain clattered as the tricycle glided down the road. They entered a shady bamboo grove. There scattered squat tombs, some covered in weeds. A cold draft made Bao shiver. She slid her hands into the wide sleeves of her blouse to keep them warm. The tricycle slowed to a halt. Tong got down and stood with his legs apart and his back to the road. He might want to pee, so she waited. She glimpsed shriveled fruits amidst green leaves of a tangerine tree. They might taste bitter for the lack of sunlight.

Tong lit a cigarette.

"What're you doing?" She pointed at her left wrist, where she forgot to wear a watch. "We have to save Orchid."

He flicked off ash from the cigarette. "I can't help you."

"Why?"

"I'm not a good actor like you."

"What do you mean?"

He kept on smoking, as if he hadn't heard her. She climbed off of the tricycle. Her apron caught on the iron rack and she nearly tripped.

"What's your problem, Tong?"

"I'm sorry." His eyes brimmed over with tears.

"For what?" She felt like crying, too. Suddenly he became dear to her, like a real husband.

"Who was I to yell at you? I'd bought the tiger hat that aroused suspicion. Your grandpa told us to be cautious on the mountain, but what did I do?" He squatted down and held his head in his hands. "I promised him to take care of you."

"I forgive you." Kneeling on one knee, she pulled up the

apron to her lap. "But this isn't about us."

"I went looking for you earlier but didn't find you. At least I can stop you from doing this crazy thing." He reached out a hand to touch her hair. "If a barefoot doctor laid a hand on you—"

"I can take care of myself, thank you." She walked to the tricycle and climbed onto the seat.

Tong twisted the handlebars around. "Listen to me this once."

"Why should I?"

"I'm older than you and I . . . love you." His tears fell to the ground. Yellow daisies stood out amidst weeds like shiny stars. "You're my flower."

"I'm not a flower." She tried to pry his hands from the handlebars, but his fingers seemed to have taken root. In her frustration she started to cry. "You made me a woman. At least I can do something about it. I'll go by myself if you won't help." She pedaled the tricycle against his body.

"Hold on a minute." He tried to push the tricycle backwards. "Maybe we can rescue Orchid and run away."

"It won't be safe. When the guard finds her gone, they'll pursue her and she may go into labor. It'll endanger her and the baby." She smiled through her tears. "It's better that I take her place. What can they do to me? I'm not pregnant. When I tell them I'm a student, they will leave me alone."

"Bao, you're no match for Childless Du. He drove a tough man mad, and he tricked us. He's dangerous!"

She started to pedal again and cut him short.

"All right," he said. "Let me stay with you. I'll make sure

they don't harm you."

"No. You must take Orchid away, or all this—everything we've risked—will be for nothing. Nothing!"

He didn't reply. She saw red clouds in the sky, a golden full moon rising in the east. He took off his hat and dusted it inside out as if he had nothing better to do.

"Do you hear me?" Her angry voice resounded in the graveyard.

"I hear you all right, but I don't understand you. Why do you go to extremes? There must be—"

"Extremes? What could be extreme about saving a baby? Do you want him to end up in a jar like Soybean?"

The plea in his eyes didn't deter her. On the contrary, she grew warm with aggression. Tong had to see that they were not doing this merely for Orchid's benefit.

"We put her in this miserable lot. If you refuse to help, for me Soybean dies a second time." She strutted toward Tong, who stepped back before their chests touched. "I can never put Soybean back in my womb. Thanks to Orchid, she gave me an alternative. I'm not going to the extreme, think again. This is like asking you to put on a condom on our first night, can you refuse me?"

She'd never seen such naked pain in a man's eyes. Tong stood mute, his head sinking into his chest. For a long moment, she was torn between sympathy for his despair and the thrill of her own power. As the blood drained from his face, he seemed to fade like a shadow at nightfall.

"You may feel left out of the student movement. That's no reason to get ruthless. Other people have feelings, too." His voice was so gentle it embarrassed her. He rotated the hat with his fingers, around and around. When he raised his head, his eyes were dry, his face devoid of emotion. "Sure, I'll pedal the tricycle for you. I'll help you be the heroine you want to become." He put on his hat and straightened it.

She climbed onto the back of the tricycle. When they left the bamboo grove, a flock of crows rose from the treetop. Their black wings spread across a setting sun that emitted little warmth. She wanted to apologize to Tong but decided not to, for fear that it might weaken her resolve to save Orchid.

Chapter 15

ON THE BACK SEAT of the tricycle, Bao straightened the pillow tied around her waist underneath the beekeeper suit. A familiar brick wall appeared, illuminated by lamps. A poster featuring a family of three displayed the slogan, "It is good to have one child." Tong stopped the tricycle in front of the hospital. The bungalows were mostly dark, except for a few windows. Orchid must have been in one of the cells.

"I'll return and get you within an hour," Tong said, "after taking Orchid to your grandparents."

Bao nodded, suddenly frightened by the prospect of being held hostage by strangers. Perhaps Tong was right to stop her. She wanted to lean against him for courage.

"Look, there's Comrade Fang's jeep." He held out his hand to Bao, as she climbed out of the tricycle. "If they brought Orchid here in it, they must be treating her case seriously." He jostled her. "We're just pretending to be a married couple, for goodness sake! Don't lean on me as if you expect me to carry you."

"Sorry, I was trying to find my footing."

She grew teary as she made the excuse. Tong was all business now, and it served her right. Nothing should deter her from achieving her goal to save Orchid, least of all her fears. She covered her short hair with a kerchief and tied a knot over her nape. Then she smoothed the apron over her protruding belly.

"Let's go in." She put her hand in the crook of his arm and wiped her wet eyes.

They went to the gynecology office where she had seen Doctor Li three weeks ago. The light was on, and the bamboo curtain was drawn. She knocked.

The door swung open. "About time, you'll make me miss supper." The guard stood dumbstruck. "Who are you?"

"I came to see my sister, Orchid." Bao felt her cheeks burn as she stumbled over the lie. Luckily the kerchief draped over her forehead, and her face was covered in dust.

The guard, a lanky man about twenty years old, barely bothered with a perfunctory glance. Tong handed him a pack of Marlboros.

"Have a cigarette," Tong said. "Marlboro is the best, made in USA."

The guard sniffed the cigarettes. "Don't I know it?" He examined the pack, sealed, and he slipped it into his pocket. "What do you want?"

"Let me see my sister." Bao had calmed down. With Tong's help she'd be able to execute her plan. "I want to give her fresh honey." She lifted a glass jar.

"I'll take it to her." The guard reached for the jar, but Tong intercepted it.

"Little Brother, this one is for you." Tong offered the jar to the guard with both hands. "See this yellow creamy stuff? It's royal jelly. We only harvested two bottles like this for the whole season." He leaned forward and lowered his voice. "A tip for you: Royal jelly promotes male function."

"Really?" The guard peered at Bao's belly, his eyes bright with curiosity.

"Just think, what does a queen bee do all day? Lay eggs. Where does she get her strength? Royal jelly is her love potion." He grinned at the guard like a conspirator. "Your wife will tell the difference after you eat royal jelly."

"I'm not married." The guard's face was flushed like a ripe tomato.

"You're not?" Tong feigned surprise. Bao bit her lip to keep a serious face. "Don't worry, you'll get married soon to a pretty girl. After you eat royal jelly, she'll give you a fat son within the first year."

The guard scratched the back of his neck. His furry upper lip pouted as he considered Tong's words.

"Let me see my sister," Bao said.

"She is . . ." The guard stared at his olive green rubber-tipped sneakers. "She's indisposed."

"I know you have a job to do, Little Brother, but a security guard also needs to eat supper. Chairman Mao said it best, 'Food is heaven.'" Tong eyed the chopsticks lying atop two empty bowls on the desk. "Let's go to the canteen while the sisters have their talk. We'll be back in ten minutes."

The guard gazed into the darkness. "I was supposed to be off-duty twenty minutes ago."

"Why don't you lock me in with her?" Bao patted her protruding belly. "I don't have wings to fly away!"

Tong cast her a sidelong glance. He was obviously concerned about her safety. If the guard looked closely, he'd suspect Tong's true intentions.

"Have pity on my elder sister." Bao bent forward to insinuate herself between the guard and Tong. "Her tubes will be tied, it's a terrible thing. Nobody deserves it, especially my sister." She felt warm tears in her eyes. "My sister set her mind on having a baby boy. She said she'd kill herself if she had another abortion. You have to let me comfort her, her life is in your hands." She blew her nose into her palm. "I'll tell her to be a good mother to Daisy. Since her family depends on her, she must think of them and recover quickly. You know, fresh honey helps heal scars."

The guard rubbed his sole on the cement floor, his eyes downcast. "Forgive me for being rude, ma'am. Why do you worry about her, when you're almost ready to pop yourself?"

Startled by the question, Bao couldn't think of an answer.

"I'll be frank with you, Little Brother." Tong lit a cigarette and thrust it into the guard's half-open lips. "My sister-in-law is headstrong. We all told her not to have more babies, it's against the law. You know what she said? That she wouldn't get caught." Tong slapped his thigh. "I'm a soldier, I knew this day would come. There's no place to hide from the law. I hate to be right about it." He gave Bao a look to tell her to continue.

Bao spoke up. "You mustn't see her. If you say 'I told you so,' she'll bash her head against the wall." Bao dabbed the corners of her eyes with a crumpled hanky. "Our parents died when we were young. My sister is my only kin. She raised me when I was a little girl—"

"Don't say any more." The guard raised his hands in a surrendering gesture. "Bring her the honey, and I'll let you two talk awhile."

"You're a good man, Little Brother." Tong fetched two bottles of honey from the tricycle.

The guard led them to the back and unlocked a side door. Bao entered after the guard turned on the light. Tong put the honey bottles on the floor.

"Keep your voices down. I'll be back after supper." The guard locked the door.

Bao blinked her eyes as she scanned the room. The fluorescent ceiling light flickered. A cot took up most of the space. At its foot was a covered spittoon, used as the portable toilet. On the other side was a footstool, which held a bowl of rice, topped with overcooked bok choy and fatty pork, and a bowl of radish and rib bone soup. The food was cold and jelled with grease. A woman lay on her side, her head covered by a pillow. Bao recognized her black cotton shoes and maroon socks, winter accessories that Orchid had worn in the cave. Bao lifted the pillow slowly.

"Keep your hands off me!" Orchid windmilled her arms and kicked hard.

Bao retreated to press her back against the wall.

"It's me, Little Sister." She took off her headpiece and pulled out the pillow from underneath her bee suit. "I came to take you out of here."

Orchid stared up through the tangled hair that hung in front of her face. Her bloodshot eyes bulged from their sockets.

"Liar."

"I'm not here to harm you, I swear." Pressing a hand upon her heart, Bao felt a pang. How could she prove her innocence?

"What're you wearing?"

"I pretended to be your sister, so that the guard would let me in. We'll exchange clothes. When the guard returns in ten minutes, you'll leave with Tong and he'll take you to my grandparents' house."

"Why?"

"So you can give birth in safety." Bao raised her voice in spite of herself. "The one-child policy worker team won't touch you. We'll make sure of it." She took off her apron and beekeeper suit and threw them on the cot.

"Why are you doing this, Little Sister?"

"I owe it to you." Bao reached out her hands. "Now give me your clothes."

Orchid clutched her own collar. "I haven't bathed in a while."

"Hurry up! We can't waste any more time."

"Did your fellow tell you to do this? Don't listen to him." Orchid beat away her groping hand.

"Tong didn't ask me to do anything. This is my idea, all my own." Patting her chest, Bao felt giddy, reckless, and heroic.

"Do your grandparents know you're here?"

Bao didn't want to be scolded, so she took the offensive. "Don't you want to go home and have your baby?"

"More than anything in the world." Orchid wiped her eyes with her palm. "But Little Sister, I can't leave you in the hands of Childless Du."

"He can't touch me, because I'm not pregnant."

"You're very young, Little Sister."

Bao took a deep breath. "I went to your house. Your old aunt was there, crying her eyes out, and so was Candor. If you lost your baby son—"

Orchid jumped down from the bed. "Take me out of here. I want to go right now." She flailed her arms like a blind woman.

"Give me your clothes." Bao unbuttoned Orchid's blouse and peeled it off her back. Inside she wore several layers of tattered clothes, which had been reduced to moldy rags. Her swollen torso gave off an odor like a dirty chicken coop. Bao held her breath as she tied the apron around Orchid's belly. She combed back Orchid's hair and tied it up with a piece of string, then covered her head with the large kerchief. "The guard barely looked at me. You'll do fine if you keep your mouth shut. Tong will talk for you."

Orchid stood like a lump of wood, her face blank and bloodless.

"Did you have lunch?" Bao took the rice bowl from the footstool.

Orchid shook her head. "I want to go home, I want to see Daisy."

"You'll see them tonight, I promise you." Bao picked up

some rice with the chopsticks. "You need to preserve your strength. Now eat."

Orchid opened her mouth as Bao fed her rice. She chewed slowly. Bao picked up a bok choy leaf, which Orchid ate obediently. The act of feeding gave Bao a rush of satisfaction. She felt like a mother feeding her pregnant daughter who would give birth.

"Thirsty," Orchid said.

Bao lifted the soup bowl to her mouth. Oily soup flowed down the corner of her mouth and dribbled onto her beekeeper suit. Orchid held onto the bowl while chewing a piece of radish, as if she was afraid that Bao might take it away.

"It's all yours." Bao withdrew her hand.

Orchid tore a rib bone with her fingers and chewed the meat. Bao heard Tong's voice outside.

"You must leave with Tong. He'll buy you food if you're still hungry." She snatched the bowl from Orchid to put on the stool, as the office door unlocked.

"Get your wife out quickly," the guard said. "I won't let that bastard accuse me of slacking."

Bao pulled the string to turn off the light as the guard unlocked the closet door. She said loudly, "You take care now, Sister!" and pushed Orchid toward Tong.

Tong took her by the hand. "Don't cry, silly! It isn't good for the baby." His voice was affectionate. "Here, I got you a pork bun, eat it while it's hot."

Bao heard the office door close and open and the muttering of men's voices. The guard must've been talking to his night shift replacement.

"You owe me a big one." He sounded indignant.

"I didn't mean to be so late," the replacement said. "My old lady was having a fit. Her imbecile brother wants to open a grocery store, and she asked me to lend him money. I tried to talk her out of it—"

"How will you make it up to me?" the guard said.

"I'll set up a date for you, how about that? The girl next door has grown up to be a pretty flower." Guffaws drowned out the rest of his words.

"Man, you're 'all thunder and no rain.' Set me up a date this month."

"Why are you so horny—" The man groaned. He must've gotten a punch.

"Shut your dirty mouth!" Chuckling, the guard slammed the door.

The night guard turned on a transistor radio, switching from pop music to news, to storytelling, to Chinese harp, and to a classical concerto. Finally he settled on Sichuan opera. Bao was disappointed. Shrill singing made it hard for her to relax after a trying day. She was hungry, but she couldn't ask the guard to bring her food. Nor did she dare turn on the light. She took the rice bowl to eat the cold leftovers. To her surprise, it didn't taste bad.

She sat in the dark and listened to *The Cowherd and the Weaving Maid*, which was based on a legend about a once-happy couple who became stars separated by the Milky Way. Bao missed Tong. She had coaxed him into helping her. Only when he broke down, had she discovered how much he loved her.

Could she make it up to him afterwards? Hopefully Orchid would soon give birth to a healthy baby boy. Then she would have no regrets about having her tubes tied. After all, it was mandatory for women with two children.

Having eaten a few bites of food, Bao reached for Orchid's smelly rags at the foot of the bed. She picked up the vest with her fingertips. Its front spread open to show a large armhole. She slid a hand through the armhole without touching anything. Her wrist looked white and delicate in the shadow. She sniffed at the vest but didn't detect any unpleasant odor. Perhaps she already smelt like a dirty chicken coop.

Bao swung the vest around her back and buttoned it up. It hung like a sleeveless robe. She was free to move in it, as if she weren't wearing it at all. She took off the vest, picked up a blouse, and put it on outside her jacket. The magenta blouse floated about her body like a silky cape. This whole getup wasn't as ugly as she had imagined. Too bad she didn't have the voluptuous curves to fill up the sexy outfit.

She put on every piece of the clothes, stuffed the pillow underneath, and lay on her side, imagining what it would be like to be enormous, if she had carried her baby to the ninth month. She would have lower back pain and swollen feet. She might crave chicken soup and roast pork. Perhaps Orchid wanted to lie on a large bed with a pillow between her legs and fall asleep watching television. Instead she had to hide in a mossy cave. She couldn't get much sun for fear of being discovered. The constant water dripping sound must have reminded her of a torture chamber. Day and night she woke to hear poachers' gunshots. Daisy asked all the time when Mama would come home. The girl's hair was uncombed, her face and neck covered in dust and grease, and her socks needed mending. Candor brought dry, coarse food, until he hurt his knee and had to stay home.

She had a dainty name, Orchid, and lived in Crystal Village all her life. She wanted a boy, who would grow up to be a strong man and work in the fields. When she and Candor grew old, they would live with their son's family and help take care of their grandchildren. She didn't envy Bao, who had aborted a baby without finding out if it was a boy or girl. On a fateful day three weeks ago, she had risked her life to leave the cave because she was worried that the crying girl might jump off the cliff. She had offered Bao a handkerchief and comforting words. Never had she expected Bao to lead Childless Du to her cave.

The pillow's bumpy soybean filling gave way with a rustling sound, as Bao laid her head on it. Tong was right again that she was emulating the students in Tiananmen Square. Unlike them, Bao would succeed, because she had on more than a perfect disguise. She had finally transformed herself into Orchid inside and out.

Bao woke up to hear the door being unlocked. Someone pulled the string to turn on the light. Childless Du entered with two men. She recognized one, a stocky man with bristling hair and a pockmarked face. She had met him at the hot pot stand, where he had scolded Brother Liao for begging. A scrawny older man in rimless glasses moved like a marionette, his clothes reeking of tobacco. Somehow he reminded Bao of her father, also a chain smoker.

"It's time," Childless Du said.

Bao turned toward the wall. "No," she said in the Pingwu dialect. She had to hold out until Tong would get here. How long had she slept?

"It's your third time, Orchid. I don't put up with nonsense."

"You could turn the other way."

"And let the likes of you run wild?" He reached for her foot.

She kicked his hand away. "Don't touch me."

The bed jolted as Childless Du sat down. She clutched the metal headboard with both hands and shut her eyes.

"You bumpkins don't see merciful Buddha even when you trip over him." He crossed his legs and made the bed squeak. "Have some financial sense, won't you? Raising a child is a great burden. You'll have to toil ten more years just to feed him. Why do you hold the feudal idea that a boy is better than a girl? You're a woman. Would you forgive your own mother if she'd abandoned you because she was hell-bent on having a boy?"

Childless Du tried to reason with her, so Bao must've fooled him. She loosened one hand on the headboard.

"Since this is our last run-in, let me be honest with you, so you won't feel too bad about losing it all. Everyone knows a son is a heavier burden on the family than a daughter." He took out a cigarette and tapped one end on the case. "A girl only needs to be pretty to marry well. Daisy is cute. She'll have no trouble getting a man to look after her."

He lit the cigarette and took a long drag. Bao felt itchy and sweaty around her neck. She might've put on too many pieces of clothing. Even Orchid would have taken off a few layers. Would Childless Du be suspicious if she wiped her brow?

"With a boy, you have to give him some schooling. He won't help you much in the fields. Candor, with his bad knee, will have to slave for the family. The little emperor is bound to have gigantic tantrums. Think about it, can you really live with a son's family? Everyone knows girls are more affectionate and loyal. Daisy will take care of you in your old age. The boy? He'll suck you dry and later submit to his darling wife, so an old lady like you will be ordered about by someone else's daughter."

Childless Du was silent for a while, dragging on the cigarette. He might get suspicious if she didn't respond.

"A life is priceless." She raised her voice. "You have no right to murder my baby."

"Priceless, huh." Childless Du snorted. "What if I tell you, I was worth a burlap sack of rice and some dried beans?"

"Be grateful to your foster parents—"

"I'm doing you a favor—giving you my sincerest words." He threw the cigarette butt on the floor and put it out under his heel. "You'd be grateful to me if you were smart. City women your age don't pop out children like piglets. They take good care of their bodies." The bed board clunked when he stood up. "Look at that soldier with his slutty girlfriend—they know how to have fun. Don't you envy them?"

Where on earth was Tong? She raised a hand to cover her face. "Go away and leave me in peace."

"Some people could be enlightened, while others are donkeys. No matter, they're all the same to me. Believe me, I'm doing you a favor." He paused. "Daisy deserves a mother who indulges her, not someone who uses her like a little slave."

"Don't talk to me about Daisy." She clenched her fist.

Childless Du cleared his throat. "Let's go then."

Bao grasped the headboard so tightly her stomach muscle ached. "I'll report you to Comrade Fang. She's your boss, and she owes it to Candor to help us."

"Have you lost your mind?" Childless Du called the two men. "Let's put her out of her misery."

Tong should have walked in by now! Where did he go wrong in his plan? When someone tugged her vest, she beat away his hand and sat up on the bed, a corner of the pillow jutting out from her waist. She pressed a fist into the pillow to keep her hand from trembling.

"Can I . . . have . . . one more night? I want to say goodbye to . . ." Her voice broke.

"She's toying with you." The stocky man stepped forward.

Childless Du raised a hand to stop him. "Say your goodbyes. I give you two minutes."

Bao buried her face in her hands. In a moment she would have to submit to the inevitable. Could she fend off their filthy hands? A shudder ran through her body. She mumbled incoherently and rocked back and forth, praying for Tong to arrive.

"Look here now." Childless Du bent down to peer at her face. "Who are *you*?"

The shock brought along a great relief. Bao managed to

catch her breath. "Not the one you're looking for, obviously."

Childless Du glanced at the office door. "What did you do with Orchid?" he asked the guard.

"Nothing." The man peered into the storage room. "She looks fine to me."

"She's *not* Orchid. Are you blind?"

"I don't know Orchid. I've never opened the door, I swear."

"No need to argue, you won't get paid for your shift." Childless Du glared at Bao. "Confess now, where's Orchid?"

Bao said nothing. Childless Du stepped toward her.

"Aren't you the smart one, playacting with me." A deep grin etched wrinkles on his hollow cheeks. "I can have you locked up as an accomplice."

A whiff of his sour pickle breath almost made her gag.

"It's your last chance to confess." Childless Du pushed up his glasses with two fingers. "Where is Orchid?"

"You won't find her."

"Do you want me to search your grandparents' house and turn it upside down?"

Bao looked at the floor. "She's gone, on a train to Chengdu. The maternity ward at the First People's Hospital is excellent."

"The First People's Hospital requires a couple to present their marriage license. Your boyfriend with the milk breath doesn't speak a word of the dialect." He stopped talking. Bao realized her expression must've betrayed her. Childless Du chuckled in triumph. "We won't let some meddling children come and lead our villagers astray. Who do you take us for?"

There was a tremor in his voice. Bao smelt his fear and

grew excited.

"I'm a witness to your crime," she said.

Childless Du took off his glasses and put them inside his breast pocket. No wonder he wore flat-lens glasses. His eyes were so deeply set he looked blind at first glance.

"You want to beard the lion in his own den. Now you go down, Orchid."

The guard stepped forward. "But you said she isn't—"

"She *is*!" Childless Du spun around. "You never opened the door, right?"

The guard nodded, winking at Bao as if he had eye pain. Childless Du patted his shoulder.

"Pardon my earlier mistake. You'll be paid double for doing a fine job. Orchid has repeatedly violated the one-child policy. It's time to tie her tubes." He slapped his thigh. "What're you waiting for?!"

Bao leapt up and started to run, at first slowly because she couldn't believe what was happening. Of all the punishments she'd prepared herself for, sterilization was never one of them. She pushed a man so hard he fell against the doorway with a thud. Was Tong approaching the hospital gate? The night air was cool outside, moonlight spreading on the ground like a thin layer of frost. Sharp gravel hurt her heels, as she tried to keep ahead of the pattering footsteps behind her.

Why wasn't there an office with the light on?

She ran past the sinks and garbage dump, before realizing that she should head for the gate. She passed the billboard with the slogan, "It is good to have one child." She barely had a glimpse of Chairman Mao, before a hand grabbed her collar

and yanked her backward. She swung her fist and punched a shoulder. A man grabbed her wrist and twisted her arm to her back, while another man took hold of her legs. Together they carried her to the bungalow. Looking past her abductors' shoulders, she saw the guard's enormous eyes.

"Help me please, Big Brother, help me!"

She kicked her legs and fell to the ground. A rock scraped her knee as she tried to crawl. Someone grasped her hair. She had never had a fistfight with anyone—now she was fighting for her life. She should have brought a knife, gun, or even a grenade. If these men overpowered her, she would kill herself before they mutilated her body. She bit into a wrist and tasted salty skin. A slap nearly deafened her. She opened her mouth and flailed her arms but couldn't grab hold of an immobile object. She was being carried to the operating room.

"I'm *not* Orchid!" she shouted at the top of her lungs. "How dare you kidnap a university student—"

"Shut up, Orchid!"

When the door was kicked open, she had a glimmer of hope that it wasn't real, and she would wake up from the nightmare.

"Lock me up if you must. I pretended to be Orchid, so I'm guilty of it. Just lock me up!"

"Too late, you should've knelt down and begged me in the first place."

She glimpsed Childless Du's lopsided smile. "Monster! Pigs! You're breaking the law. I'm not even pregnant—"

"We'll make *sure* of that."

Childless Du and his men held her down on the table,

where Doctor Li had performed the abortion three weeks ago. There were dark smudges on the ceiling, the likely remains of squashed mosquitoes. She clawed at her captors but was slapped in the face so hard her teeth rattled in her mouth.

"Give it up and cooperate!"

Her pants were pulled off with the ripping of seams. When her knees were pried open, she felt her hipbones being yanked out of their joints. The sharp pain deepened into dull spasms. No, she wouldn't let them tie her feet to the stirrups! She resumed kicking and roared like a caged lioness.

"Knock her out."

"Don't overdo the anesthesia—I want her to be awake." Childless Du's face, white and blurry, became as big as a toilet bowl.

Then she remembered Hongzhi—had he looked at his murderer's face before he fell?

"Kill me if you must. Just don't sterilize me. I'm only eighteen—"

"Look at it this way, you'll have fun with your boyfriend without ever getting into trouble again."

Bao spat in his face. "Pig! Tong will kill you, if you dare to touch me."

Childless Du wiped his face with a sleeve. "Fix her." He nodded at the men.

"You deserve to die without offspring, Childless Du."

The air became too thin to fill her lungs, so she had to stop cursing. The ropes around her wrists and ankles were tight enough to cut off her blood circulation. Her scalp tingled. Her eyes stung, but she held back tears. She wouldn't give them the satisfaction of seeing her cry.

Bao felt a needle sting, but she couldn't tell where it pierced her skin. The ceiling seemed to float down and drape her like an eiderdown. When a knife cut the skin of her belly, she was too tired to kick. She thought she wasn't bleeding, that inside was dry and clean, like an overstuffed cotton coat. She prayed they would make a mistake and kill her instead. She would rather die dreaming that one day she could still have a baby.

Chapter 16

OUTSIDE A MAN POUNDED a door and kicked it hard. There was no answer, so he went on to the next door. His voice echoed in the courtyard.

"Where's Gu Bao? Tell me where she is!"

Tong was here. Bao opened her mouth. Hurry, stop them, she wanted to shout. But her throat was constricted and she couldn't make a sound, her eyes brimming with hot tears.

Childless Du lifted a corner of the bamboo curtain to peer outside. Bao heard the guard's mumbling voice as the key turned in the lock. The door flew open and bumped against the wall.

"Bastards!" Tong brandished the police baton, his face red and shiny with sweat. "What're you doing to her?"

The marionette-like man dropped the scissors, pressed his shoulder against the wall, and moved toward the door. Tong leapt at the stocky man and smacked the back of his thighs with the baton. Falling backwards, the man made a guttural sound and jerked his arms in a vain attempt to grasp the air. Tong flipped a stool to press on his chest.

"We're just following orders." The man whimpered

through chattering teeth.

"This is a hospital," Childless Du said. "Drop your weapon."

"I'm a soldier and will take out enemies like you!"

The stocky man gripped the legs of the stool but couldn't pull it up. "She pretended to be Orchid, so things got out of hand."

Childless Du cleared his throat. "Comrade Fang doesn't condone anyone meddling with our local affairs and attacking the workers with a weapon!" When Tong lunged at him, Childless Du pushed the marionette-like man out of the doorway and escaped into the night.

Tong prodded the guard's chest with the police baton. "Now you keep a good watch. If anyone lays a hand on her, I'll kill you first!" He stomped outside to look for Childless Du.

The guard lifted the stool from the floor. He didn't bat an eyelid when the stocky man got up and stumbled outside. The guard came to Bao and cut a dead knot with a pair of scissors. His buckteeth bit his lower lip as he tore open the rope. She gazed at his triangle-shaped eyes and several hairs poking out of his nostrils. The words "Big Brother" were on the tip of her tongue. The guard took the chair to sit in the doorway with his back to Bao.

Although her legs were free, her feet felt broken. She tried to wiggle her toes but was unable. A glimpse of the open wounds on the right side of her belly made her feel faint, clammy, and thirsty. No wonder the guard had averted his eyes. She must've looked frightening, like a mauled animal with her entrails hanging out.

Crickets chirped in the warm summer air. She had heard them all her life, but now she was grateful for the peaceful sound. After the fistfight and terror, she lived to hear the male crickets attracting the females with their lusty songs. Small, fragile creatures flourished in every corner of the world. If she hadn't come to Pingwu for a secret abortion, she would never have met Orchid, much less experienced her plight. Now lying on the operating table, she knew her life would never be the same. If she could stand up on her feet again, she had to go on living with dignity.

She heard footsteps. Tong entered the room and stood against the wall, panting and coughing so hard his body shook.

"Go find her a doctor," the guard said.

"How could you let them do this to her?"

"I'm only a guard. Who knows half of the things that are going on around here?"

"I'll petition to Comrade Fang. She can have all of you fired and Childless Du thrown in the prison!"

"You need witnesses, the village chief and other local cadres, to testify. Mind you, Comrade Fang has rewarded this one-child policy worker team for two years in a row. You can't win in the Pingwu Courthouse. If you go to Comrade Fang's boss, the lawsuit will take you years. What good does it do either of you?" The guard shook his head. "I'll get you the nurse."

Tong pounded the wall and then dug in with his knuckles, as if he wanted to drill holes through the whitewash. Bao felt ashamed that he should see her in this state of grotesque helplessness. Where was that shy girl, who had cried after their first kiss? Now, her mutilated body was not a thing to be pitied. No, she'd rather bear his anger, that he should scold her for being foolish. How could a woman stand up to an evil man with no weapon but her own flesh?

Tong turned his body around, first his hand, followed by his shoulder. His eyes looked down as he approached the bed. "I should have protected you."

She reached a hand toward him. He took her fingers and folded them inside his palm.

"I want to kill Childless Du." He shivered, unable to meet her eyes.

Was this the Tong who couldn't speak of combat? But she didn't want him to kill. There were better ways to avenge injustice.

"How's Orchid?"

"We moved her to an old temple. Her water broke, and she was delirious." He stole a glance at her lower belly. His cheeks turned crimson, and even his ears became red. "I searched the hospital ground before I left. Childless Du wasn't here. I came back as soon as I could."

"You gave me a good scare."

A warm tingling sensation returned to her fingertips when she opened her hand. She touched his stubble and felt a tiny electric shock. His hair was damp with dew. His clothes smelt tangy as if he'd walked through a grove of orange trees. She traced the downy hair that connected his eyebrows in the middle. What a blessing it was to have him by her side!

"Don't leave me," she said.

"Never." He squeezed her hand.

The door flung open. A nurse clutched in her hands a half-finished vest, threaded with bamboo needles. "What're you hollering about, murderers and all that nonsense? She's not dead." Yawning, she rubbed her eyes.

Her loud voice made Bao nauseous. Where had she been when Bao shouted for help? She might be an accomplice to Childless Du's team. The woman had a strong chin and prominent teeth on a longish horsy face. Bao moaned when the nurse examined her wounds.

"What a mess. Who did this suture?"

"Help us." Tong grabbed the nurse's elbow. "She's not even nineteen, her parents are in Nanjing. We can't let her die!"

"Get Doctor Li. He's due back today and probably home already." She called out to the guard. "Come and bring your flashlight. We'll take the back road."

Tong followed them outside and told them to hurry. Then he closed the door and paced the room. Every now and then he looked out of the windows into the darkness, where shadowy shapes loomed. Crickets chirped in the grass, and occasionally a croaking frog broke the monotony. He hooked a thumb in his belt buckle, raised his heels, and bent his knees slightly forward.

"You saved my life."

"Sweetheart." He rested a heel on the bottom of the wall.

The anesthetic must've been wearing off. She was freezing and feeling nauseous. Her body shaking, her tongue felt heavy and stiff around the edges. A serrated pain gnawed at her lower belly, but she could bear it, because something else weighed on her mind.

"If I'm barren, do you still care about me?"

His face became creased as the blush drained from his cheeks.

"I'd give anything to have a baby with you." After saying this, she felt as if a heavy load were lifted off her chest. Why hadn't she said this to her parents? They might have let her keep Soybean, if she had admitted to loving Tong so deeply.

He came to her bed and knelt on one knee. "I'm with you, Bao, no matter what happens." He pulled the blanket over her legs.

"Hold me."

Tong put an arm around her shoulders. She opened her mouth in search of his lips, but he turned his face aside. Their arms intertwined, they huddled like a pair of birds encased in a hard white shell. He wiped his eyes on her shoulder and trembled with the effort to muffle his sobs. She took comfort in his tears, knowing that when grief took over, he wouldn't attempt to kill Childless Du. The pain in her lower belly was flaring up. It seemed to tear open her flesh, like unzipping a jacket. She moaned, a bitter metallic taste in her mouth.

Bao woke up and squinted her eyes in the bright fluorescent light. Tong held her hand, weeping quietly. She saw the leathery skin of Doctor Li's face. Under bushy eyebrows, his eyes were bloodshot and stern.

"I had to perform a second operation on you," Doctor Li said. "Some quack did a terrible job—he should be locked up. I removed your scarred fallopian tubes and used the electrical conducting forceps to coagulate two adjacent sites. You lost five centimeters of the fallopian tube. I'm not sure if you'll recover the use of your right ovary. You're young, so your body will heal. The good news is your left ovary is intact."

He put a thermometer in her mouth. Feeling the brittle glass with her tongue, Bao turned her head and saw Grandpa. Was he wearing a beekeeper jacket? He held onto the windowsill, as if his knees would buckle. His face ashen, he almost blended in with the lime washed wall. She blinked to make sure that he didn't fade away like a ghost. Doctor Li pulled out the thermometer to read her temperature.

"Grandpa, I'm all right. Don't worry about me, I'm fine."

"If I had known this would happen, I'd never have let you come here." Grandpa squatted and held his head in his hands. "I'd rather not see you as long as I live."

"It wasn't your fault, Grandpa." She longed to embrace him and stop his tears, but she couldn't move a finger. Under the coarse sheets, her body felt like a pile of immobile flesh and bones.

"Doctor Li said you'll recover in a couple of weeks." Tong stroked her hair. "You'll return to the university and finish your studies, graduate and become a lawyer."

She missed the simple life of moving from lecture halls to dining halls and back to the dorm. Her seven roommates, all virgins, could only have privacy by hiding behind their mosquito nettings. Could she return to that haven? She had aged ten years overnight. One side of her body had been killed, while the other half waited for its time to bloom. How could she piece herself back together into a whole woman?

A smile took so much effort it might have become a grimace. "I will put Childless Du in prison, even if this takes the rest of my life."

"We have a victory." Tong whispered into her ear, "Grandpa said Orchid had her baby." He kissed her earlobe. "Childless Du can't kill a healthy baby. They're finally safe."

Tears of joy flooded her eyes. She had saved a life. The child would grow up and stand up to Childless Du. She raised her head and moaned, as a deep ache radiated from her lower back to her left thigh.

Doctor Li put a hand on Tong's shoulder. "I'll prescribe her some pain medication and antibiotics. Herbal remedies can be used for long-term care. You call me if she gets worse or has any adverse reactions."

"Any tonics to help with healing? Money isn't an issue." Tong walked with Doctor Li to his office. They talked in low voices and closed the door on their way out.

When Grandpa looked up from his folded arms, Bao bit her lip to stifle her moans. He wiped his eyes and rolled up a sleeve of his beekeeper jacket.

"Your grandma is cooking you a meal, a special treat that you'll enjoy."

"I'm not hungry, Grandpa."

"I wish your parents were here—they could talk some sense into you." He grabbed onto his thighs to push himself into a standing position. "Women lose babies every day. Bao, you can't save them all, not in this part of the country, not anywhere, as a matter of fact."

"That was my third one, Grandpa."

The blades of the ceiling fan rotated noiselessly. Her hair quivered and tickled her cheek. Outside the crickets were silent, and not a frog was croaking. There was a touch of rosy light in the transom windows above the doorframe. A new day was dawning.

"Grandpa, you remember the earthquake, don't you?"

Nodding, he sat on a stool beside her bed.

"It was an early morning, like this one, but in the winter, when snow covered the mountain slopes."

"The coldest winter I can ever remember." A smile crept onto his lips. For a moment he seemed to forget about her troubles. "We lived in the earthquake shack and had little to eat, but we were happy enough. You 'cured' your grandma's back pain and headache. Every night you sang and danced for us."

"One morning I got up to use the toilet. I saw two pandas in our backyard, a mother and her cub."

Grandpa squinted his eyes, as if straining to see his backyard more than a decade ago.

"The panda caught Cauliflower Tail. I watched her tear apart the hen and eat it, feathers, bones, and all."

Bao thought of the mother panda she had freed from the snare a few days ago. Her black-goggled eyes were wistful and sad, as if Bao had known her since childhood.

"I feel like Cauliflower Tail. Grandpa, can you understand that?"

"Little Bao." He took off his beekeeper jacket and placed it atop her thin quilt. It was stained with blood that must have come from Orchid's delivery. "We have grown old, but you haven't changed a bit."

But I have, she wanted to say, I'm not the same girl you carried into the house after the abortion.

She sniffed the pipe smoke from his calloused fingers. When she had lived with her grandparents more than a decade ago, she used to crawl into Grandma's lap and rattle on about everyday goings-on. One day Grandpa had pulled her onto his lap and asked her, "What do you talk about to your grandma all day?" She had yelled and struggled to get away. Now she gazed upon his ruddy face, which hardly aged a day aside from the deepened crow's-feet and thinning gray hair. She longed to return to the hillside cottage, have a warm honey drink, and shell roasted peanuts with her grandparents.

The door opened. Tong folded a few pages of prescriptions inside his breast pocket. "We're lucky to have Doctor Li. He could be a renowned doctor if he worked in a big hospital in Nanjing."

Grandpa gave Tong his seat. He smoked a pipe outside, leaving them to talk in private.

"So we *can* have a baby one day." He lowered his voice to a barely audible whisper. "Do you regret the promise you made to me?"

It took her a moment to realize what he'd meant. Then she burst into a smile. "Was I too forward?"

"I like to be pursued." He pressed her hand against his stubbly cheek. "I want to quit the army and start all over again. Would you accept a deserter without a future?"

Tong had wasted many years on a dead end career path, but

he was a decent, capable man.

"I'm going to knock my head against a stone wall." She squeezed his hand. "Don't we deserve each other?"

"Your father begs to differ." He gnawed at the fleshy part of her palm, tickling her a little.

"We can move here and look after my grandparents." She rubbed his nose with her fingertip. "Mind you, I'm a beekeeper's apprentice."

"A barefoot lawyer needs to make a living somehow."

"We can make beeswax candles and hand cream." She winked. "If you get stung enough times, you won't ever get cancer."

Grandpa knocked the brass bowl of his pipe against the windowsill. The loud noise startled them both. "Go away, greedy cat."

Tong stood up and asked what was going on.

Grandpa pointed to the eaves. There was a sparrows' nest on the protruding edge of a molding. While the mother was away, a cat had come to prey on the baby birds.

"Can I have a look?" Bao said.

Tong pulled away her quilt and slid his arms under her. "Hold on tightly."

She reached up to put her arms around his neck. When he lifted her from the bed, she felt as if she'd grown wings, defying gravity and leaving the pain behind. He turned aside to go through the doorway. She breathed in dewy morning air. A light mist enveloped everything as far as her eyes could see. Under the eaves, tiny heads bobbed up and down inside a fluffy teacup-sized nest.

"Three baby birds." Just then the mother returned with food in her beak. "Am I heavy?"

"Light as a feather." He nudged her bottom with his thigh to keep her from slipping down. "You should eat more."

Grandpa brought a chair from the room. Tong stumbled back to sink into it and let out a sigh of relief. They looked at each other for a moment and then pulled away simultaneously. Grandpa was watching them.

"After you get well, you'll study so hard you become the top student in your class. I'll help you bring a team of lawyers to Crystal Village. Childless Du will spend the rest of his life behind bars."

"Easier said than done."

"Am I missing something?"

Bao averted her eyes.

Tong lifted her chin. She saw his sheepish smile, before he pressed his lips tightly to her mouth. When their teeth clattered, she stole a glance at Grandpa. He stopped in front of the portrait of Chairman Mao with his hands folded on his back.

Tong muttered under his breath, "A baby?"

It'd be selfish of her to wish for a daughter. She nestled up against him and pecked him on the cheek.

Bao woke up and found herself in the sickroom. With the bamboo curtains drawn halfway, the afternoon sun baked the west-facing windows. Dust particles floated in the beam of sunlight. Alongside her bed, there were two empty beds with rusted iron frames. Their wooden boards were bare without any bedding. Had they received more brutalized victims than Bao could ever imagine? The room looked shabby in the daylight, though open and airy. Her pain had subsided to a mild throbbing. She felt a little hungry.

Grandpa dozed by her bedside. His head dropped toward his chest. He was about to topple onto the bed, before he jerked awake with a start.

"Did you ask for me?" He wiped a trace of drool from the corner of his mouth.

"No, Grandpa."

Footsteps approached. There was a flutter of tapping on the door before it opened. Daisy burst into the room holding up a string bag knitted with red, green, yellow, and purple threads.

"Auntie Bao." Daisy climbed into the bed and opened the string bag. A red egg popped out and rolled onto the white bedding.

"Congrats on your new addition." Bao signaled to Grandpa, who propped up her pillows and lifted her onto them.

Candor's family couldn't wait a whole month to hand out the red-dyed eggs that celebrated the birth of a son. The festive treat for a baby girl was sugary noodles, satisfying but less costly. Bao cupped the red egg in her palms. It was still warm.

Bao's stomach growled. "This is too beautiful to eat."

"Get down, Daisy. Let Auntie Bao rest."

Candor held onto a cane and hobbled into the room. He wore a yellow shirt with miniature dragons embroidered on the pockets, the bronze buttons fastened all the way to his throat.

His clean-shaven face looked a little raw and flaky, the result of zealous scrubbing in a long hot bath.

Bao brushed Daisy's loose hair to the back of her ear. "Where is your little brother?" Daisy put her mouth to Bao's ear, and her whispering tickled Bao. "I can't hear you." She pulled back with a smile.

Grandma entered with a swaddle in her arms. "Orchid was detained and waiting for her tubal." She sat on the bed to show Bao the baby.

He had the tiniest face Bao had ever seen. His skin was red and tender, covered with fine hair. His flat nose and creased cheeks resembled a doll more than a person, and his eyes were shut. Grandma took off the tiger hat to show his abundant dark hair.

"Look, how pretty she is."

"A beautiful baby." Bao burst into laughter. "But he's a boy!"

"I'll let her sister tell you."

"Sis is my baby doll. I helped dress her, it was fun!" Daisy reached out a hand to squeeze the end of the swaddle. "The tiger shoes are big. She wears them inside so she won't lose them."

"We named her Bao," Candor said.

Bao folded her hands under the quilt. "Why the red eggs? Are you disappointed that it's not . . . it's a girl?"

"How can we be anything but grateful?" Candor plopped down to kneel on one knee. His injured leg stretching sideways, he held onto the bed board to maintain an upright position. "Look how beautiful she is. Our family is eternally indebted to you."

"Please get up." The baby was so fragile and perfect Bao couldn't help reaching out her arms. "May I?" Grandma handed her the swaddle. She held the baby, a soft warm creature that was almost weightless. "Darling." She pursed her lips to coo at the baby.

Tong entered the room and placed a cotton thermos bucket on the empty bed. He stood behind Candor, who was still bowing, put his hands under Candor's armpits, and lifted him up from the floor. Grandpa moved a chair for Candor to sit down.

Grandma took out a bowl of porridge from the thermos bucket. She fed Bao a spoonful. The corn porridge was warm and smooth, imparting a mild tang of duck egg and succulent chewiness of lean pork. She gulped it down and licked the spoon to get every drop.

Suddenly a loud shriek startled Bao so much she almost dropped the baby. The small face in the swaddle turned deep purple as she squawked like a bird. Large tears squeezed out from the corners of her shut eyelids. Her lower lip quivered uncontrollably with each wail, as a red tongue flickered in her mouth.

"What does she want?" Bao looked up.

"She needs to suckle." Candor took the baby to rock her. "Little Bao is hungry."

Tong fetched a bottle from the thermos bucket. The baby wiggled and yawned, tossing her head about in search of the nipple, before clasping it in her mouth and sucking with gusto.

Candor stroked her gossamer soft hair. "Thank God she's

healthy, so Childless Du can't harm her. Otherwise, the village chief has to answer for the crime. He's afraid of losing his job and going to hell in the afterlife."

Although Bao had won a battle, the war against Childless Du was just beginning.

"How could he give her a tubal, after he did this to me?"

"Childless Du may say yours was an unfortunate mistake. He might even apologize to you and offer some form of compensation to settle the case, because he's an unconscionable man." Candor raised the bottle for the baby to feed. "Once he tried to kidnap a pregnant woman. She wasn't home, and neither was her husband, so he arrested an old vet who gave shots to their pigs. The vet was released after paying a fine of eight hundred yuan—he didn't even get a receipt."

"You need a good lawyer to put Childless Du in jail." Tong patted Bao's shoulder.

"I'm only a student." She plucked off his hand and held it in her palm.

Tong sat at the foot of the bed. "Bao, you taught me a lesson. Saving one woman is nothing. You want to do much more: change the system, and why should you wait? If not for yourself, you'll do it for Daisy and Little Bao."

How he trumpeted her secret! Now her diffidence could be seen as false modesty. Bao blinked her eyes.

"Has Childless Du been sued before?" she asked.

"There was some talk of compensation after Brother Liao's wife died." Grandpa dusted his sleeve. "When Brother Liao went mad, people just got more scared."

"We have all suffered, so many families, each on our own."

Candor pulled out the nipple from the baby's mouth, propped her up, and rubbed her back. "We helped each other when we could. There comes a point when you have to think for yourself. What have you got to lose if you can't keep your baby?"

Bao sank her fingernails into her thigh. There was a time when she could have begged Tong to kill Childless Du.

Grandma folded up her apron to place inside the thermos bucket. She reached out to take Daisy's hand. "How about the two of us taking a walk in the yard?"

Daisy shook her head.

"You haven't looked at a hospital before. The pharmacy has big, tall cabinets with dozens of drawers. You want to open one and see what's inside?"

Daisy clutched onto Bao's leg, for fear that she might be dragged away.

"I almost forgot, Daisy!" Grandpa patted his forehead. "The baby sparrows."

"Hatchlings?" Daisy knelt on the bed.

"See for yourself." Grandpa wagged his head with a smile. "Their mother catches worms to feed the babies, mouth to mouth."

Daisy leapt off the bed and left with Grandpa.

When Tong moved to sit beside Bao, she pulled his arms around her body. They clasped their hands like tying a bow. He put his chin on her shoulder. They rubbed cheeks without saying a word. Neither could speak of the abyss of despair they had shared. She was grateful that Tong had stood by her side.

The horse-faced nurse entered with a basket of white

bedding. Grandma moved their things from the empty bed. The nurse spread a plastic covered cotton mattress on the bed board.

"We want to take Childless Du to court," Tong said. "Will you help us, Nurse Ma?"

"Doctor Li detests those barefoot doctors." She flung the bedsheet over the mattress to let it settle. "I'm sure he'll help."

"Will you help, too?" Tong said. "You're a witness of sorts."

She took her time to fluff the pillow. Then she sat on the newly made bed, crossing her feet at the ankles.

"To be honest, I've seen worse."

Bao swallowed. "What could be worse than forced sterilization?"

Candor craned his neck and pushed himself up on his fists. If not for his limp, he might have run outside to join Daisy.

"One woman had an abortion on her due date," the nurse said. "A rivanol shot didn't kill the baby. We were told to inject potassium chloride on its temple when the mother was pushing."

"It was a boy, too." Grandma's soft voice raised gooseflesh on Bao's arms.

Bao slid a hand under her shirt to touch the gauze bandage. She would have an ugly scar after she healed.

The nurse walked over to coo at the baby. When she put out an index finger, the baby grabbed it in her fist.

"You made it, kiddo."

Little Bao, now satiated, licked her lips, her eyes drowsy. Bao reached out her arms, and Candor handed her the baby.

She kissed the small face, soft as pudding. The baby opened her eyes and yawned. Her mouth stretched sideways, revealing her pink gums. It wasn't exactly a smile, but it melted Bao's heart.

"What a treasure you are!"

"When she grows up, her elder sister will teach her to sing, 'Finding a Friend.'" Tong straightened her tiger hat. "Happy birthday, Little Bao."

He picked up the red egg from the quilt, cracked it on the bedpost, and peeled it. Bao bit into the gray-green egg yolk. The egg was overcooked, its yolk firm and a little powdery. Chewing slowly, she relished the minty yolk and silken egg white.

Tong put the last bit of egg in her mouth and wiped his fingers on his pants. "When we return to Nanjing, you should work with your father. He'll give us professional guidance."

"What about you?"

"I'll do anything—street peddler, salesman, substitute PE teacher—as long as I can be with you."

She reached up to touch his chin. The warmth of his face comforted her. "I won't give you up, even if my parents disown me."

"Look at it this way." He drew illegible words in her palm. "If we had a daughter, I wouldn't give her to a man unworthy of her. Why should Professor Gu be any different?"

A rush of warmth coursed through her body from her head to her toes. Perhaps it was the red egg. Tong was right: Food is heaven. In her mind's eye, Bao saw that snow-covered mountain slope more than a decade ago. She came out of the earthquake shack, after the panda had trotted into the woods with her cub. She picked up a brown feather from the ground, put it to her nose, and sniffed the vane of barbs. Its quill dark with the blood inside, the feather had been growing until it was plucked off Cauliflower Tail's wing.

Now Bao slid a hand into Tong's sleeve. He raised an eyebrow. When she said nothing, he bowed his head to rub his cheek against her temple. His stubble tickled her, and she burst into a fit of giggles. This seemed to encourage him. He nuzzled her neck. She laughed so hard her eyes welled up.

About the Author

Born and raised in mainland China, Yang Huang came to the U.S. shortly after taking part in the 1989 student movement. She lives in the San Francisco Bay Area and works as a computer engineer for UC Berkeley and as a writer by vocation.

Huang has had short stories and a feature-length screenplay published in literary magazines including the *Asian Pacific American Journal*, *The Evansville Review*, *Futures*, *Porcupine Literary Arts Magazine*, *Nuvein*, and *Stories for Film*. Her short story was nominated for the Pushcart Prize. *Living Treasures* is her debut novel and a Bellwether Prize finalist.

To learn more about Huang and her writing, visit www.yanghuang.com.

Acknowledgments

I owe a debt of gratitude to my agent, Barbara Braun, for her vision and support.

Thank you to my writing group: Amy, Clare, Susan, John, Bill, and Joe for their support, inspiration, and friendship.

Thank you to wonderful teachers who nurtured and challenged me: Elizabeth Graver, Barbara Kingsolver, Elizabeth Evans, C. E. Poverman, Jonathan Penner, Robert Houston, and Vikram Chandra.

Special thanks to George B. Schaller, whose book *The Last Panda* opened my eyes to the beauty and mystique of this endangered animal that graces the mountains of Sichuan.

Finally, I want to thank my family for their love and unconditional support. This is our book.

More books from Harvard Square Editions:

CPSIA information can be obtained
at www.ICGtesting.com
Printed in the USA
FS0W01n0817281114
3608FS